Freddie Petford

The Death of Conscience

By

Frederick Petford

CW00822232

Published by The Claverham Press Ltd
London

ISBN 9798355002503

By the same author

The Ghosts of Passchendaele

Book one in the Great Tew supernatural thriller series

Dedicated to my wife Marguerita
and my daughters Milly and Imogen.
The three graces in my life.

Interested readers can explore more about the themes
covered in *The Death of Conscience* and its prequel
The Ghosts of Passchendaele
on Facebook and Instagram at
Frederick Petford.
Come and join us!

Prologue

Dawn. The British lines near Delville Wood, Northern France, 9th August 1916.

The deafening barrage that had been falling onto the German lines through the night died away, and the two young men pressed together in the crowded trench looked at each other. It was a snatched moment of calm and connection in the sudden, shocking, silence.

They knew what came next.

'Get ready,' a sergeant behind them bawled. His cry was taken up by others, their shouts fading into the distance over the shadowy sea of helmets and fixed bayonets that filled the front line as far as the eye could see in both directions. The colonial twang of South African accents sounded from men further down the line.

The older of the two men was aged twenty-one, dark haired and blue eyed, with a sardonic smile. His brother was two years younger and had his mother's blond curly hair. A good looking boy. They shook hands, as they had done many times in the last year.

'Good luck then, mate. Try to stick together, but if not, I'll see you in Berlin.' A sly grin cracked the older brother's face. 'Don't worry, we'll be back poaching Langford trout by Christmas.'

A whistle sounded in the distance. Then another, and another. A fresh-faced nineteen-year old lieutenant climbed onto an ammunition box and turned towards them as, with a great roar, the newly arrived South African troops surged towards their ladders. He blew long and hard on his own whistle and shouted, 'Come on then, up we go lads! Don't let the colonials get all the glory. Onward the Oxfords, follow me!'

Then he turned, pulled his revolver out of its holster and climbed.

Grim faced and shoulder to shoulder, the men shuffled towards the ladders. Some prayed, others cried, but there was no hesitation, no shirking.

Death waited for many of them, they knew that. But they went anyway.

It won't be me. Not this time…

Up above, the chatter of German machine guns started and so did the screaming.

*

An hour later, what remained of the Oxford Light Infantry was retreating under heavy fire. They had managed to penetrate the barbed wire and reach the German front line in the shattered remnants of Delville Wood and in hand to hand fighting, had pushed the Foot Guard Regiment that opposed them back towards their supply lines. But a strong counter-attack had forced them to give ground and they were now exposed in no-man's land.

The older brother wriggled past a shattered tree stump as trench mortar rounds exploded around him. There were bodies everywhere and he saw the lieutenant who had led them up the ladders lying on his back, apparently uninjured, but clearly dead. Cursing, he got to his feet and sprinted, bent over, through the sucking mud towards a shell hole ten yards away.

Ten yards closer to safety. Come on, keep going.

A bullet plucked at his sleeve, and he threw himself forwards, head first. The hole was thirty feet wide and half-filled with water, and he frantically dug his feet into the slime to stop his slide. Men drowned in shell holes. Momentarily safe from the bullets, he lay on his back and took stock. He reckoned it was another hundred yards to the British lines and wondered whether his best bet would be to wait until nightfall. There were hours to go, but at least he'd get back.

He cleared his rifle barrel of mud, lighted a cigarette and looked around. There were two bodies with him. One was lying half in the water with an arm missing. He turned to look at the other and his blood ran cold. He knew straight away. Just by the shock of blond curly hair showing beneath the helmet. Dropping his rifle he slid over and pulled the man onto his back.

'Oh, mate. What have they done to you?' he whispered, the words carried away by the gunfire and screaming that drifted over the battlefield.

His beloved younger brother had taken a cluster of machine gun bullets to his chest. He counted them. Four in all, from top right to bottom left. Death would have been instantaneous. He slid his arms around the body and held him close and, as the sounds of battle faded from his mind, he raised his head and howled like an animal, raw with grief.

And a mile away a dark and ancient thing that haunted the battlefields and fed on death and pain, noticed, and turned towards him. Because of all the human emotions, it was utter despair that made a man's soul most vulnerable.

Invisible to all, the wraith crossed the shattered ground in seconds. It approached the man cautiously and watched as he held his brother, eyes closed and keening. Then it slipped past his defences and buried itself close to his heart, unseen and unnoticed, an evil parasitic presence that would feed on his soul, and weaken and corrupt it so that, in the end, death would come, and the crying man would be like he was.

*

The long hours of daylight slipped past, but for the soldier in the shell hole time had stopped. And still he cried. The last vestiges of hope and humanity were leaving him. His friends from the village were there one moment and gone the next, strong, vibrant, men blown to pieces in shell bursts or left jerking on the murderous barbed wire as German machine gun bullets rippled into them.

And he had taken lives too. Four men he knew of, the last just a few hours earlier. As the remnants of the Oxfords had burst into the German trenches in a killing fury, a guard had come running round the corner almost straight onto his bayonet. All he'd had to do was thrust forward. As though astonished at his temerity, the man had met his eyes, then silently pitched forward into the mud.

As dusk fell he eyed the man with his legs in the pool. He recognised him vaguely, from over Whitney way. Unbidden, an idea came to him. He slid down to the water and unbuttoned the dead private's uniform. Slipping his fingers inside he grasped his identity tags and eased them over his head. He read the name – Nathanial Downs.

He quickly changed his own tags with the dead private's. Then he rifled his uniform pockets, and swapped their pay books, letters from home and one or two other personal possessions including an engraved cigarette case and lighter. When he had finished he studied the man carefully.

The poor sod even looked at bit like him. Two brothers who died together in the same shell hole. Tragic. We might even get a mention in the Oxford Evening Echo.

Heart beating with a strange, wild, exhilaration, he crawled to the rim of the shell hole and peered cautiously towards the German trenches. Nothing stirred in the darkness, but as he turned to look back at the British lines he saw a line of men moving slowly forwards, crouching and wriggling alternately. The leaders were only twenty feet away.

Christ, they're coming back for more.

Left with no choice he played dead, lying on his front to hide his face. He sensed a movement and then heard a whispered exchange right next to him – barely more than breath in the air.

'How far now do you think Sergeant?'

'We're half-way I reckon, sir.'

'All quiet so far then, follow me.'

There was a quiet sucking of mud as the line of men slid on into the night. The new Nathanial Downs barely noticed. The men had Scottish accents. They must have pulled the Oxfords out during the day. His heart leapt. Back in the trenches no-one would know his face.

He turned to look at his dead brother one last time and whispered, 'Goodbye, mate. Don't worry. We both know who needs to pay for this. I'll set things straight.' And with that, he eased himself over the rim of the shell hole and set off on his stomach across the mud, his rifle slung across his back.

Fifteen minutes later he slid into the British front line trench, having narrowly avoided being shot by a sentry peering through a slit between two sandbags.

'Jeez,' the kilted private exclaimed in broad Scots, 'it's a wee mud baby. I nearly put a bullet in your heid son. Where've you come from then?'

'I'm with the Oxfords, I got stuck in a shell hole and had to wait till dark before getting back.'

The sentry resumed his position, both eyes glued to the slit that looked out over no-man's land. 'Aye, well, they've pulled you back,' he said out of the corner of his mouth.

'He's right.' A lieutenant appeared out of the gloom. 'There've been a few stragglers. You need to head up the supply trench and make your way to the Wellington reserve camp. Ask at the command post on the Ypres to Lille road. They'll direct you. Try and clean yourself up as well, man. I can barely see your uniform and your face is covered with mud.'

Saluting and only too happy to be on his way, the private walked to the junction with a trench that ran westwards away from the front line. As he did so a volley of shots and shouting carried over from the German lines and a flare burst high in the sky. Machine guns started firing as he hurried away into the night.

6

For the next half hour he worked his way through multiple layers of defensive trenches. There were soldiers everywhere and he was challenged a couple of times, but his story was accepted without question, and no-one asked his name.

Finally he climbed up to ground level and arrived at what was left of the main road. He stood for a moment and looked around the god-forsaken landscape. The ground had changed hands three times and only shattered tree stumps, the sand-bagged mounds of defensive strong points, and mud were left. In the moonlight the pockmarked road lay thirty feet ahead of him and a long column of troops wearing South African bush hats was approaching from his left. He ducked back into the trench and let them pass, then re-emerged.

What now?

He stared to his right as the sound of an engine carried across the wasteland. The faint light of a headlamp slit showed on the road and as he watched it seemed to stop next to a ruined building. He stared as the moon came out from behind a cloud and revealed a motorbike despatch rider wearing a long leather coat standing in the shelter of the one remaining wall. There was the brief flare of a match as he lighted a cigarette.

No-one stops a despatch rider.

Barely aware of what he was doing, he drew his razor-sharp bayonet from its scabbard and, concealing it up against his side, he walked over.

'Evening mate, got a spare fag?' he asked.

'Blimey, what happened to you?' the rider asked as he felt in the chest pocket of his coat.

'I got lost in the push yesterday, just trying to find my regiment again.'

The man nodded. It was hardly an unfamiliar story. He handed the packet over and, as he looked down at his pocket and felt for a match, the soldier drove the bayonet into his neck and wrenched it to one side.

The rider stared at him in astonishment, choked briefly, and died standing up. And deep inside the mud covered soldier, the wraith rejoiced, and took a bite out of his soul.

Shortly afterwards, Nathanial Downs, despatch rider, was driving carefully towards Ypres and the junction of the road to Paris.

*

Two weeks later there was a knock at the door of a modest home in Witney. Mrs Downs opened it to see a grave-faced telegram boy standing there. Tears welled in her eyes as she reached out and took the small buff-coloured envelope. She ripped it open and read the contents of the form, turning to her husband who had appeared from the garden.

'Missing, believed killed,' she whispered.

'Who?' he asked.

'Nat, my darling Nat.'

The Downs family had three sons in France. The other two survived the war and came home, but nothing more was ever heard about her youngest son.

Mrs Downs wondered what had happened to him every day until she died.

Chapter One

Great Tew, Oxfordshire. September 1920.

'Cheerio gentlemen, safe home now.' Stanley Tirrold, the statuesque proprietor of the Black Horse public house, pronounced his customary valediction on two farm workers who had finished their cider and were heading for the door.

'See you on Friday,' the shorter of the two replied. With a sweeping nod to the others in the bar, he led the way outside.

Out of the corner of his eye, Bert Williams saw them go and raised his hand, but his main attention was focussed on the lively conversation he was having with the Reverend Tukes. The amiable parson of St Mary's Church was a regular patron of the ancient inn, and the discussion was a familiar one, namely the role of the church in country life.

It had become apparent some time ago that their views were not fully aligned.

As the pub door closed, Bert, who had the countryman's benign contempt for an indoor man, remarked, 'It's all very well with your MA from Oxford, parson, and being landlord of the Glebe allotments, but you're preaching about spiritual mysteries, while my 'taters in the garden are full of disease. I looked up your stipend in Smith's Directory. Half of it would suit me and the missus.'

'Really Bert, I am not in charge of my remuneration and, believe me, I am as concerned about your 'taters as I am about your immortal soul.'

'My immortal soul? I reckon Eve Dance can keep an eye on that for me.'

Tukes sighed and drank some cider. Eve's position in the village was well established and he knew many of those who attended his church did so out of habit not belief. Nevertheless, he rose to the challenge. 'Do you really think that is true? Are you sure?'

'Sure as hell is full of parsons,' Bert replied with satisfaction, clearly feeling he had got the better of the exchange.

Many years earlier the vicar had boxed as a flyweight for Oxford and had been known for his steely ability to carry the fight to his opponents. Some of that light showed in his eyes. 'Regarding the allotments, I've been meaning to mention that Mr Hawkins came to me the other day and said he would be giving up his plot at the end of the season. He's in his eighties now and can't manage it any more.'

Bert came to attention like a pointer spotting game. The plot in question was the most coveted in the Glebe, by a distance. It had the best soil and the most sunlight, and Mr Hawkins turned a tidy profit from selling his surplus fruit and vegetables around the estate.

'Is that so? And me being next on the list.'

The parson hesitated. 'Well I suppose technically you are the next on the list, but I don't think I can let you have it.'

Shock showed on Bert's face. 'What?'

'The Glebe allotments are only available to practising Christians. St Mary's is a broad church, Bert, very broad in fact, but sadly our many spirited discussions on theological matters have led me to believe you reside beyond its walls.'

'Eh?'

Grinning widely, Stanley Tirrold eased up to them on his side of the bar. 'I think he means all those years of sinning and poaching when you should have been singing hymns and praying have come back to haunt you, Bert.'

'But I've bin waiting for him to d…, I mean, that's a bit harsh, parson. I've done plenty of praying in my time and it's not my fault if the best time for a bit of lurcher work is when the gamekeepers are in church.'

'It is a question of compatibility Bert. I find myself unable to bridge the gap between the qualities required of an allotment holder in the Glebe meadow, and your own, er…,' He tailed off, sipped his pint, and eyed him over the glass.

'There's Mrs Sutton too,' the landlord added cheerfully.

Bert glared at him. 'That's not helping, Stan.'

Two other men left the pub leaving the three of them alone. There was a long moment of silence, then the padre unsheathed his sword and applied it with exquisite grace.

'What's needed is a sign that you are prepared to embrace the church with the same enthusiasm with which I understand you embrace your wife's sister up at the hall.'

Bert stirred, 'Look Parson, I don't know what you've heard…'

But the vicar interrupted. 'No, hear me out. If you will agree to attend bible classes with me every week between now and Christmas then I may be able to reconsider my decision.'

The man opposite swallowed. 'Really?'

'Yes. In fact, to give us something to work towards, let's say the arrangement will be that you give us a ten minute sermon on the blessings of the church in rural life, at the service on Christmas Eve. I and my fellow members of the church council will then vote on your suitability for the Hawkins plot.' Tukes beamed at him as a loud burst of laughter sounded from the landlord.

Bert looked stunned. 'But that's not fair, Parson. I'm next on your list,' he said. Then he lowered his voice and added meaningfully, 'Isn't there something else I can do for you? A trout or two, regular like?'

'I've enjoyed a Langford trout up at the hall on many occasions, but I fear my conscience would ruin my enjoyment of one obtained illegally.'

The poacher stared at him, outraged. 'But that's not true, your cook's had a good few from me at the kitchen door, and no complaints.'

'Is that so? I really couldn't say,' the churchman observed vaguely. 'The point is that it is my list, under my jurisdiction. The church will be delighted to embrace you. No-one is more welcome than a heathen convert.' He beamed encouragingly.

Bert turned his gaze onto the publican. 'I'm being blackmailed by a vicar,' he said, his tone a combination of bitterness and wonder. Stanley Tirrold's grin almost split his face as he nodded slowly.

'God works in mysterious ways,' the parson remarked.

*

The two farm workers who had left the inn earlier were a mile away, on a footpath that led up the Cherwell Valley. Their route took them through dense woodland, and they had just entered a clearing surrounded by towering trees. The last rays of evening sunlight angled down through the thick canopy of leaves like yellow bars of light penetrating a deep green pool.

The taller of the two nodded ahead through the gloom. 'That's Innes Knox.'

His companion looked up to see a pale, almost ghost-like figure standing uncertainly on the far side of the clearing. She had seen them. He raised his hand in recognition and called across.

'Good evening, Miss Knox.'

She gestured back. 'Hello.'

They came up to her and stopped. Innes smelled cider on their breath and felt a momentary flash of anxiety as they looked at her with interest.

'I came out for a stroll and missed my way. I'm staying with the Dances you know,' she said, thinking that the reminder would do no harm.

'Yes we know.' The shorter man appeared to be the spokesman of the pair.

'Would you be kind enough to direct me back to the village? I fear it will be dark soon.'

'Yes, I reckon it will be.' There was a short silence.

'And the way?' she prompted.

There was a curious hesitation in the man before he answered. 'The most direct way is straight back along the path,' he turned and gestured in the direction from which they had come, 'then turn right at the track and Rivermead will take you back to Great Tew. Not more than a mile.'

'Thank you, I'm grateful.' The men continued to stare at her in a hollow sort of way that she found both irritating and unnerving. 'Was there something else?' she asked, rather against her better judgement.

'Do you want us to walk you back, miss?' The taller man finally spoke.

Innes met his eye. She had been brought up amongst the tenements of Glasgow and was no innocent. 'That is a generous offer but I'm sure I can manage. On down the path and right at the junction.' She waved vaguely past the men.

'You'll be alright on your own then. You're sure?'

'Certainly. Of course I'm sure,' she replied firmly then moved to her left to pass them. After she had gone less than five yards a voice sounded behind her.

'Miss Knox.'

She turned. 'Yes?'

'Don't you stop now, not for anything. Just keep walking. You hear me?'

What an extraordinary thing to say.

'I assure you I am keen to get back to the village. Thank you again gentlemen.'

A minute later the path turned a corner and she glanced back. The men were still there, staring silently after her as the light faded from the sky.

Ignoring a feeling of unease she pressed on, making good speed, although it was increasingly hard to see where to put her feet. Ten minutes later with the heavily leafed trees meeting high overhead it became fully dark, and she tripped

14

and fell flat on her face. Climbing back to her feet with a muttered curse, she stood still for a moment rubbing her aching wrist and took stock.

Her senses were unpleasantly raised. There was a heavy feeling of expectation in the air, and an absolute silence that seemed artificial. None of the small comforting night time noises that she had become used to hearing though her open bedroom window penetrated the darkness. A prickle crept over her skin and a thought suddenly chimed in her head.

Something is coming. Something malign.

Heart beating hard, she pressed on painfully slowly, forced to place each foot carefully in the darkness. She sensed the path rise and swing to the right a little and was hugely relieved to see that, a hundred yards ahead, the trees formed a pale arch where it emerged from the wood.

Then she stopped and gasped in shock. A huge dog was standing side-on in the gap. It turned its head and stared directly through the darkness at her.

As she watched it leapt effortlessly out of sight and seconds later a stealthy rustle sounded behind her. Shaking with fear she slowly turned to face the noise, heart hammering against her chest. It was pitch black and yet she knew it was standing there. Close to her. Not six feet away.

A creature of the old places. The thought was instinctive and confusing.

All reason deserted her and that most fundamental of human instincts took over. Screaming loud and long she whirled round, lifted her skirts with one hand and sprinted through the trees towards the light, head up and going like a thoroughbred hunter in a steeplechase.

Somehow she stayed on her feet and then at last she was out of the woods and into what seemed like daylight by comparison. Fifty yards away she could see the junction with Rivermead and screaming *right, right,* in her head, she dashed around the corner and saw with unutterable relief the light of Great Tew market cross not far ahead.

She didn't stop running until she was on the high street but, once there, she paused and tried to regain her breath and her composure, before walking up to Marston House where she and Jaikie lived as long-term guests.

'Ah Innes, we were just about to send out a search party,' Colonel Dance joked as she appeared in the drawing room.

'Yes I am sorry, Jocelyn. I wandered too far and lost my way. Fortunately a couple of men pointed me in the right direction.'

'Are you all right?' his wife Eve asked, noting her drawn expression and high colour.

'To tell you the truth I had a rather intimidating meeting in the woods. I think it was a dog. It chased me and I really had to run for it.'

'A dog?' the colonel was looking at her with a strange expression.

'Yes, huge. A horrible black thing.' She shivered.

'Where were you Innes?' Eve asked.

'I'm not sure exactly. On a track in some woods. When I came out of them I turned right onto Rivermead and was soon back in the village.'

She saw the colonel and his wife exchange glances. 'I think you were in Hanger Wood. At least that is what it's called on the map. Around here it's known as Black Dog Spinney.'

'Well someone should keep the infernal creature locked up. It nearly scared me to death.'

'That's the thing. No-one around here owns a big black dog. They wouldn't dare, I'm certain of it.' An uneasy expression appeared on the colonel's face as he looked at her then added quietly, 'Tales of that dog go back hundreds of years. Its appearance is said to presage a death. A bad death. Infernal creature might be closer than you think'.

*

Muttering darkly about the declining probity of the church, Bert Williams left the Black Horse and walked down the high street to the market cross, then turned towards his cottage on Rivermead, unaware that Innes Knox had sprinted in the opposite direction earlier. A deal had been struck with the vicar and he was committed to his bible classes and sermon.

Preoccupied as he was, he failed to notice a sharp-featured boy standing in the shadow of a thatched cottage further down the high street. As Bert passed out of sight, he slid a dark canvas bag over his shoulder, eased out of the doorway, and drifted past the window like a ghost, before hopping over a gate and disappearing down a narrow footpath that led into woodland.

Twelve year old Thomas Dunn was the man of the house now, and he was going poaching.

In 1916 his mother had stood in the same doorway, twenty two years old and pregnant, and bravely waved her husband off to war. She hadn't seen him since. The dreaded telegram boy had arrived seven months later, leaving Mrs Dunn to cope with three children on a seamstresses' wage that left them poor and sometimes hungry. The Langford Estate had helped, but with twenty seven such telegrams having arrived during the four years of war there was a limit to what could be done.

The boy made his way downhill through thick woods towards the river. He could smell autumn coming in the night air and his pulse quickened with the thought of returning with a couple of fat trout in his bag. He'd just put them on the kitchen table and creep back to bed, leaving his mother to find them in the morning. *Supper for a night, maybe two. She'd be pleased.*

As the slope flattened out he left the path and slowed down, moving silently and with great care through the trees, every sense alert for either of the estate's gamekeepers. Downstream, the famous Lath Pool was one of the best waters on the Cherwell and a favourite for Lord Langford and his house guests. The wide grassy meadows on either side made casting with a fly rod easy.

But young Thomas Dunn carried no rod. Here, where the woods came right down to the river's edge, he was going after trout the way his dad had taught him. He stood motionless in the trees for twenty long minutes, staring across the rippling silver and black water. To his right rapids rattled musically, forcing him to rely on sight alone.

When he was satisfied no gamekeeper lurked in the shadows he took off his jacket and shirt. His lean body glowed pale in the moonlight, every rib showing as he wormed his way forward through the narrow margin of long, wet grass until he was right next to the river, then gently lowered his right arm shoulder-deep into the cold water. Working by touch alone he gently wriggled his fingers and

18

slowly moved his hand upstream to the spot where he knew a trout often lay under the bank.

There it was. A thrill ran through him.

Moving his fingers with exquisite sensitivity he tickled the fish, eyes shut and mouth open in concentration as its cold flesh sent coursing signals up his arm.

It's a big one, he thought delightedly, imagining his mother's face when she saw it on the kitchen table. He stiffened his body, braced his boots against the grass and, in one smooth movement, gripped the fish and flicked himself over.

A muted cry echoed between the trees as a sharp pain shot up his arm and across his shoulders. His body had moved but the fish had not, and his muscles had paid the price. As the ache subsided, he rolled onto his stomach and leant over the bank.

The water rippled enigmatically. Curious he slipped his hand under the surface and felt around. The thing was still there, and he gripped it again and pulled steadily. It moved a little and he redoubled his efforts. Suddenly it came away and he saw a dim white shape moving underwater. A moment later a wrinkled hand appeared, attached to a bare forearm around which his own hand was tightly wrapped. He shrieked and let go, but the horror continued as a face bearing an appalling rictus grin rose to the surface and showed clear in the moonlight, hair weaving gently in the current.

Thomas shuffled frantically backwards on his hands and feet then stared transfixed as the body drifted lazily out towards centre of the pool, slowly rotating, and looking for all the world like an old man floating on his back in the last swim of the season. It hit a rock and turned, then flicked backwards against another. For a moment the water held it there and Thomas gave a low moan as the man's open eyes stared across the pool and met his gaze. Then its arm came up and over in a ghoulish parody of a farewell gesture and it slipped away down river and out of sight.

'Holy Mary,' the boy whispered. But then his face tightened. As his eyes had met the dead man's he had recognised him.

'You got it in the end then. Good riddance, you coward,' he said out loud.

Chapter Two

The prime minister's Rolls Royce took seven minutes to drive from Downing Street to Buckingham Palace, where it was admitted via a side gate and came to a halt next to a door which opened as he emerged from the car.

'Good afternoon, Prime Minister.' The equerry's greeting was as familiar as the route along two long corridors and up one flight of stairs. During the war the prime minister and King George the Fifth had met every week and, when peace had been declared, they had continued this arrangement by mutual agreement. The two men entered an ante-room and Lloyd George came to halt as his escort crossed the room, opened another door, and announced, 'The prime minister, Your Majesty'.

'Come in, will you.' The reply carried to the politician who obeyed the instruction, entering a simply furnished study dominated by a large desk with three chairs facing it.

The two men greeted each other with a combination of familiarity and caution. During the latter stages of the war the prime minister's open feud with General Haig, the senior British commander had finally led the exasperated general to approach the king directly for support. In Lloyd George's opinion His Majesty had overreached his constitutional position as a result. The resulting tensions had never boiled over, but the memory remained and both men exuded a certain wariness as the footman served tea and then withdrew, leaving them alone.

After a brief amount of small talk the king asked, 'How are the negotiations with our allies on the reparations committee going? Have you reached an agreement about the bill the Germans will have to pay?

'We are making progress Your Majesty, but the French are pushing hard for a very high figure and the Belgians are with them. As you know, in public I too am demanding a tough settlement, but in private I see no merit in presenting the Germans with a bill they cannot possibly pay and have instructed the foreign secretary accordingly. He is meeting me tomorrow morning so I will be better able to update you next week'.

The king nodded and sipped his tea, then remarked, 'I have received a letter from my cousin'.

Lloyd George raised his head in surprise. 'Your cousin, the Kaiser?'

'My cousin the ex-Kaiser, who now lives in exile in the Netherlands,' the man behind the desk corrected.

The prime minister smiled inwardly. He had no doubts about the king's patriotism but was well aware that the head of the British Empire had only jettisoned his German aristocratic titles and changed the family name from Saxe-Coburg-Gotha to Windsor in 1917, three years into the war.

The king continued, 'You'll recall he was forced to abdicate at the very moment the ceasefire was being negotiated, and it fell to Ludendorff, the German supreme commander, to decide whether to accept the allied terms for a ceasefire. Apparently when he read them he was appalled but told Ertzburger to do the best he could, and then sign.'

Lloyd-George nodded. 'He had no choice. The German people were starving due to our naval blockade and the country was on the verge of a full scale revolution.'

'Yes, I think you are right. Anyway, in his letter cousin Wilhelm has clearly intended to communicate something specific, and it is relevant to you and Curzon.'

'I am all ears, Your Majesty.'

'Apparently there is continuing widespread unrest in Germany, directed at one of the articles in the Treaty of Versailles. It is number,' he peered at a notepad on his desk, 'Two hundred and thirty-one. The one where they acknowledge they caused the war.'

'Yes. The guilt clause, as I believe it is nicknamed.'

'Just so. Ludendorff is stoking the fires of public outrage by claiming that Germany didn't start the war and was not defeated. My cousin's message to me is that the German government will pay to rebuild the infrastructure destroyed during the conflict, but not the costs the allies incurred in fighting the war. Politically and socially they can go no further. The people will not take it.'

'I doubt they can afford it either, Your Majesty. Even with that proviso the bill is going to be enormous. Germany was our second largest trading partner before the war. The empire will not be well served by driving them to financial ruin in the longer term.'

'Agreed. Anyway, I trust this will help to inform your discussions with our allies.' He hesitated, then strode to the and stared down at the Buckingham Palace garden. 'This letter may be the precursor to more horse-trading about who exactly was responsible for the Great War. There can be no doubt about that. It was Germany and they must pay. And be seen to pay. You are with me on that I am sure.'

'I am, sir. We will hold the line, believe me.'

*

The following morning Sir Anthony Kerr, permanent secretary at the Foreign Office, stood in his impressive office and stared out of the window. The first floor room looked out over the back of the building and below him a mixture of horse-drawn and motor vehicles passed along Horse Guards Road. On the far pavement he could see two Norland Nannies in their brown uniforms pushing identical perambulators. One was talking animatedly and, as they turned onto a path that led into the trees of St James's Park, the other threw her head back and laughed with delight.

Simple lives and no cares, he thought, rather wistfully. Hearing the door open, he turned and greeted the tall thin young man who entered. 'Morning, Halley.'

'Good morning Permanent Secretary, here is your personal post.' He placed the bundle on his desk and added, 'The Foreign Secretary is heading down to the foyer, he will meet you there.' He glanced at his watch. 'Twenty to ten, sir, you'd better be on your way.'

Kerr nodded and shortly afterwards emerged from his office and joined Lord Curzon by the front door. They walked from the Foreign Office to Downing Street. For once the prime minister's day was running to schedule and at ten o'clock precisely they were shown into his office.

Once they were settled he said, 'I've been informed privately that the Germans will undertake to pay for the damage caused by the war, but that is all. They insist that they are not solely responsible for starting the conflict and will not cover the costs the allies incurred in fighting it.'

He shuffled the papers in his desk and found what he was looking for. 'This damned article two three one in the Versailles Treaty is causing a great deal of trouble over there.' He read it out.

'Germany and her allies accept responsibility for causing all the loss and damage to which the Allied and Associated Governments and their nationals have been subjected as a consequence of the war imposed upon them by the aggression of the Enemy States.'

'We are familiar with the clause, Prime Minister,' the foreign secretary remarked dryly.

'Germany descending into chaos will do the British Empire no favours. I want you to persuade the French to give ground.'

Curzon looked at him. 'They have been intransigent so far.'

Sir Anthony added, 'It is looking as though the total account presented to Germany will be the equivalent of around seven billion pounds Sterling.'

Lloyd-George stared at him in astonishment. 'Good lord, that'll break them. The country will be bankrupt within two years, and we'll have another war on our hands.'

Kerr nodded gravely and said, 'We have an idea about how to address the issue so that everyone's needs are met.' He went on to explain.

When he had finished the prime minister nodded briefly. 'Alright. I will leave the pair of you to persuade the French. But remember, article two three one establishes Germany's moral responsibility to pay reparations, and nothing must dilute that, or they'll try to wriggle off the hook completely.'

Curzon and Kerr walked back to the Foreign Office and parted on the first floor landing. The permanent secretary returned to his office and made some notes, then picked up the bundle of letters that Halley had delivered earlier. He flicked through them and one with a Paris postmark caught his eye. It was addressed to him personally, and marked 'strictly private and confidential, addressee only'.

Curious, he opened the envelope, withdrew a single piece of paper, and began to read. A minute later he put the letter down on his blotter and leaned back, his face grey with shock.

'My god,' he whispered. 'Oh my god.'

*

In Great Tew the discovery of the body rattled around the village like a bee in an empty milk churn.

Lord Colin, father of Piers Spense the current Lord Langford, had worked hard to balance tradition with improved efficiency and perhaps his greatest triumph was the introduction of electrical power across the 20,000 acre estate. When a new steam-powered mill opened in Banbury the old watermill upstream of Lath Pool had become redundant, and the noble lord had commissioned a hydro installation that drove a generator in a newly built power house on the river bank.

26

The hall had been the first beneficiary of this innovation, followed by the cottage hospital. But in the following years cables had been laid across the estate, so when he died in 1916 Lord Colin knew that that Langford was well placed to take advantage of the new wave of electrical appliances that were appearing for use in homes and on farms,

A taciturn but efficient engineer named Givell was employed to look after the electricity supply. So when, at half past six the morning after Thomas Dunn's adventures, Mrs Sutton, the cook up at Langford Hall, flicked the light switch by the kitchen door to no good result, she was surprised, then irritated. Turning, she called down the corridor to the scullery boy who had just emerged tousle-haired from his room.

'The electric is off Harold. Run down to Mr Givell's house and tell him, will you. And look sharp, Lord Langford is off to London this morning and his breakfast won't wait. If he can't mend it quickly, I'll have to light the range.'

The boy disappeared out of the back door. Fifteen minutes later the engineer emerged from his cottage and strode quickly downhill towards the power house. A row of sweet chestnut trees edged the stony footpath and his boots pushed through their fallen leaves, filling the early morning air with a wet, ripe, smell as he turned over possible problems in his mind.

He arrived at the power house and unlocked the door. Inside all seemed normal but a glance at the gauge showed that no current was being produced. He checked some basics but, finding no obvious fault, he walked upstream to the mill where the Archimedes screw was installed. Even as he approached he had an inkling of what was wrong. Normally the outfall produced a busy sound of rushing water, but nothing carried to him through the still air. As he passed, he could see that there was barely a trickle emerging from bottom of the screw casing.

Grunting in acknowledgement, he climbed a flight of wooden steps to the head of the inflow pipe where a narrow gauge mesh was bolted into place to stop any floating branches or leaves blocking the machinery.

One glance was all it took. One glance, and a sharp intake of breath.

Four hundred years earlier, the builders of the leat had known their business. There was no weir by the mill, the channel from the river upstream was six hundred yards long and narrowed steadily so the flow at the end was powerful. Strong enough, in fact, to pin and hold the corpse so that it rested with its back against the intake grid, arms outstretched to either side and head and shoulders raised up out of the water. Its dead eyes stared upstream as though waiting for Charon the ferryman to come into sight.

'Holy Mary,' muttered Mr Givell, unaware that young Thomas Dunn had used the same expression just nine hours earlier.

He looked up as a pair of crows landed on the bank and eyed the corpse speculatively. 'Oh no you don't!' he said. And, taking off his jacket, reached across and draped it over the man's head, shielding his eyes. Then with another quick glance around, he set off at a fast pace back uphill towards the village. He went straight to the police house and disturbed Constable Burrows at his breakfast.

Ten minutes later, aware that the power was off, villagers noticed the hasty passage of the engineer and the policeman carrying a folding stretcher back down the track. Sensing something was amiss, those who had nothing better to do followed them.

The upshot of this was that when, forty minutes after his momentous discovery, Mr Givell and Constable Burrows prised the unfortunate corpse off the intake pipe, a small crowd had gathered, alerted by that strange news-transmitting osmosis that permeates close-knit communities.

The Reverend Tukes arrived five minutes later and took command, the dead being his business. 'Do you recognise him Burrows?' the clergyman asked, as the crowd stared in silence. They knew who it was, and what it meant.

The policeman had a long look just to make sure, but there was little doubt in his mind. 'It's Dunstan Green I reckon, Vicar'.

'That's him for sure,' a woman's voice sounded behind him. 'Drowned himself, most likely. And for good reason.' A stir of agreement sounded through the crowd.

Burrows frowned. 'Alright, that'll do.'

'I agree, it's Dunstan Green,' Tukes said. He looked at the constable, 'Have we got a sheet to cover him?' he asked quietly. 'Best get him up to the hospital, so Dr Knox can have a look.'

Turning to the crowd of deeply absorbed villagers he announced, 'As you can see there has been a terrible accident. It appears Dunstan Green has drowned in the river.' Would four of you help to take the body up the hill. The rest of you please return to your normal duties.'

Directed with quiet authority by the elderly vicar, the volunteer bearers lifted the corpse onto the stretcher and led the remainder of the crowd towards the track up the hill.

As they followed the mournful procession, Burrows took Tukes' arm for a moment and held him back. 'An accident you reckon, Vicar?'

'Well you're the policeman but I couldn't see any other indications, could you?'

'No, nothing obvious. It's just… well, you know, with it being him.'

But the vicar just shook his head and paced on up the hill, deep in thought.

*

Half way down the main street in Great Tew a wide gravel gap gave on to a pair of handsome black wrought-iron gates topped with gold spikes. From there the red Tudor bricks of Langford Hall were just visible through the mature trees that dotted the parkland. At half past eight nineteen year old Lilly White, lady's maid to Claire Spense, the Dowager Lady Langford, climbed the back stairs in a state of considerable excitement. As usual she carried a breakfast tray for her mistress bearing a copy of the London Times, a single brown boiled egg, two rounds of toast, and Mrs Sutton's home-made marmalade.

But, perhaps more importantly, she was also bearing deliciously exciting news.

She entered her mistress's bedroom without knocking, placed the tray on a bedside table then crossed to the bay window and drew the curtains. As light flooded into the room she smiled affectionately at the gently stirring lump under the covers and said, 'Good morning my lady.'

'And to you Lilly.' The grey hair and refined features of the mother of the current Lord Langford emerged into view. She raised herself up and leaned forward as her maid organised the pillows and placed her breakfast on a bed tray. 'Anything in the paper?' she enquired.

'Nothing of note on the front page, my lady,' Lilly replied.

Her mistress grunted. 'Just another new day then.'

'Not for everyone, madam.'

Lady Langford caught the barely concealed excitement in her tone. 'Has something happened?'

The maid's words tumbled out in a rush. 'They've found a body in the mill leat. The electric was off this morning and Mr Givell went to the power house and found the corpus wedged across the pipe so it blocked the flow. Constable Burrows and the vicar have been down there, and they've brought it back up to the cottage hospital. The doctor will be having a look I reckon.'

Her mistress nodded thoughtfully. The building's cool, brick-lined, cellar was used as a morgue. 'Who is it?'

'It's Dunstan Green, my lady.'

'Oh really? Did he drown?'

'That's what they're saying, yes.'

Lady Langford frowned, then picked up the teaspoon and tapped it down firmly on her egg. The shell broke and a trickle of bright yellow yolk oozed down the shell. 'Perfect,' she said with some satisfaction. 'Alright Lilly, run my bath and come back in twenty minutes.'

The maid bobbed and disappeared into the adjoining bathroom to carry out these instructions. Left alone, Lady Langford set about the boiled egg with her usual gusto, but after a couple of mouthfuls she sighed and put the spoon down.

A premature death on the estate was always unwelcome, but this time she felt a particular sense of unease. She stared out of the window pensively and then slowly resumed her egg, but for the rest of the morning she was unable to shake off a lingering feeling that the young man's death wasn't the end of something, but the beginning.

*

Innes Knox arrived at the cottage hospital at the same time as the stretcher-bearers. She noticed the corpse had been carried through the village uncovered and wondered if it was a conscious act of disrespect, or a simple lack of a sheet. Putting the thought to one side she directed the men down the stairs to the cellar where a wooden table lay below a single unshaded light.

In a few short sentences the engineer explained the chain of events, while Burrows and Tukes looked on. A couple of the men who had carried Dunstan Green up the hill loitered in the shadows, clearly intent on picking up as much of the finer detail of the discovery as possible and she dismissed them with a no-nonsense, 'You can go now, thank you gentlemen'.

No-one spoke as they climbed up the stairs, and the constable couldn't help noticing how the stark shadows from the bulb picked out the angular beauty in the young doctor's face. He wondered if she was going to marry Edward Spense, Lady Langford's youngest son, as was strongly rumoured amongst the villagers. As the cellar door at the top of the stairs clicked shut, his idle speculation was interrupted.

'Is there anything to indicate his death is suspicious, Constable?' The doctor's Scottish accent seemed more noticeable in the quiet of the informal morgue.

He shrugged slightly. 'Not as of this moment, but we thought you ought to have a look.'

'But for now the assumption is that he fell into the river and drowned. Or possibly took his own life?'

He nodded. 'Either of those.'

'Very well, I will examine him. Do you wish to stay?'

No-one did, and they left the doctor to her work. Tukes headed back up the hill to the vicarage and Mr Givell returned to the mill to check for damage. Burrows was intercepted by Laura, his wife, as he called into the police house. He outlined what had happened and said he was going to Marston House to inform Colonel Dance. The colonel was the chief constable of the county of Oxfordshire and, although technically Burrows reported to a sergeant in Banbury, for obvious practical and diplomatic reasons he ensured that Jocelyn Dance was kept abreast of events in his own village.

'Did he kill himself do you think?' his wife asked.

Her husband put his helmet on and checked it in the mirror. 'It's most likely an accident. But all possibilities remain open.' He kissed her on the lips as the wail of a baby sounded from upstairs. They had married the previous Christmas Eve and Laura had given birth seven months later, a fact which had been noted with amused satisfaction and no judgement by the villagers, and Matilda Hermione Burrows had rapidly established herself as the most important member of the household.

The policeman smiled. 'Duty calls. For both of us.'

An hour later Innes made herself a cup of tea and drank it in the little two-bedded ward above the cellar. There was just one occupant, an elderly woman who had fallen and broken her hip and was under observation for a day or two. She chatted with her and the volunteer nurse who was tidying up, but in the main her mind was occupied with the results of her examination.

Innes was a dedicated doctor and furiously self-critical. She was well aware that she had made a mistake the previous year, when she had delayed too long before expressing her doubts about another corpse that had lain on the wooden table in the cellar. The chief constable's subsequent reproach had been painful, and she was anxious not to repeat her error.

When she called in at the police house looking for Burrows, Laura directed her up to Marston House. 'He was round there earlier, and the colonel telephoned asking him to come back.'

'How are you, and how's the baby?' the doctor asked with a smile, thinking her friend looked tired.

'Wonderful. Exhausting and wonderful,' the dark haired young woman replied.

After a short conversation they parted, and Innes walked up the high street to the handsome Georgian house. The colonel and Burrows were in his study, and she knocked and entered.

'Innes, come in. You have news?' the grey haired chief constable asked.

'I do. I've completed a preliminary examination of the body and one fact has become apparent straight away.'

'Which is?' The colonel's keen intelligence showed on his face.

'There is no water in Dunstan Green's lungs. He did not drown.'

Chapter Three

It was nine in the evening and Sir Anthony Kerr and Lord Curzon were still in the Foreign Office. The letter that the permanent secretary had received had horrified him and they had discussed it at length. No-one else was present and neither man was making notes.

As he poured another drink for the pair of them, Curzon remarked, 'You were there weren't you, when the ceasefire agreement was signed?'

'Yes, I was. In a railway carriage deep in the Forest of Compiégne. Admiral of the Fleet Sir Rosslyn Wemyss led the British delegation and of course Marshall Foch, the Supreme Allied Commander was there as well. At times I almost felt sorry for Ertzburger, the German negotiator, facing all that military top brass.' He smiled faintly and added, 'The French softened him up by making sure the train that brought him went on a circuitous route through all the devastation. So he understood the impact of the war on France. When he finally arrived, Foch and Wemyss simply laid out a series of demands and told him to take it or leave it. They even refused his request for a ceasefire while they worked out the terms.'

'Yes, I'd heard that.' Curzon handed him the brandy and Kerr nodded his thanks and continued.

'It was all finally agreed at five in the morning on the eleventh of November. Hostilities were to end at eleven o'clock. The haste to get the ceasefire agreement completed was so great that the last page of it was typed first, and they all signed that, without an official version of the rest of the document attached,' he remarked. 'Incredible really.'

'They were in a hurry. Nearly three thousand men died on that last day of the war.' Curzon met his eye, his face grimly serious. 'We need that document, Kerr. Whatever it takes. Otherwise there will be another war and we may well find ourselves fighting it alone'

*

Sir Anthony travelled to Oxford by train. He was alone and in haste; an uncharacteristic mood of melancholy possessing him. Lord Curzon had a reputation for arrogance and was inclined to bluntness, but his most senior civil servant was a dapper and twinkling man whose keen intelligence and charm normally adorned him like a glittering cloak. But as he neared his destination, he found his mood darkening.

The human cost of the Great War in terms of death and injury from gun and shellfire had been appalling, but the level of physical destruction was also hard to conceive. The Red Zone as the French called the area of complete devastation was twenty miles wide and stretched for two hundred miles from the Belgium coast to Verdun. Four hundred square miles where there was simply nothing left apart from mud, barbed wire, and abandoned trenches. And the unrecovered bodies of hundreds of thousands of men.

37

Lord Curzon was right, another war in Europe was unthinkable. He pursed his lips and stared out of the window as the train slowly rolled into Oxford station.

Lady Langford sent Fenn in the Alvis to collect him from the station and at twelve thirty the estate car rolled across the gravel turning circle and stopped below the main entrance to the hall. As the chauffeur opened his door, Dereham appeared, followed by Lady Langford.

She was shocked at his appearance, thinking he looked strained and much older than she remembered, but smiled graciously and said, 'Sir Anthony, what a pleasure to see you again'. She shook his hand and gestured to her two sons who had arrived in the doorway. 'You remember my boys, Piers, who is Lord Langford now, of course, and my youngest, Edward.'

'Yes indeed, I'm sorry it's been so long and thank you for seeing me at such short notice,' the formally dressed man replied. He looked back down the drive to where the tower of St Mary's rose above the trees and inhaled the sweet late summer air. 'I'd quite forgotten how beautiful it is here.' And with warm expressions of mutual regard, the party retired into the house and made their way to the drawing room, a handsome chamber adjacent to the small dining room.

'I thought we'd lunch at one-thirty if that suits, so we can deal with whatever matter is at hand first. Do have a seat. Sherry?' His hostess smiled and indicated a pair of large settees which were placed opposite each other in front of the fireplace.

Once drinks were served and Dereham had departed, Sir Anthony wasted little time in getting down to business. 'I'm sorry to say that I am the bearer of news that you will find upsetting.' He looked at them gravely. 'The truth is we may be at the start of a chain of events, the conclusion to which I cannot see clearly at this moment,' he said. 'It involves your family and the defence of the realm.'

As Piers and Edward stirred in surprise, Lady Langford raised her eyebrows and replied in her surprisingly low voice, 'Either you have developed a taste for the dramatic since I last saw you, or I fear we must brace ourselves. Well, out with it then Sir Anthony, what has happened?'

But instead of replying directly, he asked her a question. 'How much did you know of your husband's work, Lady Langford?'

She gestured vaguely. 'As much as the next wife, I imagine. He worked in the Foreign Office of course...'

Kerr nodded. 'He worked for me, in fact. I am the permanent secretary there and we liaised closely on many matters.' He looked at Piers and Edward. 'Your father was a capable man with a particular flair for, well, frankly, skulduggery. He was heavily involved in the collection of information about the activities of our enemies overseas, normally through our embassies but also sometimes directly. He worked with a wide range of individuals who saw reason to work for us. Some of those people were motivated by patriotism or finer feelings, others by money, but whatever their reasons, Lord Colin was their commander. He was, in modern parlance, the chief spy of the British Empire.'

'Good lord,' Piers muttered. 'Did you have no idea at all, mother?'

Lady Langford had drained her sherry in a single gulp and was heading across the room for the decanter. 'No I did not. I assumed he was in some administrative role of course, but I had no idea what he was administering.'

Edward was smiling. 'Good old father, batting for Blighty all those years, and he never said a word about it.'

Kerr smiled wryly. 'As you can imagine, never saying a word is a key component of the role.'

'So why are you here now?' asked Piers.

There was a pause as Lady Langford returned with the decanter. I'll leave that there,' she said putting it on the coffee table. 'I fear Sir Anthony is just getting started.'

'Thinking back to 1916, when your father was discovered in his study the morning after his heart attack, were there any concerns, any anomalies at all?' the Whitehall man enquired.

The three of them stared at him. 'Meaning what exactly?' asked Piers.

Kerr sighed. 'We have received information which suggests that your father was murdered. I am sorry.'

There was a profound silence in the drawing room. 'I beg your pardon?' Lady Langford said finally, in a small voice.

'The death certificate was signed by a Doctor Hall. I presume he is the local man? He didn't express any concerns, confidentially perhaps, to you?' Kerr looked at the woman opposite.

She shook her head, visibly still trying to come to terms with what she had heard. 'No, nothing. Colin had been working late. The maid found him at eight o'clock the following morning lying on the study floor and raised the alarm. The assumption was that he had had a heart attack.'

'Were his papers still on the desk?' Kerr leaned forward.

'There were some there I think, scattered around. We sent them back to London eventually.' She hesitated for a moment and then said, 'Look, what exactly is the nature of this suggestion. Who has made it?'

'Quite. Good question,' Edward added.

Sir Anthony looked at the three of them. 'Of course it is a good question, and you deserve an answer. Before I do so, I have to ask for a solemn undertaking that you will never speak of it outside this room, unless it is to me directly. Your discretion is of the utmost importance. Do I have your oath on that?'

'I notice you are asking before we have the information that you are about to disclose. I hope in making such a commitment we will not be putting the Spense family or Langford at a disadvantage.' Lady Langford's quiet voice was clear in the room and, as she returned his gaze, Kerr saw the poise and depth of character that his hostess possessed.

These people are part of a long, long, line. They've weathered many things.

'I do not believe that is the case, Lady Langford,' he replied, 'and I should tell you that I had to obtain specific permission from the prime minister to discuss the matter with you.'

'The Welsh wizard himself? Did you indeed,' She glanced at her sons. 'Very well, you may proceed.'

41

'Thank you.' The man opposite paused, then began to speak. 'If you'll forgive me I will recap a little history. Does the date 28th June 1914 strike a chord with you at all?'

His question was met with blank looks. 'Nothing particular springs to mind, but it was six years ago,' Piers remarked.

'Sarajevo?' Sir Anthony prompted.

Edward clicked his fingers in satisfaction. 'It's the date that the heir to the Austro-Hungarian throne was assassinated.'

Kerr nodded. 'Yes, you are correct Mr Spense, Arch-Duke Ferdinand and his wife were on a state visit to Sarajevo, the capital of Bosnia-Herzegovina, which had recently become part of the Austro-Hungarian empire. Serbia was furious with the Austrians for taking control of their neighbours. Unfortunately, the date of the visit was also the anniversary of Serbia's defeat in battle by the Turks – a black day in their history.' He shrugged, 'Perhaps it was accidental, perhaps not. Either way, the Serbs took it as a deliberate slight and that was enough to inspire violence.'

He paused and sipped his sherry, eyeing them over the top of his glass before continuing.

'History turns on such mistakes. There were two attempts on their majesties' lives. As they progressed through Sarajevo in an open top car, a bomb was thrown which missed their vehicle but caused damage and casualties to the one behind. Later that day they insisted on visiting the injured in hospital and it was on that unplanned trip that a young activist from the nationalist Serbian Black Hand movement saw his chance. He shot both Ferdinand and his wife as they sat in their car. She died on the spot, the Arch-Duke an hour or two later.'

'Yes I remember now,' Lady Langford said. 'My husband was very distracted by it at the time.'

'As well he might have been,' Kerr observed. 'The young assassin was a man called Gavrilo Princip and he worked for the British government.'

'What!' Edward's startled exclamation struck a discordant note in the quiet drawing room.

Sir Anthony nodded gravely. 'He had been passing back useful information about Balkan politics and at the time it suited our purposes to support the Black Hand people, but we had no inkling that he had gone rogue. And of course his actions regarding the Arch-Duke were not at our behest. Far from it.'

'But he was one of my father's men?' Edward said.

'Just so. And therein lies the difficulty.' Sir Anthony spread out his hands in a slightly embarrassed gesture. 'Paperwork is the bane of the civil service and in order to release the funds for any such enterprise there had to be an agreement. Your father had written a letter in secret to Princip proposing the terms on which he would be retained, and the remuneration could expect. The man accepted by countersigning a copy and returning it to London, via the British consulate in Sarajevo. Once it was in the file matters could proceed.'

'So there's even red tape in the spying business,' Piers observed. 'Who'd have thought it?'

Sir Anthony continued, 'The night your father died he had the Black Hand file with him here at Langford. In due course, it made its way back to the office in London and there matters rested until yesterday morning, when I received a rather alarming letter. It has been written anonymously but the sender makes two claims. One is that he was present in your father's study that night and murdered him, although he offers no explanation as to how, or why. The second is that he is in possession of the countersigned letter from Princip that shows beyond doubt that the man who killed Arch-Duke Ferdinand was working for the British Empire. It would have been in the file here at Langford but is not now in the file in Whitehall.'

As the others digested this, Sir Anthony reached over and refilled his glass. They watched in silence. Then he looked at them, his face grim, and spoke quietly.

'The writer's intention appears to be some form of blackmail. Already, historians are writing about the origins of the Great War. On one side there was the triple alliance of Austro-Hungary, Germany and Italy. Facing them, the British in an entente with the French, and the Russians. When Arch-Duke Ferdinand was killed Austria declared war on Serbia believing that the Serb's ally, Russia, would keep out of it. This was a tragic miscalculation. Russia declared war on Austria, Germany came to its aid and subsequently threatened Belgium and France. The British were drawn in through our alliances and little over a month later the Great War had started.

The emerging consensus is that the assassination of the Arch-Duke set in motion the train of events that led to the conflict. And they are right. There is a clear line of sight from the slaughter of the Somme and Passchendaele, that leads all the way back to Gavrilo Princip's actions that day in Sarajevo.'

'My god,' Lady Langford whispered, her hand at her throat.

44

He met her eye. 'Oh yes. If the letter is true, the writer is in possession of a document that proves the man who caused the Great War was a British agent.'

*

The morgue at the Radcliffe hospital in Oxford was one of the most advanced in the country and it was to there that the body of Dunstan Green was sent. The accompanying letter from Colonel Dance was admirably succinct.

Dear Sir,

I would be grateful if you perform an urgent post mortem to ascertain the cause of death of this man, who was recovered from the River Cherwell yesterday. A preliminary examination suggests that he was dead before he entered the water.

I look forward to hearing from you.

Yours faithfully,

Col. Jocelyn Dance,

Chief Constable, Oxfordshire County.

The doctor in charge was called James Ferguson and he was an experienced pathologist. He quickly established that the man's lungs were devoid of water, confirming that death was not due to drowning. He then examined the body thoroughly for any evidence that might indicate a killing blow or stabbing but found nothing. There were some cuts and abrasions, but his conclusion was that these had been caused post-mortem, probably due to its immersion in the river.

He examined the stomach contents, which were normal, and took blood samples for analysis, asking the laboratory to check for a wide range of common poisons. The results came back negative. He also looked for signs of a heart attack, or cancer, but there were no such indications. Dunstan Green had been in excellent health.

At this point Dr Ferguson paused. The vast majority of corpses would have given up their secrets by now and he was momentarily stumped as to how to continue. He went to lunch to think about it.

In the hospital dining room he met a colleague and admitted to the impasse that the morning had presented him with. 'I've tried every obvious or common test and, frankly, drawn a blank. Any ideas, Worthing?'

They discussed the matter for some time, but Dr Worthing had little to offer beyond the actions Ferguson had already taken.

'The indications are that death was immediate,' the pathologist observed. 'Almost as if the poor man was struck by lightning, although that would have been obvious of course. The only anomaly is that the lab reported high levels of adrenalin in his blood. As though he was severely shocked or frightened immediately before he died.'

'Facing a threat, or possibly an attacker you mean?' Worthing spooned a piece of apple pie and custard into his mouth and chewed appreciatively before gesturing downwards. 'Very good this, you know. I always come in for it on a Thursday.'

'Yes it is,' Ferguson nodded rather distractedly before continuing, 'The police obviously want to know if it's murder but unless I can come up with something I'll have to admit that we simply don't know.' He frowned and added, 'You know it's an odd place, Great Tew. There have always been

46

rumours. It really does look as though the poor man died of shock. Almost as though something terrible confronted him…' he tailed off.

'Things that walk in the night?' Worthing smiled. 'Look, perhaps more prosaically, something else occurs. I don't wish to ruin your lunch, but have you considered the fate of King Edward the Second?'

His friend raised his eyebrows in surprise and stared at him. 'Good lord, I hadn't. I suppose it's a possibility but surely there would have been signs, and there were none.' He drummed his fingers on the table, thinking hard. 'Mind you, that does give me another possibility to check.' He pushed his chair back and stood up. 'Excuse me, Worthing. And thank you, you might just have put me on the right track.'

*

The report from the pathologist was delivered to Marston House at ten o'clock the following morning. The chief constable read it with interest, and considerable surprise. Later in the afternoon he chaired a meeting in his study with Burrows and Innes Knox to review the findings.

'You can both read the thing at your leisure, but for now I'll précis the formalities and get to the meat of the thing. Dunstan Green didn't drown,' he nodded approvingly at the young doctor, 'but also, he wasn't poisoned, shot, stabbed, or beaten to death. Nor did he have any medical condition.'

He beamed across his desk. 'Any ideas?'

Always keen to present himself well, Burrows thought hard, but as Dr Knox looked stumped, he didn't think it likely that he would solve the mystery. As she shook her head, the colonel said, 'I'll put you out of your misery then,' and read out the relevant passage.

'*Examination of the left ear of the corpse indicates that a long, sharp, needle-like tool, was driven with precision through the ear canal directly into the brain, resulting in immediate death. The probability of this occurring as a result of a natural accident is so remote as to be irrelevant. The conclusion must be that Dunstan Green was murdered by an assailant who intended to conceal the wound and therefore the manner of death. In this respect his subsequent immersion in the river may well have been deliberate as the water had removed all traces of blood, and water-related swelling to the flesh had concealed the wound to a great extent.*'

The colonel put the report down on the desk and said quietly, 'There we have it then. He was murdered in a fiendishly cunning way and his attacker then chucked him in the river in a further attempt to conceal the crime.'

'So it was pre-meditated then,' said Innes.

Burrows' brain clicked and whirred. 'Not necessarily,' he said slowly. 'It's possible that the actions were spontaneous. If it happened close to the river.'

'That seems unlikely. What about the weapon?' asked the chief constable.

A fleeting image ran through the young policeman's mind, and he chased after it, trying to bring it into focus. Aware of his abilities, the other two observed his efforts and waited in silence. And their patience was rewarded as Burrows finally caught up with the picture.

'What about a thatching needle? From what the pathologist says, that would fit the bill.' He warmed to his task. 'I'm not saying definitively, sir. Just suggesting that if Green met a thatcher who had reason to attack him, then the fellow would be equipped as is suggested in the report.'

'It's a possibility I suppose,' the chief constable admitted doubtfully. 'Plenty of farm workers carry them routinely. So we cannot at this point say whether the attack was premeditated, or someone simply saw a chance and took it.'

'Probably a thatcher,' added Innes helpfully.

'Possibly a thatcher,' corrected the constable.

'Either way we need to consider the motive,' the colonel remarked. 'Who would want Dunstan Green dead? I fear in that regard there may be a rather wide field. Twenty seven families in fact.'

There was a short silence then Burrows remarked, 'Twenty five actually, sir, two local families lost two sons in the war.'

Colonel Dance nodded slowly. 'True. To be honest anyone who sent a son to France had good reason to dislike the man, but the ill-feeling among many bereaved families about Green's behaviour places them at the head of the queue – certainly in the absence of any more significant evidence.'

He stared out of the window. Further up the street the cobbler's van from Banbury was pulled up outside the Black Horse. As he watched, a man leant down from the back and handed a box to Stanley Tirrold, who turned and carried it into the pub. His wife emerged and took another. The agricultural labourers bought one pair of boots a year and they did it in September, with their harvest money. By now, last year's would be worn thin and before long the bar of the pub would be full of men joking and trying on new boots.

49

It was a mutually convenient arrangement for the landlord and the cobbler, as the men took the opportunity to have a drink or two while they were there. He pictured the familiar scene. *Good men, who worked hard and had done their bit in the war.*

He cleared his throat. 'Look, we'll have to get to the bottom of this but I'm damned if I'm going to have a cloud of suspicion thrown over decent families who are still struggling to deal with the loss of a loved one. Maybe one of them did it, maybe not, but frankly Green was hardly a person of the highest calibre himself.'

'Shall we keep quiet about the murder for now then, sir?' asked Burrows.

The colonel nodded, his mind made up. 'Yes. As far as the public are concerned the man drowned in an accident. Or maybe took his own life in a moment of regret. I don't really care. But behind the scenes we will instigate enquiries. Or rather you will, Constable. There's a murder charge to be brought here and we must make every effort to bring it to fruition.'

He glanced at Innes and raised his eyebrows speculatively as an impish grin crept across his face. She leaned back and raised her hands. 'Oh no. No you don't, Jocelyn.'

Burrows turned to her. 'It would be a help, miss. You're not in uniform. You've got good reason to circulate around the estate, and people trust you. They might say things to you that they wouldn't say to me.'

'He's got a point you know Innes. You could get Edward involved again too. Just like last year,' the colonel added.

Her eyes narrowed. 'Yes, that ended well, didn't it?'

'Lessons learned and all that,' he replied blithely. 'The more I think about it, the more I feel this is a job for that discreet and reliable detecting firm of Burrows, Knox and Spense.'

He glanced at his watch. 'Well I'm glad that's agreed. If you'll excuse me I have to see a man about a pair of boots.' With that he rose and strode out of his study. Moments later the front door slammed shut and they watched him pass the window and cross the high street, clearly aiming for the Black Horse.

Burrows looked at her, mute appeal on his lugubrious face. Then he said, 'It's a big job for one man, miss. And you did have some good ideas when we were after Christian Freeling's murderer.'

'Did I, Constable? I really can't recall', she replied coolly. Then a pleasing idea came to her. 'What about Edward?'

'Well you have been spending time with him, miss. If you'll pardon my forwardness, I was thinking that you could persuade him.'

'Oh yes, there was a falling out between you wasn't there, Burrows?'

A pained look appeared on the policeman's face, and he stirred uneasily in his seat. 'There was. He stole my helmet and paraded round the market cross wearing it, when under the influence of drink.'

Trying to hide a smile, Innes said carelessly, 'You arrested him I believe? Finally'.

'He was rather lively, miss, but he spent a night in the cell, as I suspect you well know.'

'The whole village knows Burrows, and thoroughly enjoyed the incident. I believe one could have sold tickets. But at least your black eye has cleared up. Tell me, do you recall your price for assisting me with the Freeling investigation last year?'

The constable opposite her sighed. The young doctor waited. 'I do,' he said eventually.

'You knew I had fallen out with Edward, but you ruthlessly forced me to go cap in hand to ask him to join us. It was a most uncomfortable meeting.'

Burrows nodded glumly, it was all too apparent what was coming as an expression of benign malice appeared in the Glaswegian's face. 'Well what goes around, comes around,' she said briskly. 'That is my price Burrows. I'll come in if Edward comes in. I suggest you go and ask him.' She stood up. 'And you'd better do it nicely. Let me know, won't you.'

And with that she left the room, leaving the policeman sitting forlorn and alone in his chief constable's study, his helmet on his knees.

Chapter Four

Claire Spense and Eve Dance walked arm in arm across the wide parkland at the back of Langford Hall. At the top of the slope behind them, late afternoon sun glowed on the red walls of the three-storey Elizabethan mansion, while up ahead cropped grass ran flat for half a mile through widely spaced clusters of trees, before disappearing steeply downhill to the River Cherwell.

On the far side of the valley autumnal colours were starting to show in the chequerboard of fields and woods that covered the lower slopes, while high above the cultivated farmland the great whaleback ridge of Green Hill showed as a long, clean, line in the sky.

It was a favourite walk, which the close friends had taken together many times, and in many different moods – from deep grief over the death of Claire's husband Lord Colin and, less than eighteen months later, utter despair at the loss of her middle son Hugh at Cambrai, to delight at the news of a long-awaited grandchild for Eve, and joyful relief of the end of the war.

'That is a very fine hat, Eve,' Lady Langford observed as she linked arms with her.

'Isn't it splendid. My five year-old granddaughter also wholeheartedly approves. When I visited her up in town she asked if she could have it when I die.'

'Good heavens!' Her friend laughed. 'What did you say?'

'I suggested she wait until nearer the time. She asked me again an hour later.'

They strolled on chuckling, then Lady Langford addressed the most pressing business of the day.

'You heard about Dunstan Green of course?'

Eve nodded, 'Jocelyn told me that they found no water in his lungs. Apparently it means he didn't drown, but that is not public knowledge and must remain so.' She squeezed her friend's arm, although the trust between them was absolute and there was very little that they did not know of each other's lives.

'The implication being that he was dead when he entered the water? Possibly murdered?'

'Yes.' There was a short silence. Eve watched a group of the estate's Red Devon beef cattle grazing peacefully beyond a copse to their left. The sun on their russet-brown coats contrasted beautifully with the leaves on the oak trees and, not for the first time, she marvelled at the foresight of the men who had planted the beautiful parkland, in the certain knowledge that they would not be alive to see it in its prime.

Not in that life anyway, she thought.

'I'm not sure whether to feel sorry for him or not,' Lady Langford remarked.

Her friend nodded silently. She'd read in the paper that there had been around sixteen thousand conscientious objectors, once conscription started in 1916. Most had been

54

motivated by long-held religious or pacifist beliefs and many had served bravely in France as stretcher bearers or in labour battalions. But some had simply refused to have anything to do with the war at all. Dunstan Green was one of those and he had passed the last two years of the conflict in the safety of Dartmoor prison, working in a quarry gang with similar men.

When he had been released in 1919 and returned to Great Tew, he had been widely ostracised, particularly by families whose sons had not come back.

'Good heavens, there'll be plenty of grass here in the spring,' Eve smiled as the two women changed direction to avoid a series of large cow pats and Lady Langford continued her train of thought.

'I do hope someone from the estate hasn't taken matters into their own hands. Desperate grief can drive people to desperate acts,' she paused before adding dryly, 'as I should know'.

Eve gave her a small smile of recognition, before remarking, 'There will have to be an investigation I suppose, although the thought of suspicion falling on those bereaved families is intolerable. Many of them are barely managing as it is.'

'I know.' Claire stopped and turned to her friend. 'Eve, I must confess to feeling uneasy. Something about this death has rung alarm bells. Almost as though it's part of something bigger. And perhaps much worse. Do you sense anything?'

Eve looked at her thoughtfully. The previous evening she had gone up to one of the standing stones that formed the huge outer ring around a smaller Neolithic stone circle called

Creech Hill Ring. The inner and outer circles of stones marked a junction where two of the streams of energy that run across the earth collide and, for people like Eve Dance, it was a place of extraordinary power concealed in plain sight. It was her habit to spend time there, letting her mind drift in the clean white air high above the ancient landscape.

'I was at the Litha stone last night, occupied with other things, but I did feel something. Like the echo of thunder on a Summer's night. Or gunfire.' The final two words were out before she realised.

Gunfire? Distant gunfire? Was that what she had heard?

'Was it something to do with Great Tew do you think? Or the war?' her friend asked.

'I'm not sure,' Eve replied uncertainly. She smiled at Claire. 'Nothing to worry about anyway.'

'I hope not. After that business last year, the last thing we need is more trouble.'

They walked on, each occupied with their own thoughts. Then, changing the mood, Eve asked, 'And what of Edward? How is the relationship with Innes going? I'm afraid she is rather tight-lipped about it at Marston House, despite my best efforts to draw her out.'

His mother smiled ruefully. 'The same here, I'm afraid. Since he moved back to the hall I had hoped to work on him a little, and I am still convinced that the pair of them would be happy together. Of course events last year delayed things greatly. Innes was very ill for weeks and weeks, although at least she did finally jettison those dreadful glasses.'

Eve nodded. Both Innes and Edward had suffered life threatening injuries the previous year and there had been a long delay before any idea of romance had been realistic. But summer had come and gone and, whilst they had spent time together and seemed happy in each other's company, an engagement announcement had been stubbornly absent.

'Innes had her doubts about getting involved romantically with anyone. Do you think she still feels the same?'

Eve frowned briefly and said, 'I think she might be persuaded, indeed she indicated as such to me, but it will take a committed and patient suitor,'

'And there lies the problem,' the older woman sighed. 'As well as the shell shock and his breakdown, Edward was also deeply affected by the grief amongst families that lost loved ones during the war. And he felt Hugh's loss dreadfully. I do think he cares for Innes, but I suspect fear of exposing himself to more pain is holding him back.'

As she finished speaking, five strokes of the great bell of St Mary's sounded mournfully over the parkland. 'Shall we turn back?' Eve suggested.

'Yes, come and have a sherry before I dress for dinner,' her friend replied.

As the two friends walked back towards the hall, the low sun throwing long shadows across the grass, Edward Spense was standing in the rick yard at Home Farm, a quarter of a mile away. Although the majority of the farms on the estate were let to tenants who been there for generations, five of the closest farms to the hall were run directly by Giles Stafford, the land agent. Since recovering from his wounds, Edward had been helping out, and they had just returned from cutting hay in three north-facing fields that were always the last to be cropped.

Samson and Delilah, the two great steam engines that were shared across the estate were hissing in the lane and the four fully laden hay wains that they had pulled from the fields were lined up neatly along the far wall. A dozen tired men waited for their instructions. They had left for the fields before dawn and not been back during the day.

'Edward, I think I'll send the men home and build the hay rick tomorrow,' Stafford said. Then raising his voice, he called out, 'Get a tarpaulin over each of the wains please gentlemen, then back here tomorrow at half past seven for the rick building. You'll find a barrel of cider in the small barn, if you'd care to refresh yourselves when you're done.'

Edward looked down the yard to where one huge haystack had already been built. To reduce the danger of a fire, a vertical pipe had been buried in its centre and, with its thatched roof and chimney, it looked like a cottage. On the opposite side to the barns, eight large circular ricks were lined up along the wall. These were the corn stacks, built with sheaves made in the fields and tied with unique knots that identified each farm, so the yield could be tallied as the stacks were built. These too were neatly thatched and watertight and would sit through the winter until the corn was threshed and sent to the mill in the Spring.

All is safely gathered in..., he was just allowing his mind to drift back to the first harvest festival he'd organised as the newly ordained vicar of St Mary's in 1914, when he saw his older brother Piers appear from the track that led to the hall.

'Good evening, Lord Langford,' Stafford smiled as he approached. The men had an easy but respectful relationship, each aware of the fact they needed each other, and during the war they had worked closely to keep the estate functioning as men had gone off to fight.

'Hello, Piers,' Edward added.

'Stafford, Edward,' the plump dark-haired man replied. He was wearing a comfortably worn but beautifully cut tweed suit and a dark brown trilby. 'All in?'

'Yes, we're just getting these wains covered and then they'll build the rick tomorrow.'

'Excellent. I imagine there's a barrel of cider lurking somewhere is there? I'll just have a drink with the men.' He crossed the yard to a chorus of 'Afternoon, My Lord,' and disappeared into the small barn.

Edward watched him go. 'Good at that sort of thing isn't he,' he remarked to the land agent.

'Better than many,' Stafford agreed. 'He inherited the common touch from his father, as did you, incidentally.'

'Well, maybe, but in the days before I had my breakdown in the trenches I lost the respect of the men. They could sense their padre was just going through the motions. The effect of these things lingers long after the events.'

'Is that why you shut yourself away at Holly Cottage when they shipped you back?'

'That and other things.'

The men completed covering the wains and clattered across the yard to the small barn. Stafford said, 'Well, I think I'll have a drink too. Are you coming?'

'In a moment.' Edward nodded vaguely. Left alone he stared down the yard, a familiar acrid smell in his nostrils. Forty yards away a heavily bearded man wearing a Victorian farmer's smock, trousers, gaiters, and boots had appeared from between two of the corn ricks. Hands on hips he stepped back and ran his eye up towards the barn where Edward stood, then transferred his gaze to the huge haystack, before slowly nodding in satisfaction.

Inspecting the harvest. Edward knew instinctively what he was doing. And he knew who he was too because he'd seen his photograph alongside the other previous land agents in the estate office.

His name was James Ritton and he'd died in 1897.

*

Bert walked slowly to the vicarage and rang the bell. His sense of grievance lingered but it was clear that the hour-long class into which he had been ruthlessly coerced by the Reverend Tukes was something to be endured for the greater good.

'You pay attention Bert, and no skiving. We need that allotment,' his wife had remarked with a smile as he departed gloomily.

Mrs Vane the housekeeper showed him into the clergyman's study where a bright fire burned. Tukes rose from behind his desk and beamed. Bert eyed him warily. He had learned not to judge by appearances.

'Come in, come in. Now I thought we'd sit at the table here, side by side and then each week we can look at a passage from the holy book and discuss its meaning. Will you have a cup of tea?'

Dragging his gaze from the well-stocked drinks trolley in the corner, the countryman nodded slowly. 'Thank-you, two sugars please, Bonnie'.

The housekeeper nodded. 'Edna, all right?'

'Better than nothing,' he replied with a smile.

'You don't change, Bert Williams,' she said, although her look of disapproval was tempered with a brief softening of her eyes.

'But that is the reason Bert is here, Mrs Vane. To change.' The reverend bustled about collecting bible, notepad and pencil and placed them on the table, then they took their seats. He opened the book at a marked page and added, 'I thought we'd start with the story of the feeding of the five thousand. Otherwise known as the miracle of the loaves and the fishes.'

'Yes, I know that one.'

'Good. I'll read it through out loud to begin with.' He was a good as his word and Bert listened in silence, although the recitation was briefly interrupted by Mrs Vane returning with the tea. As she closed the door their eyes met, and Bert saw a gleam of amusement on her face.

'What's your reaction to hearing that then, Bert?' the vicar asked, as he completed the reading.

'What sort of fish were they?'

'Eh?'

'I'm just asking what sort of fish they were. I mean how big for starters. My cousin's in the navy and they caught a marlin that fed the whole ship for two days.'

'Well, whatever size they were, I think we can safely assume that two of them would not be enough to feed five thousand people.'

'What about the bread. How big were the loaves?'

'One imagines the same principle applies. Especially as Jesus also filled twelve wicker baskets with the surplus.'

Bert sniffed and reflected. 'So how did he do it exactly? I mean, did the extra grub just appear out of nowhere?'

The parson's neck muscles tightened fractionally. 'It is generally acknowledged that Jesus performed a miracle in order to feed all the people who had come to see him.'

'Right. What's the difference between a spell like Eve Dance does and a miracle like Jesus did?'

'Oh Bert, they are very different things.' Tukes sipped his tea to gain time.

'How's that then, Vicar?' the countryman persisted.

'Jesus was proving the living power of God. Five thousand people bore witness. Tell me, why do you think he performed his miracle that day?'

'Maybe he was just showing off. Because he could. You know... like a magician doing a trick.'

A pulse showed at the parson's temple, and he wondered if he had made a terrible mistake. 'No Bert, Jesus was not showing off, I can assure you of that. Try again.'

'Because the people were hungry.'

'Exactly. And Jesus took the opportunity to demonstrate his power in a spectacular way, in order that they might be fed.'

'Assuming it wasn't two marlin. And five of those massive loaves the baker in Banbury does for the Summer fete.'

'For heaven's sake Bert, the five loaves and two fish were in a boy's basket.'

'How big a basket?'

While the vicar was wrestling with the finer details of the story of the loaves and fishes, the wooing of Edward Spense by Constable Burrows took place in The Black Horse. The policeman was in mufti, it being his regular practice to lean on the bar for a few hours every week in order to listen to the latest gossip and present an informal face to villagers.

His wife had noticed that, with the presence of a baby with colic at home, these visits had increased in regularity, but she loved him and said nothing. For the moment.

Seeing Edward sitting in the corner with a newspaper, the constable bought two pints and ambled casually over.

'Another one, Mr Edward?' he enquired, standing over the table.

'Evening Burrows, how's the black eye?' The man did not move his gaze from the sports page of the Oxford Evening Echo.

'All cleared up now, thank-you.'

'Sore was it?'

'For a day or two, yes.'

A look of satisfaction appeared on Edward's face. 'Well I served my time for it, Constable. A long dark night of the soul on the hard bunk of your cell. And refused breakfast too, as I recall. I'm not really in the mood for further conviviality with the boys in blue at this precise moment.'

Burrows swallowed and attempted to dredge up a smile as he muttered, 'Faults on both sides, sir, you know how it is.'

'Not really. I presume you want something?'

The policeman hesitated and glared at the openly grinning and toothless elderly man at the next table, who was clearly enjoying their conversation.

'The fact is, I would appreciate a quiet word. That's why I've brought the beer. It's in the manner of a peace offering.'

Edward sighed and slowly folded the paper, then leaned back and met his eye. 'Beer? You are attempting a reconciliation with a pint of beer?' he asked loudly.

Intensely aware that he was still standing over the table holding the pints, and that most of the pub was now watching the exchange, the policeman lingered uncomfortably in the extended silence that followed the question.

'Oh alright then,' Edward said finally and called across the bar, 'Two large brandies please Mr Tirrold, on Burrows' slate.' He shuffled along the bench. 'For heaven's sake man, don't stand there waiting like a seaside donkey. Put the beer on the table and sit down. Now tell me, what can I do for you?'

*

In London, Sir Anthony was briefing Halley, his aide. 'We must move this thing along. In his letter the writer proposes the exchange at Great Tew but does not specify a particular location or date. If we agree, we are to place an advert in the personal columns of The Times on the 20th of October. He even gives us the wording for heaven's sake.'

He glanced at the letter. *'Trixie, I love you. Teddy.'* One assumes we will receive a further communication following its publication.'

'It's interesting, sir. A single code word would have been sufficient wouldn't it, something like 'Trafalgar' or 'Oxford'. I wonder why he chose that phrase?'

'Yes I see your point. Has he plucked that from thin air, or does it mean something? Is that what you're suggesting?'

'Perhaps. But then we have no idea about the man at all. The letter is typed and unsigned. There's no address and it was posted in Paris. That phrase is all we have.'

'Indeed.' The permanent secretary nodded slowly and crossed to the window that overlooked St James's Park. Hopkins knew it was his favourite place to reflect on the challenges that confronted his great office every day.

'I've briefed Lord Curzon,' he said, his eyes on the tree tops. 'I told him our belief is that the man is an opportunist blackmailer, rather than a professional. And that his reasons for murdering Lord Colin, if indeed he did so, remain shrouded in mystery. His exact words to me were, 'Put it to bed Sir Anthony, no leaks, no loose ends. Tell me when it is done.'

The aide hesitated, and then replied cautiously. 'Does that mean a terminal solution is required, sir?'

'It means exactly what it means,' came the oblique reply. 'Place the advert Halley. We will wait to hear more from our correspondent.'

*

A mile up the Cherwell valley from Great Tew, in a little hamlet called Upper Barn, Mr Reginald Bennett sat in his kitchen and stared at an unopened parcel that had been sitting on the table since the sub-postmaster had delivered it a week earlier.

Tears showed at the corners of his eyes and slowly trickled down his cheeks as he stared at the label. He imagined a War Office clerk somewhere writing the address and sticking it on. Wrapping the box with string.

Had they wondered what he had been like? How vital and strong he was? Or how funny and endearing they both had been? Probably not. Such things were the preserve of mothers and fathers.

He reached out and cut the string. The first thing he saw was a letter addressed to him. The envelope had a smear of mud on it. French mud he guessed. He opened it.

Mr R Bennett,
Upper Barn,
Great Tew,
Oxon.
26th August 1916
Dear Mr Bennett,

By the time this reaches you, you will have been officially informed that both your sons were killed in an attack on the German lines at Delville Wood on the 9th of August 1916.

I am writing to express my deep regret and commiserations at your loss. I can only imagine what the impact of the news will have on you and your wife. If it is any consolation, I can tell you unequivocally that both men were popular members of the platoon and good soldiers. That they volunteered for service before conscription was brought in, says much about their steadfast characters.

I am enclosing this letter with your eldest son's personal effects, which will be sent back to you in due course.

My sincere condolences again.

Yours sincerely,

Lieutenant Michael Ross

Mr Bennett put the letter down in the table and stared out of the window. He imagined the officer writing it in a dugout somewhere in the British lines and wondered if he had survived the war. Sudden, bitter, rage flowed across his face, and he reached out, screwed the piece of paper into a ball and threw it across the room. The darkening kitchen echoed to the sound of wet sobs as the grief caused by the arrival of the two telegrams four years earlier came flooding back.

Chapter Five

The following day Burrows, Innes, and Edward met in the snug in the Black Horse to commence the investigation into Dunstan Green's death. It was something of a reunion – as the colonel had observed, they had worked together the previous year on another murder enquiry and, in consequence, they naturally re-assumed their respective roles.

This meant that Innes, through intellect and sheer force of personality, was the leader, Burrows offered guidance from the Oxfordshire police manual and Edward provided local knowledge. It was a surprisingly effective combination.

Once they all had a drink, Innes leaned forward and opened proceedings, speaking quietly so the hum of conversation from the other bar covered her voice.

'To recap then, Dunstan Green was killed by a person or persons unknown, close to the river, upstream of the power house. The perpetrator took care to try and conceal the murder by stabbing him in the ear, possibly with a thatching needle,' she nodded at Burrows, 'and by throwing him into the water, so the blood was washed away. For now we will assume he was trying to pass the thing off as an accident or suicide.'

'Yes I think we're agreed on that, miss,' Burrows replied. 'When I attended Mr Green's parent's house they were good enough to acknowledge the ill-feeling about him on the estate.' He pursed his lips and added, 'Apparently he went out for a walk when it was dark most evenings, it being the best way to avoid attracting attention to himself.'

'Oh really? Well that's hardly surprising,' Innes replied. 'Did they say what time he went out that night?'

'No, they were visiting friends. He was there when they left the house at eight o'clock and out when they got back at ten past ten. They went to bed and only realised he hadn't returned when I arrived at the house early the following morning.'

'Hmm. The post-mortem says he had been in the water for at least six hours, but no longer than ten. The body was found in the leat at seven in the morning so, working backwards, we can assume the murder took place between nine p.m. and one a.m. the previous night.'

'Yes, that would fit,' Edward said, 'so as far as the establishment of alibis is concerned we have a reasonable time frame.'

Burrows nodded firmly, 'Exactly. And we're going to need a lot of alibis. Anybody who disapproved of Green's efforts to avoid the war is a potential suspect. That's pretty much everyone on the estate and by ten o'clock most of them were in bed, I imagine. We'll have no way of proving otherwise.'

'That still leaves the hour between nine and ten I suppose,' Edward remarked.

The constable nodded again. 'True. Also, I think the King's Head darts team were away at the Carthorse Inn in Banbury, in which case they can alibi each other.'

'Ah. You make a very good point Burrows,' Innes interjected, 'It would be a sensible idea to find out if anything else was happening that evening. Wasn't it choir night at St Mary's for example? We may well find we can clear a lot of people out of the reckoning quite quickly, at least for the bulk of the evening.' She leaned back and took a sip of her cider. 'Edward, would you put a list of collective events together and try to find out who was attending?'

He nodded. 'Right-ho.'

'Thank-you. It occurs that we're also going to need a complete list of possible suspects, otherwise we will rapidly lose track of who was where, and when.'

Burrows smiled at her. 'You'd make an excellent detective, miss. The Oxfordshire police manual is quite definite about the need to keep detailed, accurate, notes during a case.'

Edward said, 'Stafford will have one of those I imagine. The tenant farmers pay their own workers, but every household on the estate pays a small contribution towards the pension scheme and the costs for the cottage hospital. There will be a master list somewhere, I'll have a word with him.'

Innes nodded briskly. 'Good. Well that's progress.' She paused for a second then asked, 'We are sure that the murderer is a man, are we? I mean we're making that assumption, but is there any actual evidence?'

Burrows looked at her. 'It's hard to see a woman putting a thatching needle into a man's ear and chucking him in the river, miss.'

Innes visibly hesitated. Growing up among the tenements of Glasgow, she had seen and heard violent women and had no illusions about what the fairer sex was capable of when driven to it. 'Alright. I accept that for the moment,' she said, 'but let's bear it in mind, especially if we get stuck.'

Edward said, 'There's something else too. We're automatically assuming that Green was killed because he was a *conshie*, but what if there was another reason? Something unrelated to his war record – or lack of it.'

The other two looked at him. 'Good point,' said Innes.

A pensive expression appeared on Burrows face. 'You're right to mention that Mr Edward, but we have a large and obvious motive sitting in the middle of the case and I'd say we're duty bound to pursue that first. If we draw a blank…' he shrugged.

'I tend to agree,' Innes observed. 'It's possible something else might emerge as we investigate but, when other families sent their sons to war and lost them, his cowardice is hard to ignore.'

They continued to talk for twenty minutes then Burrows departed. Left alone in the little room, Edward looked at Innes. Her clear blue-grey eyes and sensuous mouth were spellbinding and, not for the first time, Lady Langford's youngest son thought she was the most beautiful woman he had ever seen.

Sensing a sudden change in the atmosphere, she returned his gaze with a wary smile that seemed to say, *Yes, I'm here, but you must make the running Edward.*

He slipped his hand under the table and took hers. 'How are you?' he asked.

They'd shaken hands before, but it was the first time he'd touched her in that way, and Innes felt as though electricity was running up her arm. Her heart surged, but she controlled her voice, and kept hold of his hand.

'I'm fine Edward, and if I may say so, you are looking well yourself. A summer's work on Home Farm has done you good.'

'Yes I almost feel back to normal. Although my little problem remains a constant companion. I saw a man called James Ritton in the rick yard as we were getting the hay in.' He looked at his friend and smiled. 'The only trouble is he died twenty-three years ago.'

'Oh, I see. As you hadn't mentioned anything for a while I did think that perhaps you'd stopped seeing ghosts.'

He shook his head. 'Far from it. I think I must accept that they will be with me for the rest of my life.'

As I would like to be.

The thought arrived in the young woman's head like an express train emerging from a tunnel. Undeniable. Impossible to ignore. It must have showed on her face because Edward said, 'You look as though you've seen a ghost yourself. Are you alright?'

'Yes, yes, I'm fine.' She smiled back at him.

Blithely unaware of her turmoil, Edward continued, 'I have enjoyed our rides around the estate, it's been a great pleasure spending time with you, Innes. A great pleasure. I do hope we can continue our excursions together.'

Innes gave his hand a gentle squeeze, realising he was inching forward and trying to express emotions that he found difficult. 'I've enjoyed getting to know you better too. I respect you greatly Edward, you know that. You've faced war and a breakdown bravely.'

72

If you cross the line I will gladly follow you, my darling. But I will not lead.

For a minute or so they sat without speaking, hand in hand, enjoying their secret intimacy. It felt as though they had gone through a hidden gate together and emerged into a new place. Then Edward said, 'Your parents are coming down aren't they?'

'Yes. They're staying at Marston House but I'm sure you, Piers and Claire will be invited over for supper. In fact I know that is the plan.'

'I look forward to meeting them. I'm sure they're delightful.' He squeezed her warm hand. 'Just like their daughter.'

*

Eve Dance climbed the uncarpeted stairs to the attic at Marston House. It was eleven o'clock in the evening and everyone else was in bed, but her recent conversation with Lady Langford about the Dunstan Green murder was weighing on her mind and she had decided to act. She unlocked the door with a small brass key, the only one in the house, and entered.

This was her domain. Her spiritual sanctuary. As an adept of the natural, her instincts were always to be outside and surrounded by the elements when at her devotions, but sometimes, especially in the dark half of the year, this wasn't practical. Put simply, it was a chilly damp night and the prospect of an hour of astral meditation inside Creech Hill Ring was not an attractive prospect.

But her instincts told her not to delay. So here she was. It would do.

73

The room was about twenty feet square with a sloping ceiling and two small dormer windows which faced the back of the house. It was pleasantly warm, heated by the remains of a fire which Eve herself had lighted an hour earlier. There wasn't much furniture - a dark green chaise-longue that could accommodate her when stretched out, a richly coloured Turkish rug that covered most of the floor and, at its centre, a large crimson cushion sitting in front of a wide shallow brass dish, some eighteen inches across. It was from North Africa and very old, perhaps her most treasured possession.

Crossing to a small side table she took four tall candlesticks and arranged them in a semi-circle around the dish. Then she opened a drawer and withdrew a silver dagger in its scabbard and a paper bag filled with dried herbs. An aromatic mixture of sage and lavender. Finally she picked up a handsome jug and a matching bowl. Taking everything to the cushion, she poured water from the jug into the wide dish and tipped the contents of the bag into the bowl.

She lighted the candles and turned off the ceiling light. The room was instantly transformed as the four flames reflected on the still water in the dish. Starlight appeared in the windows and the red embers of the fire glowed.

Kneeling down on the cushion she put a match to the herbs. They flared briefly in the darkness and their heady smoke caught in her nostrils, sending a shiver of anticipation through her body. *A good sign.* She smiled and unsheathed the dagger, then paused for a moment, gathering her concentration, before starting to speak in a low voice. It was an ancient tongue and one of the language scholars from Oxford University might perhaps have recognised the Norse

74

roots that lay buried deep in her words. Their rhythmic cadence seemed to fill the room and sink into the walls.

The chant went on and on, punctuated by the gentle chime of the dagger as she repeatedly touched the four sides of the wide dish.

At last she rested and placed the dagger on the floor, then leaned forward over the dish and stared directly onto the candle-lit surface. Freeing her mind from her body, she opened herself up to all the hidden places, and the liquid seemed to glow and shimmer in response. Even though her body was motionless, she felt herself moving forwards towards the water, pulled deeper and deeper until it became a wide dark sea, and she was floating over it.

Show me. Show me the gunfire, she asked.

The surface dissolved into the grey light of dawn, and she heard the crump of heavy artillery shells landing. *Delville Wood.* The name was suddenly in her mind. And an image of a deep trench filled with men from the Oxfords. A sea of helmets. She shivered, feeling their fear.

Then the soldiers were out of the trench. Running. Shouting. She sensed their exhilaration and aggression. Fighting men. *It won't be me, not this time.* But for many it was, and as they fell she saw their souls rising into the air like grey twists of cloth before disappearing across the horizon.

She drifted over the battlefield, seeing what was happening in individual places at different times, like a torch beam shining onto pictures in a darkened art gallery. Her gaze passed over a shell crater where three men lay in the hole. Two were dead and the third was holding one of them. She couldn't see either face, but she could feel his raw, aching, grief very clearly, and knew his soul would be fully occupied helping him to deal with the pain

She stiffened. Something was wrong. There was another creature down there, something malign, standing looking at the three men. Unable to do anything, she watched, sickened, as the wraith, which had once been an untainted soul too, slipped into the man and hid. She stayed for a moment then drifted on. But as she did so a thought was suddenly clear in her mind.

That was why I was brought there. That's what I was meant to see.

*

A week later the investigators convened again, this time in the morning room of Langford Hall. It was an unpleasant day. A cold wind was blowing from the north and gusts of rain lashed against the windows as a footman placed a tray of coffee on the table.

'Shall I be mother?' Innes asked, in her broad Scottish accent, then poured a cup for all three of them. As Burrows reached happily for a biscuit she opened proceedings. 'How has your research been going Edward?'

She watched the tall, sandy haired man opposite withdraw some pieces of paper from his pocket. He was wearing an old corduroy jacket, flannel trousers, a check shirt and dark red tie. The soft collar of his shirt was turned up on one side, but he was unaware of it, which she found endearing. She saw the concentration in his eyes as he arranged the papers. They were definitely hazel, but when the light caught them little flecks of gold appeared. Suddenly aware that she was staring, she glanced at Burrows. He was looking at her, with a faint smile on his face.

Thankfully, Edward spoke. 'I've made a list of the things that were happening on the estate the night of Dunstan Green's murder. It was choir night for example and seven men attended. You were right about the darts match too, Burrows, there were another twelve over in Banbury who didn't get back until midnight. But I'm afraid in total I've only been able to strike off thirty one from Stafford's master list, which still leaves getting on for two hundred men unaccounted for.'

Innes sighed in frustration. 'It's a huge number and if we start going round and asking them all individually what they were doing that night, word will soon leak out that we're making enquiries. And the Colonel was explicit in his desire that bereaved families were not put under any open suspicion.'

'But it's bereaved families we're most interested in, isn't it,' Burrows crunched noisily on his biscuit and added, 'if I may, I'd like to make a suggestion.'

'Of course, Constable, you're the expert,' Innes replied.

'Thank-you, miss. I think for now we should forget Mr Edward's long list and concentrate our efforts on the twenty-five families that lost sons in the war. The Oxfordshire police manual is clear on this - always pursue the obvious prima-facie evidence first. And those people have the greatest justifiable anger against Mr Green, and therefore the greatest motivation. I've written down the names of the families, it'll be mainly the fathers we need to check but I've also added the names of any other men aged over sixteen. Thirty-six names in all.'

He placed the list on the table and took the opportunity to fortify himself with another of Mrs Sutton's renowned biscuits. His wife was a goddess in every respect, but if she had a fault it was in her abilities as a cook. He had been thinking about broaching the subject with her for some time, gloriously unaware that it was dangerous territory.

'He's right you know,' said Edward, picking up the piece of paper. 'No-one on the estate had any time for the man, but there's a big difference between disliking someone, and being angry enough to kill them. Distain is hardly a motive for murder.' Glancing at the empty biscuit plate he walked over to the bell and pressed it, then returned to his seat and spread the papers on the table. 'Hang on while I compare Burrows list with the names I've been able to account for.'

The others watched in silence as a footman reappeared and Edward glanced up. 'Could we have some more biscuits.' The servant took the plate and left.

Innes looked around. Even on a dull day, the morning room was bright and cheerful. It was decorated with blue and white wallpaper in wide stripes and like all the rooms she had been in Langford Hall, there was an understated opulence that was completely at ease with the every-day comfort of a house that was lived in.

This could be your home. In time, you could be the chatelaine here. Married to that man sitting opposite. Raising a family.

Innes poured more coffee and they waited. A new plate of biscuits arrived to Burrows nod of approval, then Edward

78

looked up. 'Right, good news. Fifteen men from the families who lost sons were busy that night. Which brings our list of suspects down to twenty-one. Assuming the murderer is a male,' he added, with a nod of recognition to Innes.

'Now you're talking,' the policeman said, as he crunched a biscuit. 'That's a much more manageable number.'

Innes said, 'Burrows, do you think there's any mileage in the idea that the two families that lost two sons should be at the top of the list of suspects? Being doubly angry, as it were?'

'The Bennetts and the Reeves?' It was Edward who answered.

Burrows looked at him. 'Well you say Bennetts, plural, but there's only one left now isn't there. Old man Bennett at Upper Barn.'

'Of course, you're right. There's still plenty of Reeves though, the boys had three younger sisters. They have Spring Farm out past Little Tew.'

'Yes. There would be no harm in me dropping in to see both of them and taking their measure. I can check out their alibis, or lack of them at the same time.'

'Excellent idea,' Innes nodded enthusiastically. 'The more people we can cross off the list the better.'

''Agreed, miss,' the constable replied, visibly restraining his hand from reaching for the last biscuit.

'For heaven's sake have it Burrows, you've had nine, you might as well make it to double figures,' the young doctor observed in a waspish tone. Immune to her sarcasm, his long arm reached out like a crane's boom and collected it.

Edward hid a smile as Innes continued, 'That's the plan then. You'll visit the Reeves and Bennetts and we will continue our general enquiries. Let us know when you're ready to bring us up to date, will you.'

*

Spring Farm was one of the largest and most productive tenancies on the Langford Estate and had been in the Reeve family for three generations. The tenants were unusual in that Simon Reeve did not farm the land himself. He was a partner in a firm of solicitors in Banbury and employed a manager to run the farm's five hundred acres and its twenty-strong labour force.

The Reeves had been blessed with five children, but after the death of their two sons in the war only three teenage sisters remained. They were lively girls named, with admirable simplicity, April, May, and June. Burrows knew the family a little from their visits to church in Great Tew, so when the front door was opened by June, the youngest, he was greeting with a friendly smile.

'Hello Constable Burrows. May I help you?' she asked politely.

Before he could reply a voice sounded behind her and Mrs Reeve appeared, wiping her hands on a striped apron. 'Who is it? Oh, Constable Burrows, good afternoon.' She bustled past her daughter and smiled. 'What can we do for you?'

'I was just out on my rounds and thought I'd see how things are.' In the deep countryside where they lived, farms were widely spaced and calling in unannounced was an accepted part of life.

'And welcome too. Come through to the kitchen and I'll get Hannah to rustle up a cup of tea. We're baking today, so we might even manage a scone for you.' She led the way down the hall, glanced at the clock on the side table and added, 'Mr Reeve will be home from work in a few minutes, I expect.'

Burrows received this news with satisfaction. He had planned his social call so that it would encompass both parents, but it was really her husband that he wanted to see. And her prediction proved correct, he had only been sitting at the kitchen table with the promised refreshments for five minutes when John Reeve appeared.

'Afternoon Burrows,' the comfortably plump, grey haired, man greeted him. 'Nothing wrong I hope?'

They shook hands, 'Nothing at all, sir. I was passing and thought I'd pop in'.

The solicitor kissed his wife, sat down at the table, and nodded his thanks to the maid as a large cup of tea appeared in front of him. 'A bit of a shock, this business about Dunstan Green,' he remarked. 'Any news in that direction at all?'

'The post mortem indicated that he'd drowned. His mother and father have been informed.' Burrows sipped his tea.

Reeve shook his head. 'A sad end to a difficult affair.'

'I think there is some sympathy for his parents now. While he was alive they were rather tarred with the same brush, but as it now seems he's killed himself opinions are easing about them.'

'Well that's something,' Mrs Reeve remarked, sitting down next to her husband. 'Dunstan Green was a bad lot, but you can't blame his mother and father for all of that. And he was an only child. At least we've got the girls.'

Burrows watched her eyes move towards a picture of her two sons on the mantelpiece above the range. They were both in uniform, the younger blond like his mother, the other dark like his father had been as a younger man, he imagined.

The solicitor said, 'I suppose my wife's right. But when you've lost loved ones and seen someone else trying to save their own skin it's hard to forget it.'

Mrs Reeve said quietly, 'Edward, our eldest didn't want to volunteer at all, but his younger brother was keen as mustard. Lord Colin had been teaching him to shoot a pistol, although we had no idea they'd struck up a friendship. His lordship was in the army before he assumed the title and unfortunately filled John's head with all kinds of nonsense about life in the military. On his eighteenth birthday he caught the bus to Banbury and enlisted. We were astonished. He just came home and announced it.'

She sighed and glanced at her husband then continued, 'Edward felt he had to do the same. I mean how did it look? His little brother going off to war and him hiding away at home. That's how he saw it anyway. He was very angry with Lord Colin though, I do remember that.'

'We all were,' Reeve said. 'I served in South Africa and saw war for what it really is, Burrows. A game of chance played for deadly stakes. There's no nobility in it.'

His eyes drifted up to the photograph. 'Our boys were killed at Delville Wood like a lot of the men from round here who died. Poor Reg Bennett lost both his sons the same day, and his wife a few months later. A broken heart they said.'

He shook his head. 'There were plenty shamed into signing up because their friends or relations did so. Plenty. Look at the pals' battalions. They didn't want to go, but they did it anyway and a lot of them never came home.'

Burrows shook his head. 'You have my deepest sympathy. I've got a new baby and am only just starting to understand how being a father makes you feel.'

'I'll speak frankly, Burrows, Lord Colin might be venerated around the estate, but there isn't much regard for him in this house. He sent our sons to war, and neither came back.'

'And Dunstan Green, sir? How did you feel about him?' He looked at Mr Reeve and was surprised to see a flash of raw anger cross the man's face. He controlled it rapidly and produced a dismissive shrug that was eloquence itself.

'A coward,' he said.

Half an hour later, having established the movements of the family on the night of Green's murder, Burrows cycled thoughtfully back through the sunken lanes to Great Tew. His visit had been instructive. Spring Farm concealed strong emotions behind its comfortable façade. The pain of the loss the Reeves had suffered was still echoing round their lives and the unguarded moment of deep anger on the father's face was a clear sign of it.

Chapter Six

The man with death in his heart sat on the Marseilles to Paris Express watching the countryside roll by at forty miles an hour. Dusk was falling and the reflection of his profile in the carriage window allowed the only other occupant of the compartment, a homely twenty-five year old French widow, to complete her discreet examination with ease.

A good looking man, about her age and a fluent French speaker, although when he exchanged a few brief words with the train guard ten minutes earlier, she had deduced it was not his first language. But there was no doubt his profile was striking, and, with his swarthy sunburned skin and generous moustache, he looked lean and a little dangerous. She wondered if she dared strike up a conversation.

Was he going all the way to Paris as she was? Had he noticed her?

As it happened, the answer to both questions was yes. The man was travelling north from his home in Marseilles to a modest apartment on the Rive Gauche, which he had rented by post. When he had first arrived in the south of France he had been unsure if the sunlit city was merely a place of temporary refuge, or something more, but to his surprise he had taken to its vibrant streets like a duck to water.

His saturnine good looks were not uncommon in that part of the world and as the sun beat down he had learned French, slowly at first, and then with the help of an obliging bar maid from one of his haunts and settled down to wait out the war.

That had been four years ago. In the intervening period he had returned in secret to Great Tew twice. The first time was in 1916, not long after arriving in Marseilles. The second had been recently – the first in a series of moves intended to finish the job he had started four years earlier. However, an unexpected event had forced him to postpone matters for a few days and he had briefly returned to Marseilles.

Now he was on the move again.

Unaware that she was in the greatest danger of her short life, the widow opened her bag and withdrew two apples. Holding one out she smiled and asked him if he would like it. When he didn't reply or even give any indication she had heard him, she asked again,

'Monsieur, Monsieur…'

The elderly lady caretaker in the block of apartments in Marseilles where he lived called the Englishman *'l'homme mort'*, blissfully unaware of the irony and when, at last, he turned his face and met her gaze, a shiver of shock ran through her. They were dead eyes, expressionless, but at the same time they seemed to bore into her very soul, looking, probing, violating her most secret thoughts and leaving her defenceless.

A man with no humanity. No feelings at all.

Every feminine instinct screamed extreme danger.

The faintest of wolfish smiles showed on his lips as she withdrew her hand. 'Pardon Monsieur.' She sat rigid, her bag on her knees, and whimpered as a tear rolled down her cheek. It was at least thirty minutes before the train arrived in Paris.

Two hours later the same man sat at the kitchen table in his apartment on the Left Bank and stared out of the open window. Opposite he could see a neat, black-painted Juliet balcony, thirty feet away. The double window behind it was wide open and a woman was moving inside, her shadowy figure just visible.

The sounds of the vegetable market two floors below floated up to him as he removed a postcard from his jacket pocket and looked at the picture. It was a black and white photograph of the Eiffel Tower. He took a fountain pen out of the other pocket. It was an expensive one, the man had money and could spend on the things he enjoyed. He knew the address by heart and wrote it on the panel then paused and idly watched the woman opposite as she appeared at the window and shook a duster. She glanced briefly down to the street, then went back into the room. His mind drifted for a moment, reflecting on the unexpected event that had necessitated a delay to his plans.

What to write?

In the end he opted for simplicity and wrote a few words, then left the apartment and walked to the post office. The man serving glanced at the address.

'To England, Monsieur? Oxfordshire? Oxford is a fine city.' Something of an Anglophile, he spoke in English, but the man answered in French.

'Yes it is.' He handed over the francs required for the stamps and watched as the teller stuck them on and turned to put it straight into a sack behind him. As he did so he glanced at the few words written on the card.

The Times 20ᵗʰ October. Personal columns.

*

By the following week Burrows had completed his investigations into the movements of both Reeve and Bennett the night Dunstan Green was murdered and reported his findings to the others. They were sitting in the parlour of the police house, and he was still in uniform. Sounds of cooking carried through from the kitchen where Laura was preparing the tea and talking to little Matilda at the same time.

'Reeve first then,' he said, notebook in hand. 'His wife and two older children were at choir practice in St Mary's that night and got back to Spring Farm at eleven o'clock. Mr Reeve stayed at home with his youngest, who was asleep by ten.' He looked at them. 'So in theory there is an hour-long gap between ten and eleven when he could have left the house with no-one knowing.'

'How do you find this stuff out Burrows?' Innes asked with a smile. 'I mean about the bedtimes and so on?'

He gave her a long and lugubrious stare. 'I have my methods miss, and the Oxfordshire police manual is very sound on how to elicit information without appearing obvious.'

There was a brief pause while Edward and Innes considered this, then a clang and muttered curse from the kitchen broke into their reflections.

'So Mr Reeve could have gone out, but not necessarily with the intention of killing Green?' Innes said.

'Possibly. As we discussed before, he may have simply fancied a stroll, met him on the riverbank and acted spontaneously.'

'Or he might have just stayed at home,' Edward added.

Burrows nodded. 'Correct. All of those are possibilities.'

'Right. And Mr Bennett?' said Innes.

He flipped the page of his notebook and continued, 'Mr Bennett lives alone at Upper Barn. Both sons were killed in the war and his wife died the following year so it's a very different situation. The man is in his late fifties and works as a gardener. He's a drinker I suspect and to be honest there wasn't much cheer in the house. He's only just received his eldest son's personal effects. It's terrible really, four years on. They must have got lost in the system. I got the feeling it's brought it all back.'

Edward stirred. 'Maybe the belated arrival of his son's things pushed him over the edge' he remarked.

Burrows nodded. 'Perhaps. There's a great deal of anger in the man. It's not hard to imagine him sitting at home and brooding, then deciding to kill Green in a pre-meditated way.'

He leaned forward and continued. 'The point is, that night he was in the King's Head between half past eight and eleven o'clock when they closed, and he left to walk back to Upper Barn. There are two ways to go, both about the same distance. One option is along Rivermead, over the bridge, and then up the track on the far side of the valley.' He looked at the others. 'The other way is directly down the hill to the river and along the field path to the bridge.'

'Along the riverbank above the mill in fact,' Innes observed.

'Exactly.'

'Did anyone see him?'

'Not that I have been able to establish, miss. But it's clearly possible that they met by accident on the riverbank that night and had an argument that led to violence.'

'Right. Well, well done Burrows that's excellent investigating, if I may be so bold.'

Edward said, 'So to summarise, we know that the murder took place between nine in the evening and one o'clock in the morning, and during that period both Messrs Reeve and Bennett have periods when their alibis cannot be confirmed by other people. So they are definite suspects.'

'Given the fact they both lost two sons, I'd say they are at the top of the list, yes.' Burrows nodded.

*

Later that evening Edward and his mother dined alone in the small dining room at Langford Hall. When they had finished eating she led him into the drawing room where Dereham served them coffee and then withdrew.

She removed a small black leather pouch from her handbag, placed it on the table in front of him and raised her eyebrows meaningfully. Taking his cue, he reached out and picked it up. The leather was as soft as silk and clearly very old, and the pouch was closed at the top with a faded crimson drawstring.

He looked at her. 'What's this?'

'It's an heirloom. The Langford Ring. Have a look.'

He opened the pouch and tipped the contents into his cupped hand. 'Golly!' His exclamation of surprise was quite genuine, the ring that lay in his palm was exquisite. The gold was a deep burnished copper colour that only comes with great age and the large central diamond surrounded by five rubies glittered in the firelight. He picked it up and looked closely.

'There's some faint writing on the inside, but it's very worn. Do you know what it says?' he asked.

'It's not writing, those are Norse runes. The ring came over with your ancestors when the Normans invaded. And it was old then. The Normans were Vikings originally of course, so it must have been made well before 1066.'

He turned it over in his hand, fascinated by its beauty. 'I had no idea. Why haven't you shown it to me before? I've never seen you wearing it.'

'No, it's a little flamboyant for everyday wear but I have worn it on formal occasions with your father, when everyone is dressed up to the nines and there's royalty around. It's actually quite famous.' She reached over and slipped it onto the third finger of her left hand, next to her wedding ring and showed him. 'Nice?'

'Gorgeous. Imagine the people who have worn it over the years.'

'Exactly.' She took it off and put it back on the pouch. Then she just looked at him, smiled and waited.

You can lead a horse to water…

The silence went on for a while, so she finally said, 'Your father gave it to me the night he asked me to marry him. It's a Langford tradition. It goes to the eldest daughter if there is one, if not, the first bride to marry into the family. And on that occasion that was me.'

She put her hand on his knee and said, 'I really think that Innes should be wearing it don't you?'

He met her eye and said warily, 'Do you?'

'Really, I do my darling. She is beautiful, intelligent, and loyal. I cannot imagine a better partner for you, or for Langford.'

'But does she love me? Would she say yes?'

'Well you'll never know if you don't ask her, Edward. Faint heart never won fair maid.'

He looked away and she sensed his indecision. 'I'm really not sure I'm cut out for marriage,' he said, after a moment.

Hiding a groan of frustration his mother persevered. 'Life is better lived with a loving partner. You and she would be very happy, supporting each other through life's ups and downs. Just as your father and I were.' She squeezed his hand and said quietly in her bass voice, 'Take the leap Edward. I'm sure it's the right thing.'

But he said nothing and just stared at the fire. Somehow resisting the urge to grab his lapels and scream, '*Just ask her, you idiot!*', she tried another tack.

'Your happiness is my primary concern but there are other factors too. Langford needs children. I'm afraid Piers is a bit of a busted flush in that direction, darling man though he is. And with poor Hugh gone, it really is down to you.'

He stirred uneasily. 'Really mother, that's a bit near the knuckle isn't it?'

But she didn't let him off the hook. 'I mean it. These things must be confronted. There must be an heir, preferably two or three. Look what's happened to our family, I started off with three healthy sons and there's only you left.' She turned the screw. 'If Hugh is looking down I'm sure he'd agree with me.'

He sighed. 'I'm just not sure that Innes is a suitable wife or that we would be happy. I'm sorry.'

And at this, Lady Langford finally cracked. She leaped to her feet and stood over him, five foot one inch of furious, simmering, motherhood, with a blood line that went back to Alfred the Great.

Hands on hips, she let rip in a bellow that carried along the corridor and out into the entrance hall.

'Now listen to me! I've had quite enough of your self-indulgent meanderings. It's time to stand up and be counted as a Langford.' She grabbed the pouch and thrust it into his hand. 'Take the bloody ring and don't come back until you've asked her. And if she says no, make her change her mind. Her parents are down shortly, and it'll be an ideal opportunity to settle things. I mean it Edward. Time's up. Now get on with it.'

Breathing heavily she stamped her foot and glared at him. At the foot of the main staircase Dereham paused and smiled, her ladyship's temper was legendary across the estate. And he wasn't the only one smiling. Edward's face had split into a wide grin of delight.

'What are you laughing at?' she hissed. 'I can see absolutely nothing amusing in your wilful insouciance.'

He stood up and hugged her. 'Of course I'll ask her. I was going to anyway, and as soon as I saw the ring I knew what you were up to. I just thought I'd see how far you were prepared to push it.'

'Aargh.' She pushed him back and stared. 'Edward, you utter rotter.'

He walked over to the cocktail table and poured them both a scotch. Handing one to her he raised his glass. 'To mothers with tempers and hopeful proposals. Wish me luck.'

*

Two days later Edward called round to Marston House. He was riding his black gelding and leading Miriam, the gentle pony that Innes had become used to. The ring was tucked away safely in his jacket pocket.

She emerged and mounted, and they set off up the main street towards the church.

'Where would you like to go?' she asked.

'I thought maybe Creech Hill Ring, and then down the hill towards Dipper Pool, if that's alright with you?'

'That sounds lovely.'

Nodding to various acquaintances they walked the horses through the gates of Langford Hall and then trotted along the grassy track towards the wide avenue of trees that led to the ring. Fifteen minutes later they passed between the two great standing stones that marked the entrance.

'Shall we stop for a moment?' Edward asked

She looked at him. 'If you wish.'

They dismounted and the horses lowered their heads and began to crop the lush grass as he took her hand and led her to the middle of the circle of stones. A sense that something was about to happen swept over her and she felt her heart begin to pump. Turning, he took her other hand as well, looked her in the eye, and smiled nervously.

'I've brought you here because there's something I want to ask you. You may be surprised, or you may not be. I don't know, because we have never really discussed any feelings that we might have for one another.'

No we haven't,' she said quietly, her luminous blue-grey eyes fixed on the flecks of gold in his.

'But the truth is I do have feelings for you. I realise now that I started loving you in the cottage hospital last year. You were still close to death and the thought of losing you was unbearable. But I'd seen so much suffering amongst people who had lost loved ones in the war that I think I just ignored it. Then somehow when you got better, we just went back to being how we were before. But I have loved the time we've spent together this summer and now I realise that, well...' suddenly fearful that he was babbling, he tailed off and looked at her anxiously.

She squeezed his hands and smiled, her eyes melting. 'Go on then, you lovely man. Get on with it, so you can kiss me.'

And then suddenly the ring was in his hand, and he was kneeling before her. He held it up and a ray of sunlight caught it. 'Innes Knox I am most hopelessly in love with you. Would you do me the honour of being my wife?'

'Yes, Edward I will,' she said firmly.

He scrambled to his feet, grinning wildly. 'Really? How absolutely marvellous.'

'Yes really.' Her eyes were openly watering now, and she wondered if she looked a mess.

He put his hands around her waist. 'There was some mention of kissing a moment ago.'

She raised her face to his, placed her arms on his broad shoulders, and whispered, 'Under the circumstances I think that would be perfectly in order, my darling'.

*

An hour later the two happiest people in Oxfordshire were dawdling by Dipper Pool. The horses were tied up, and they were sitting on the little beach as a gentle breeze hissed in the trees above them. The ring was safely in Innes's pocket. He'd slipped it onto her finger in Creech Hill Ring between kisses, but it was rather loose, and she was terrified of losing it.

'There's a safe at Marston House, I'm sure I can put it in there tonight and I'll go into Oxford tomorrow and have it adjusted,' she said.

'That's fine, it's yours now, but it is best to be careful, the thing is really very old and has been in the Spense family for centuries. My father gave it to my mother when they got engaged.'

Unable to resist, she got it out of her pocket again and slipped it on. 'It's absolutely wonderful.'

'So are you.' He took her hand, and she leant her head on his shoulder. The breeze was getting stronger and a hundred yards away in the rapids below the pool white ripples showed, as though small handkerchiefs were being waved by a crowd in the distance.

'This is Bert Williams's favourite poaching spot.'

'So I heard. And where he saw his water nymph last year.'

He nodded thoughtfully. 'Yes, if hc'd mentioned that earlier a great deal of trouble might have been avoided.'

She shivered. 'Well that's all over now.' There was another short and contented silence before Innes said, 'Are you sure it'll be alright with your mother and Piers? With my background I mean.'

'I'm certain. My mother cannot wait to get you started at Langford, believe me. And Piers thinks you're charming. We'll live there of course, but don't worry we won't be on top of each other. There's plenty of space and we will have our own sitting room if you like, and Jaikie can have his own playroom.'

'That sounds wonderful.' But, even as she said it, a shadow passed through her mind. *No. Not now. Not in this place, on this wonderful day.*

Dismissing the thought, she said, 'I can barely believe it Edward. A wee sassy girl from Glasgow marrying into the one of the great families of England. Wait till my mum and dad hear about it. When should we tell people, do you think?'

'Well if you want to make an announcement of it, I'd say when your parents are down. The dinner at Marston House perhaps?'

She nodded slowly, turning it over in her mind. Imagining the scene. 'Yes, agreed. After we've eaten I think.'

He laughed briefly, 'Yes, my dear. Just as you say.'

She reached up and touched his cheek. 'I can rely on you can't I, Edward? You won't change your mind.'

He leaned in and kissed her tenderly, then whispered, 'I can't think of anything on this earth that would stop me marrying you, my darling'.

*

96

Later that night Eve and her husband lay in bed. The colonel was absorbed in a book, but Eve was thinking. She had noticed that Innes had a definite glow about her when she returned from her ride with Edward – an outing from which she had returned much later than expected.

'I think he's asked her,' she said quietly.

'Who has asked what?' her husband enquired, turning a page.

She nudged him. 'Edward of course. He's asked Innes to marry him. And she's said yes. The timing's perfect, with her parents coming to stay in a few days. Claire said she was going to give him a serious prod.'

'Really? Well that's good news.'

'Is that all you can say? It's momentous news Jocelyn. It means Innes will be staying in Great Tew and, assuming they're blessed with children, the Langford line will be secure.'

With a sigh he put his book down. 'Yes, I see what you mean. And I'm delighted for her, of course. I suppose that might explain why she wanted me to put something in the safe earlier on.'

His wife turned to him. 'I beg your pardon?'

'The safe. She asked me to put a leather pouch in the safe when she got back.'

'And you didn't tell me? For heaven's sake, Jocelyn!' She thrust the covers back and swung her legs onto the floor.' As she reached for her dressing gown he watched her in some bemusement.

'What are you doing?'

'I'm going to look in the safe of course.'

'Don't you think it's private?'

She looked at him witheringly. 'Don't be ridiculous.' She crossed the room, opened a large built-in wardrobe, and pushed some hanging clothes out of the way. Entering the combination on the safe door she pulled it open and immediately saw the leather pouch sitting on some papers.

She stood stock still and stared for a moment then reached in, picked it up, and shut the safe door. A fizzing awareness ran through her whole body and her hair stood on end.

Hello old friend.

'Well, what is it?' Her husband's voice broke into her reverie.

'I know what it is,' she said quietly. 'I'm going up to the attic for a while, Jocelyn. Don't wait for me.' Then she crossed to the bed and kissed him. 'I love you, my darling.'

'Is it a ring?' he asked.

She smiled at him. 'Yes, it's a ring.'

Ten minutes later she was on the crimson cushion, the scrying bowl was full of still water and the candles were lighted. In the glow she finally turned the pouch upside down and the ring fell into her hand. Smiling, she admired it for a moment, then put it on the floor and slipped her wedding ring off.

Then, for the first time in over four hundred years, she put the Langford Ring onto her finger. Leaning over the bowl she stared at the mirrored surface, freed her mind, and let the memories flow.

Chapter Seven

Great Tew, 18th March 1643.

Lady Olivia Spense stared pensively out of a narrow leaded window on the top floor of Langford Hall. Behind her, the house's famous long gallery stretched for a hundred and fifty feet, the full width of the building. It was sparsely furnished, although the walls were hung with fine pictures. In peacetime it was a place for exercise and games when the weather was poor, but since the start of the Civil War it had become a lookout.

When hostilities commenced a year earlier, her husband, Sir Wyndham, had departed to join the King's army and had left his formidable wife in charge. The fact that this had caused him little concern was a tribute to Lady Olivia's character and abilities.

The hall was garrisoned with thirty troops sent from the Royalists' headquarters in Oxford, and their regular attacks on Roundhead movements along the high road had finally irritated Cromwell enough to order that the place be taken 'With all speed', leading to the despatch of one Captain Bulling with a hundred troopers to get the job done.

However, that had been three months ago and, under the charismatic leadership of Lady Olivia and her own wily and experienced captain, Grenville Wood, the hall had held out relatively comfortably. The pair had prepared intelligently and well. Realising that the gardens and orchards that surrounded the house were indefensible, they had focussed their preparations on the building itself. The back door and every ground floor window had been solidly bricked up and the iron-studded great door had been reinforced and was now impossible to open from the outside. Prior to this work, supplies of food and water had been placed in the cellars and, with a wide and deep moat protecting the rear and sides of the building, the Roundhead forces had been repulsed with painful losses on every occasion they had attacked.

Put simply, Langford Hall was proving a very tough nut to crack, and Bulling feared for the morale of his men who were taking casualties and had very little to show for it. The situation was not helped by the thinly veiled hostility they faced from the overwhelmingly royalist inhabitants of Great Tew, an attitude typified by the landlord of the Black Horse Inn, who kept a special barrel of sour ale for the soldiers and served it with a winning smile. The villagers were well aware that Sir Wyndham and Lady Olivia were unusually caring towards their estate workers and viewed the prospect of a commoner puritan taking residence in the hall with disdain. In fact, before the hall was finally sealed, the garrison's numbers had been swelled by a number of locals who had decided that actions speak louder than words.

But now the end was near.

Frustrated by Bulling's lack of progress, Cromwell had finally agreed to send a single cannon to Great Tew to batter the door. Lacking any defensive artillery, the garrison found itself at the mercy of the gunners and, within an hour of opening fire, the door was breached.

A subsequent frontal assault was repelled but after a second attempt the Roundhead troops gained entry to the hallway and, with pike, sword and pistol, gradually worked their way through the darkness of the ground floor and up the main staircase. Their losses were heavy, and no quarter was given as the sounds of desperate hand to hand fighting echoed around the handsome interior. Grenville Wood died, sword in hand, at the top of the stairs, his last words a despairing cry to the devoted great black war dog which fought alongside him.

'Run, Achilles. Go!' At this, the hound bounded down the stairs and across the hall. A Roundhead trooper raised his musket and saw the terrifying beast shiver as his shot found its target, then it was out of the door and away.

Lady Olivia had descended to her first floor bedroom as the cannon opened fire, and now she listened calmly to the sounds of fighting growing closer. She and Wood had always understood that if the enemy brought up artillery they were lost. Turning to the window she stared out across the fields, her eyes on the distant ridge of Green Hill as she idly touched the ornate ring on her finger. An observer would have considered her curiously lost in thought, as shouting and the noise of clashing swords sounded in the corridor directly outside her room.

Will I return to this place?

She slipped the ring off her finger and looked at it. It was truly beautiful, and priceless in a way few people understood. A gift from her husband on their wedding day, and already old when the Sir Guillaume Spense had arrived with William the Conqueror six hundred years earlier. Crowned with a single large diamond encircled by five bright red rubies, the burnished gold seemed to glow with an internal radiance.

It was too important to be taken.

She raised it to her lips, kissed it, and said some quiet words in an ancient language rarely heard in England. Then she quickly crossed to the panelling behind the bed and pressed the corner of one of the squares. Below and to her left another panel moved fractionally and she eased it open with her fingers. A cavity the size of a brick appeared. Reaching in she removed a small leather pouch and placed the ring inside it, before returning it to the hole and shutting the panel. As she did so there was a thump against the locked door of her bedroom. It shuddered but held as an agonised scream sounded close by. Returning to her earlier position she picked up a pistol from an ornate walnut table. Impeccably composed, she turned to face the invaders.

A second crash against the door moved it visibly and with a third it burst open, revealing a helmeted, bearded, soldier wearing a breastplate and carrying a blooded sword. He was sweating heavily and a gash on his forearm had soaked his white shirtsleeve in blood. Other men dressed the same appeared behind him, craning their necks to see into the room,

He stepped across the threshold then came to a halt. Backlit by the diamond-leaded bay window, a tall well-dressed blonde woman in her forties was standing side-on to him. Her arm was raised level with her shoulder and the hollow dead eye of a pistol barrel pointed directly at him.

Taking in her implacable expression and feeling his men stir, he raised his arm to still them and then addressed her.

'Madam, I am Captain Bulling. You have led your people with honour, I beg you, do not sacrifice your life. Will you not, at the last, give us your surrender and save the lives of the rest of your men?'

Looking every inch the chatelaine of a great house, Lady Olivia Spense met his eye for a long moment and then lowered her arm and quietly replaced the pistol on the table.

'If I must,' she said.

*

Pulse racing, Eve slowly came back into the room and stared at the mirrored surface of the water. She had lived many lives on earth and accepted reincarnation as reality, but in general her memories of previous events were blurred and unconnected - random pieces of a jigsaw, but never the whole picture. She believed that this was for her own protection, sensing that to be able to conjure up the entire spectrum of who she had been and would yet be, would be beyond her brain's comprehension.

But some images echoed persistently down the centuries. Her earliest memory was from a long, long, time ago and the picture was always clear in her mind – like a single frozen frame from a reel of film which she could observe, but never move beyond.

The scene was very familiar. She was standing alone in a shallow valley, on the edge of marshy fenland. In front of her the ground stretched away across limpid reed-lined pools, separated by occasional clumps of elder and birch. In the distance she could see the edge of a thick reed bank. White clouds showed in the sky and on the crest of a low hillside a long line of trees marked the beginnings of a forest. The sun was warm on her shoulders and a ripe breeze from the marshes teased her nostrils. She was wearing a knee-length tunic of brown material which she suspected was woven flax. There was no threat, and she felt the presence of loved ones nearby.

And it was her. Unequivocally. Not imagination, not a dream. It was her, in that place.

But what she had just seen of Langford Hall was different. The film had kept running. Until she had seen the leather bag in the safe she had no memory of the ring whatsoever, but there had been an overwhelming pulse of recognition when she picked it up. She was well aware that she had been bound to Great Tew for many years over different lives. Now she knew that the truth was more astonishing than that.

In a previous life she had been Lady Olivia Spense.

*

The middle and upper class people in the village were regular users of the postal service and sent and received letters most days. Although telephones were increasingly in use old instincts died hard and a hand written letter was still the medium of choice for many, most of whom devoted at least an hour a day to keeping in touch.

'You can't re-read a telephone conversation can you,' Lady Langford had observed sagely to the Reverend Tukes the previous Sunday. And he had agreed wholeheartedly. The Dean at Oxford was a moderniser and keen telephoner, and the blessed peace of the rectory in Great Tew was increasingly interrupted by the infernal device, as the normally affable parson had come to view it. He'd wondered if it might be disabled in an accident, unaware that his housekeeper Mrs Vane had been tempted by similar unchristian thoughts on more than one occasion whilst dusting the hall table.

But letter-writing was rare amongst the agricultural workers, many of whom were not especially literate and whose friends and families lived within walking distance of their homes. For them letters were unnecessary. Horizons were local and many had only been to Oxford once or twice in their lives – if at all.

So, the arrival of a postcard from Paris was an event of startling interest in the rented estate cottage a mile along Rivermead, where the Wray family lived.

Beatrice Wray had been sixteen when her young man had gone off to war, and seventeen when the news had reached her that he was dead. She had grieved in a way that perhaps only a teenager can, but a year later, in truth, she was over him. Now aged twenty-one, she had taken over from Laura Bessing behind the bar at the Black Horse and had recently broken up with a cow man who lived on the far side of the estate. The rumour was that she had initiated the parting and her beau was heartbroken.

Whatever the cause, as she was an attractive young woman the news of her newly single status had been noted with interest by the unattached men of the village with the result that the inn was well attended when she was in residence.

'It's an ill wind...' Stanley Tirrold remarked to his wife with some satisfaction as he passed through the kitchen and headed for the crowded public bar to give his barmaid with the corkscrew blonde hair a hand.

She was standing across the counter from a red haired, round-faced, bulky lad. Flushed with cider and full of Dutch courage he leaned forward with a less than angelic expression and said, 'Come on then Beatrice, how about you meet me round the back later'.

But the girl was no fool. She had left her cow man because he didn't have enough ambition and wasn't going to make the same mistake twice.

'Moses never reached the promised land, and neither will you, Alan Farthing,' she snapped. Knowing guffaws sounded amongst those in earshot. Outside courting on the estate started on May the first and often culminated in a summer's night visit to a local wood known, with the ribald humour typical of people living close to nature, as The Promised Land.

But the ardent young man ignored the laughter and pressed home his suit. 'No not that, I'm just saying we ought to meet, you know…' he tailed off as she went to serve the beaming Reverend Tukes who was gently waving his pint glass at her from the far end of the counter.

His face darkened. 'Here Beatrice, don't walk away from me, I'm talkin' to you.'

He blanched as the large frame of Stanley Tirrold leaned into him. 'Steady now Mr Farthing. We don't want you meeting the Chief Inspector do we?'

The young man swallowed and glanced at the large and heavy truncheon which the landlord kept hanging next to the racked barrels in case of trouble. 'Er, no Mr Tirrold, I don't expect we do.'

'That's right. You keep it polite with my staff.'

'Yes Mr Tirrold, I'm sorry.' And with that the frustrated lothario turned and was absorbed back into his group of grinning friends, where his failure to tempt the delicious barmaid would be the source of painful but not cruel humour in the fields the following Monday.

Beatrice left the pub and walked home at half past eleven. She was not bothered by anyone. She pushed open the unlocked front door and climbed the stairs to her bedroom, assuming her parents were both asleep as they normally were at this time. So she was surprised when they both appeared at the door as she sat down to brush her hair.

'This came for you. In the post. From France,' her mother said, extracting every last inch of drama from the moment, as she brandished the postcard.

'About ten o'clock this morning it was,' her father added, being something of a details man.

'That's right,' mother agreed. 'That's the Eiffel Tower, that is.' She handed it to Beatrice who stared at the picture for a moment then turned it over and read the back.

The Times 20th October. Personal columns.

'What does it mean?' Mrs Wray asked.

But Beatrice didn't answer directly. Her mind was reeling. The writer had finished the down strokes with a curious little upward flourish. She knew it straight away. In her drawer she had a note she had received five years earlier. A note she had re-read many times as a grieving teenager. A note in the same handwriting.

Stunned, she looked at her parents. 'I don't know Ma, I don't know what it means.'

*

Mr and Mrs Knox arrived at Oxford station exactly on time and had a joyous reunion with their daughter, who they had not seen for nearly a year. Thankfully the circumstances were very different this time. Rather than lying close to death in the green-painted ward of the cottage hospital, she was clearly very well and very happy. Unbeknown to them she had dropped the Langford Ring at the jewellers to be fitted for collection the following day.

Wee Jaikie, chattering, exuberant and characterful as only a four year old can be, received his hugs and kisses with aplomb, then bounced and jumped around on the platform and stared at the hissing steaming trains, as her parents embraced their daughter and were led outside to where Fenn and the large Alvis borrowed from the hall waited.

On the way back to Great Tew Mrs Knox was struck by the radiance emanating from her daughter. She helped the wean count cows in the fields and wondered privately about this as they rolled through the attractive, hilly, farmland. At Marston House they were greeted like old friends by the Dances and before long they were enjoying a refreshing cup of tea as Ellie unpacked their things in the comfortable guest room upstairs.

We've invited the Spense family for dinner tomorrow night, I hope that's alright with you both?' Eve enquired. 'You met my friend Lady Langford last time of course, and her eldest Piers, who is Lord Langford. Now you'll have a chance to meet Edward too.'

'We'll be delighted,' Mrs Knox replied, 'he was in hospital in Oxford last time. He's fully recovered I hope?'

'Oh yes, hale and hearty these days. Isn't he Innes?' Mrs Knox caught the impish smile her host gave her daughter and felt a little thrill run through her at its implications.

Was that it? Was there news?

And in fact that was it. Unable to keep quiet any longer without bursting, that morning Innes had taken Eve out for a walk and confessed her secret. Her friend had been overjoyed to hear it from her lips, even though she had already worked out the implications of Innes being in possession of the Langford Ring.

'That is just wonderful my dear, I am so happy for you both.'

'I must admit it was a bit of a surprise, but I came round to the idea pretty quickly. In about five seconds in fact.' Innes laughed. 'We've been busy making plans ever since.'

Eve squeezed her hand. 'Of course you have. Making plans is half the fun. You'll marry at St Mary's I assume?'

'Well Edward said the Bishop of Oxford would be happy to do it at the cathedral, but I must confess that might be a bit overwhelming for a plain old Glasgow girl.'

Eve laughed. 'Plain you are not, but yes, I can see that. Well you must decide between you.' There was a pause as they arrived at Lath Pool and looked across the wide stretch of water. Then she said gently, 'And you've told him everything?'

But even as Innes turned and looked at her she knew the answer. 'Not quite, not yet. There just hasn't been a chance.'

Innes placed her hands on the young woman's shoulders and looked her in the eyes. 'I really think you must. And the sooner the better. Am I right in thinking that you're planning the announcement tomorrow night, when the Spenses are with us for supper?'

'Yes.'

'It would be better before then, Innes. While your engagement is still private between you. Really it would.' She felt the tension in her friend.

'I just haven't been able to tell him. Before we were engaged there was no reason to, and now we are, I'm terrified to do so. I should have said something that first day, straight away, but I didn't. I couldn't. I love him so much, Eve.' She stared downriver. 'Sometimes I wonder if I need to tell him at all.'

The older woman looked at her sympathetically, but her voice was firm. 'You know you do. Let's walk up to the hall together, now.'

Accepting the inevitable, the beautiful young woman with the soulful eyes nodded, and they left the riverbank. As the great Tudor house came into sight, they parted.

'Just tell him the whole story like you told me, Innes. We all make mistakes in life. If I'm any judge of Edward's character you'll get a sympathetic hearing. But either way it must be done. Now on you go.' She stood and watched as the young woman crossed the knot garden and went round the house towards the front door.

Twenty minutes later she appeared in the sitting room at Marston House where Eve was waiting nervously. 'He wasn't there,' she said without preamble.

'Did you leave a message?'

'No, it doesn't matter. I'll make sure I see him in the morning.'

'Well it'll have to be early. We're all going into Oxford tomorrow to show your parents the sights.'

'And I've got to pick up the ring from the jewellers. Very well, I'll be there before nine o'clock.'

The following morning Innes was as good as her word and as her parents breakfasted at Marston House and Lady Langford sat up in bed and ate her boiled egg and toast in the room with the secret panel in the wall, she rang the bell by the iron-studded oak door.

But she was to be frustrated again. When Dereham appeared and welcomed her with a warm smile he informed her that Mr Edward had come down early and announced he was 'Going for a long tramp over Green Hill'.

'When will he be back, do you think?' she asked uncertainly.

'Knowing him as I do, Miss Knox, I would say late afternoon. He normally takes a bite from the kitchen and a bottle of water when he goes on these expeditions.' Seeing a shadow of concern pass over the visitor's face, he added, 'Is everything alright, miss? Can I be of any assistance?'

'No it's fine, I just wanted a word with him before this evening. He's coming to dinner at Marston House with his mother and brother.'

'So I understand, miss. And I hope I am not speaking out of turn when I say that they are looking forward to it.' Along with the rest of the household, Dercham had noticed a distinct spring in the step of young Mr Edward and had drawn his own conclusions about the reasons for the arrival of Mr and Mrs Knox. And he approved wholeheartedly of the anticipated news. Like Lady Langford, he could see many virtues in the young doctor.

She nodded, clearly distracted. 'Ah well, I've missed him them.'

'I fear so. May I give him a message?'

But she was already turning away. 'No that's alright. Thank-you, Dereham.'

'Thank-you, miss.' But as he watched her cross the gravel turning circle a slight frown appeared on his face.

She's worried about something.

*

Already two miles away, her fiancé had no such concerns. With a lump of homemade cheese, bread, and a pint of water in his knapsack he was striding out. From the house he had followed the main street downhill and then picked up the footpath to the River Cherwell – the same one followed by Thomas Dunn the night he had discovered the body. From there he had turned downstream, crossed the river using an ancient packhorse bridge, and climbed the hillside opposite through a series of fields before entering a wood.

His destination was the ridge line, where a chalky trail that had been a high level route for thousands of years stretched in both directions. To the north it climbed steadily to the summit of Green Hill six hundred feet above the Cherwell Valley, where a standing stone from the great outer circle of Creech Hill Ring marked the edge of the Langford Estate. Eve knew it as Imbolc.

Breathing hard, Edward reached the top and paused to have a drink and admire the spectacular view. He walked right to the edge and looked down into the valley, enjoying the sensation of flying as the breeze ruffled his hair. Immediately in front of him the ground fell away sharply and was too steep for anything but wood and sheep - the mainstay of farms on difficult ground. But further down, fields interspersed with patches of woodland ran all the way down to the flatter land near the river.

Far below he could see two plumes of smoke rising from opposite sides of a field as Samson and Delilah puffed in unison and drew a plough across the fertile alluvial soil, their labours slowly turning the ground from stubble-yellow to reddish brown.

He raised his eyes and stared across the airy space to Great Tew on the opposite side of the valley. The village disappeared under lush foliage in the Summer, leaving just the tower of St Mary's and the chimneys of Langford Hall visible, but it was slowly re-emerging as the leaves thinned, like a green tide retreating across a beach to leave the rocks exposed again.

The fold of ground where the village lay extended towards him, and he could see the site of Creech Hill Ring and the ride of trees that led to it. Behind the village the valley side rose to the summit of Tan Hill where another of the outer ring stones stood, impassive but somehow always waiting and ready.

Innes had told him that they lined up - Tan Hill, the aisle and tower of St Mary's, the ride of trees and Creech Hill

Ring. With a slight shock he realised that it was true, and the line was pointing directly at him. Where Imbolc stood.

'The line continues in both directions Edward. It's hidden in plain sight, like the outer ring. Eve showed me. There's another one, running east to west. The inner ring marks the junction of the two lines.'

Curious, he turned and walked up to the stone and looked out in the other direction, over hilly ground towards across the Vale of Evesham. To his surprise he could see two church towers that continued the line, one the little chapel at Hampsley and beyond that the tall tower of St Joseph's in the Fields where his mother's friend Lady Mulford lived.

As he was pondering this, a voice called out. 'Edward, well met.' He looked across to see Colonel Dance approaching across the cropped grass, accompanied by a slightly built grey-haired man wearing a brown mackintosh. They shook hands as his friend continued, 'May I introduce Mr Rory Knox, Innes's father. The ladies have gone into Oxford but, on reflection, this sensible fellow said he preferred the idea of a walk. Rory, this is Edward Spense, Lady Langford's youngest son.'

They shook hands. 'How do you do,' Edward said, intensely aware that he was looking at his new father-in-law.

'A pleasure. I hear you have fully recovered from the events of last year.'

'I have, sir, it's all in the past now.'

I'm delighted to hear that, and I believe we'll be seeing you later at dinner, Mr Spense. I know my wife is keen to meet you.' He had the soft accent of the outer isles and Edward wondered fleetingly what had taken him to Glasgow and what he had made of it.'

'You will. It's a bit of an invasion I'm afraid, myself, my mother and my brother Piers.'

'Don't be silly, it's always a pleasure, you know that,' the colonel chided him with a smile and then turned to his guest. 'Well here we are Rory, it's hardly Ben Lomond, but it's the best we have I'm afraid. Behold Green Hill and the Langford Estate in all its glory.'

His guest walked to the lip of the summit and looked out over the valley. 'Magnificent,' he said feelingly. 'A worked landscape. God and man labouring in unison to produce something utterly beautiful, and quite different to what Innes was used to. No wonder she remarked upon it so much in her letters.'

They stood and chatted amicably for ten minutes and the Scotsman who was acute in his observations of other people noticed two things. Firstly, that his host and Edward Spense were close. Had he not known otherwise, he might have assumed they were father and son. But then he realised that it wasn't quite a familial relationship, more a deep trust and shared understanding of each other. As though they had been through some great trial together and emerged the victors.

He wondered curiously what it might have been, and if he could ascertain it during his stay.

The other thing he noticed was that Edward was a happy man. In this high and glorious setting he seemed to glow with purpose and anticipation and, as he reflected on his wife's private remarks the previous evening regarding their daughter's countenance, he increasingly felt she was on the right track.

Yes, Mr Spense, I like the look of you, he thought. And, staring out across the land they owned, there was no avoiding the obvious – *the man was hardly on the breadline*.

Chapter Eight

Just before eight in the evening Bert Williams rang the vicarage bell. To his surprise he was rather enjoying his lessons, in direct contrast to the Reverend Tukes, who was finding the countryman's literal interpretation of events described in the good book rather challenging.

Accordingly, when they were settled in the study he enacted a carefully thought out plan. 'Ah, Bert, I think this evening we will not reference the bible directly, but rather talk about the role of the church in village life.'

'Oh yes?'

Reverend Tukes nodded firmly. 'Yes. For example if I ask you what the advantages of having a flourishing church community are, here on the Langford Estate, what would your answer be?'

Bert pulled at his bottom lip and stared at the drinks trolley for what the country parson considered to be a depressingly long time. Finally, as eight mournful chimes from St Mary's sounded in the room, Bert looked at him and said hopefully, 'Well it's handy for knowing the time'.

'That is true of course, and historically the church bell was an important signal to the men and women in the fields. But I am thinking more about the spiritual aspects of our lives.'

'Oh right. Well you do good work with people, I know that. Visiting the sick and looking after their immortal souls and so on.'

'Ah, immortal souls. My recollection of a previous conversation is that you felt that area was best served by Eve Dance.'

'Well a lot of the villagers feel that way, but I must admit, I'm coming round to your way of thinking.'

'I'm delighted to hear it. What is behind your change of heart, may I ask?'

'Power of numbers. There's a lot of people believe in god aren't there. I mean loads and loads.'

Tukes nodded vigorously. 'Many millions, spread around the globe.'

'That's what I'm thinking. Maybe they know something I don't.'

The vicar beamed at him. 'I think we're making progress Bert.'

'They all believe the same thing then?' He gestured to the bible on the table. 'What's in there.'

There was a slight pause. Tukes was capable of great ruthlessness in the service of the church but was also, in essence, a truthful man. 'By and large,' he responded carefully.

Bert pushed on. 'But they must mustn't they? Because otherwise you've got people believing different things, who all think they're right.'

'People come to god via different journeys, but we are all part of the same blessed family.' The clergyman gestured vaguely and reflected that the poacher had an uncanny ability

118

to put his finger on some of the more difficult aspects of theological doctrine.

'When I was driving a lorry during the war I met some blokes from Karachi. They did loads of praying every day. And they were serious about it. Were they more holy or less holy than us?'

'I really don't think of it that way. We all have an individual relationship with our faith.'

Bert nodded. 'But we can't all be right can we? If I was from Karachi I'd believe what those blokes believed. Or if I'd been born into a Jewish family I'd believe what they believe.' A moment of inspiration hit him. 'It's like football teams isn't it? You support the team you've been born to, like the Arsenal, or Wolverhampton Wanderers.'

The vicar glanced at the clock and saw he had another fifty minutes to go.

'No, it is absolutely not like football teams. Perhaps we'll spend a little time reading about Noah's ark,' he said firmly. 'You can read it out and we'll discuss what you think it means.'

'Alright, but I've always had a bit of a problem with that story, Parson. I mean I've seen the Cherwell flooding over the valley floor, but it's obvious it's never going to cover Green Hill.'

'You do surprise me, Bert,' the vicar said and reached for the bible.

*

In London, Halley entered Sir Anthony's office without knocking. Seated at his desk, his superior looked up from his paperwork enquiringly.

119

'The foreign secretary is on his way, sir, he's just left his office,' the young man reported.

Kerr raised his eyebrows in surprise. An unannounced visit was rare. Normally he was summoned in the opposite direction, but the informal early warning system that the aides operated was utterly reliable. 'Anything particular that you are aware of?' he asked.

'A cable from Berlin, I understand. From the embassy.'

'Containing?'

'I'm not sure, sir. I'm sorry.'

Kerr grunted and observed, 'Well I imagine we will know shortly.' And he was correct in this prediction. Thirty seconds later Curzon entered, brandishing a slip of paper.

'Shocking news. Ertzburger, the man who negotiated the armistice for the Germans, has been murdered. Lured to a forest and shot by a pair of ex-naval officers, apparently in revenge for his agreeing to the surrender of their high seas fleet to us.'

'Good lord.' Kerr rose and came round the desk, taking the proffered cable from the minister. He read it carefully and handed it back.

'What do you make of it?' Curzon asked.

The permanent secretary thought for a moment. 'It's certainly further evidence of just how febrile things are over there at present although, as the Germans scuttled much of their fleet at Scapa Flow, we hardly benefited from its surrender. I think he'd been in trouble over his left-wing policies too, especially from the landed classes. And of course he's gone down in history as the man who signed the

120

armistice, which paved the way for the Treaty of Versailles and the German guilt clause.'

He paused and added, 'I've always thought he negotiated well, with a poor hand. He was a schoolteacher before he went into politics and my impression was that he was a decent man caught up in dreadful events. After they'd signed the ceasefire he offered Marshall Foch his hand and the general refused it.' He shook his head, 'It's very sad'.

Curzon said, 'To my mind it reinforces the need to present the Germans with their bill as soon as possible. Before there's any backsliding over their responsibility for starting the war. We must come to terms with our allies, and quickly.' He glanced at Kerr. 'I take it that other matter is in hand?'

The permanent secretary met his eyes and said calmly, 'Yes, it is Minister.'

'Good. God knows what would happen if Princip's countersigned letter fell into the hands of someone in Berlin.' He strode towards the door, then turned and added, 'I mean it Kerr. The thing must be locked up tight as a drum. We must have it.'

*

The party from Langford Hall arrived at Marston House at half-past seven and were met by Ellie who showed them into the sitting room with the French windows, where they were received warmly by the Dances and their guests.

Rory Knox had mentioned meeting Edward Spense when he and his wife were dressing for dinner, and she had insisted on a word-by-word account of their conversation, a detailed description of his appearance, and her husband's considered impressions of his character. In the end, her forensic examination of the evidence was so intense that he was forced to remark, 'Whisst woman, will you no' just wait until you meet the man yourself.'

This ill-advised suggestion resulted in a lively but muted exchange between husband and wife and a certain stiffness in the atmosphere of the guest bedroom, but as they were both on their best behaviour there was no sign of it as they descended the stairs,

Her first impressions of the tall, broad-shouldered, sandy-haired, man were very good, and she found herself anticipating the rest of the evening with increasing excitement. As for Edward, he took to Mrs Elizabeth Knox immediately. She was obviously the source of the clear blue eyes which her daughter had inherited and possessed a warm and gently inquisitive manner which made her easy to talk to. She was, he reflected rather naively, one of those people who was happy to give you their full attention.

And in Elizabeth Knox's case this was nothing less than the truth.

To Eve's pleasure, the evening progressed very well. Mrs Franks excelled herself in the kitchen and Ellie, resplendent in a new uniform, served with discretion and efficiency.

When they finished eating, Innes rose and took the ladies back into the sitting room, leaving the four men to their port. Shortly afterwards, in a pre-arranged move, Jocelyn asked Piers to join him in his study for a moment to, 'Have a look at a new book that I think might interest you', leaving Rory Knox alone with Edward.

Heart beating but confident that Innes loved him, he looked across the table and said, 'I've got something to ask you, sir'.

The man opposite met his eye. 'Oh yes? What might that be?'

'The truth of it is that I am very much in love with your daughter Mr Knox, and, with your permission, I should like to marry her.'

The Scotsman's eyes crinkled. 'Is that so? Well now there's a thing, because my wife is convinced that our daughter is very much in love with you.' He paused for a heartbeat and added, 'So from what I can see, that would be a highly convenient arrangement.'

Smiling broadly, he pushed back his chair, extended his hand and, as Edward jumped to his feet, he said warmly, 'We couldn't be more delighted, welcome to the family'. They shook hands and drank a toast. Then he asked, 'Do you have a ring?'

The colonel had returned it to the safe when Innes got back from the jewellers in Oxford, but he had retrieved it again and given it to Edward before dinner, so the younger man was able to produce the leather pouch from his pocket and show it to his budding father-in-law. 'It's an heirloom, the Langford Ring. A thousand years old probably. My father gave it to my mother when he proposed.'

And now it's going to my daughter. The schoolteacher from Glasgow turned it over in his hand as the implications of the engagement hit him. *The Spense family have things like this. Innes will be part of it.*

He handed it back. 'That's quite something. You'll be announcing your engagement this evening then? I assume you've asked her?'

123

'I have, sir. Sorry to get things in the wrong order but the moment suddenly came upon me, and I'm delighted to say she said yes.'

He nodded. 'Aye well, there's no problem with that. Best to be sure before you asked me and I'm very happy to give you both my blessing.'

Voices sounded in the hall and the colonel's head appeared round the door. 'We're going through, will you join us?' and with that, the four men re-joined the ladies. Innes was sitting on her own on one of the settees and Edward immediately took the space next to her.

She looked at him and he smiled and raised his eyebrows. *I've done it.*

He was surprised to see a faint expression of anxiety as their eyes met. *Nerves, she's bound to be a bit nervous,* he thought. Both of them missed Innes's mother's look of enquiry at her husband as he sat down. His small smile and subtle nod were all she needed, and a warm glow flowed through her as she sat back and awaited developments.

Edward slipped his hand into his jacket pocket and touched the pouch for luck, then took Innes's hand in his and cleared his throat. A silence fell on the room remarkably quickly as he stood up and his fiancée rose with him.

'Well everyone, as we are all gathered here it seems an ideal moment for Innes and me to give you our news. A few minutes ago I asked Mr Knox for his daughter's hand in marriage, and I am delighted to say he agreed. I also confessed to asking Innes to marry me a week ago and, again, I am delighted to tell you all that she said she would.'

An outpouring of cheers and cries of congratulation passed around the room, and everyone instinctively stood up as he withdrew the pouch from his pocket and tipped out the ring. Laughing and raising his voice above the hubbub, he held it up and said, 'I will now ask Innes to wear the Langford Ring in public for the first time.' Grinning widely, he gently lifted her wrist and moved the ring towards her finger.

But to his confusion, and then horror, she pulled her hand back and said, 'No Edward, I can't wear it.'

There was a moment of stunned silence in the room.

'What?' her astonished fiancé said. 'Whatever do you mean?'

'Before I put it on I have to tell you something,' she replied, anguish on her face. 'I should have told you when you asked me. Straight away. But I was a coward, and I didn't.'

Eve interrupted, her face a mask of concern, 'Innes, are you sure…'

But the young woman held up her hand. 'No Eve. I have to do this.' She turned to Edward and visibly braced herself. 'What I have to tell you…,' but she made the mistake of pausing and in that moment, she broke. Hands clenched by her sides and tears streaming down her face she wailed, 'I am not as you would wish me to be Edward. I am so sorry. The wean is mine, conceived out of wedlock. My foolish, foolish, highland fling. There was no sister, there never has been.'

As if to reinforce the thing in her own mind and his, she finished with a simple, 'I am Jaikie's mother. I should have told you before'.

Although this news came as a thunderbolt to Edward, ironically, apart from a transfixed Ellie, who was standing by the sideboard with the coffee pot in her hand, only Piers was surprised. Everyone else in the room already knew. Jaikie's grandparents had played a major role in the early years of the wean's life. And Innes herself had told Eve the previous year. Although solemnly sworn to secrecy, Eve had lost no time in telling Lady Langford and subsequently her husband Jocelyn – although thankfully the revelations had stopped at that point.

In the aftermath Eve was to reflect that it was undoubtedly a mercy that Edward did not know this, or his reaction would have been even worse. To be knowingly misled was one thing, to be made to look a fool was another.

But as it was, the damage was done anyway.

White as a sheet and stiff with outrage, he stared at her in astonishment. 'And you didn't think to tell me this before I proposed?' he said icily.

'I know I should have told you that day at Creech Hill, but I was so overjoyed I couldn't spoil the moment, and since then I've been running away from it.' She held out her hand to him in supplication, but he took a pace backwards, avoiding her touch.

'You surely must have been anticipating my proposal and yet you chose to lie by omission, Miss Knox,' he whispered bitterly, 'and it is a grievous deceit'. And as she stood hollow eyed with misery, he replaced the ring in the pouch and strode over to his mother, who stared up at him silently, her own face a picture of stricken sorrow.

He gave her the ring. 'Yours I believe, mother. My apologies, I nearly invited a liar into the family. It seems we have had a close escape.'

And with a furious glance at the young doctor he left the room and moments later the sound of the front door slamming echoed down the hall.

*

The following morning a council of war took place in Lady Spense's boudoir at Langford Hall. Present were herself, Eve Dance and Elizabeth Knox. After coffee had been served they commenced discussions.

'Where is he now?' asked Eve. There was no need to clarify to whom she was referring.

'According to Dereham he went out early. He took the Alvis about half past seven. I have no idea where he went or what time he will be back.' His mother sipped her coffee and then asked, 'What about Innes?'

'She is in her room at Marston House, packing,' Mrs Knox said. 'Last night she told me she would come home with us tomorrow as there was nothing for her here in Great Tew.'

'Aargh, what a mess. Unfortunately my son is prone to take offence and is all too eager to climb onto his high horse.' Claire Spense clicked her tongue in frustration and looked her in the eye. 'I wish to make something clear Elizabeth. Your daughter Innes is a fine girl in every respect and, in my eyes at least, continues to be someone we would welcome into the Langford family. I was aware of her difficulties before last night and had taken note of her competence and determination in finding a way through them – although

127

clearly you and your husband behaved with exceptional grace and character in supporting her.'

This compliment was received with a grateful nod of thanks from the Scottish woman, as she continued, 'One thing is clear to me. If Innes goes back to Glasgow with you I think the cause will be lost. What's needed is some more time to let emotions settle. I will work on Edward and Eve, perhaps you can ask the same of Jocelyn? They are close and I know he respects the colonel greatly.'

'Yes, I can certainly ask him to speak to Edward.'

'So how are we to ensure she stays in Great Tew, for a while at least?' Claire asked.

There was silence in the room as the sound of the bell of St Mary's chiming eleven drifted in through the window. Then Elizabeth stirred.

'I will speak to her,' she said firmly. 'There is an unpinning of good Scottish common sense in the girl and she must be told that, if she still harbours any feelings for Edward, the only way to resolve their differences is to stay in Great Tew. The rift is too deep for an exchange of letters. I will suggest she stays for a month and if there is no progress at that point, then she can come home.'

Her eyes glinted. 'Rory and I supported her greatly when she found she was pregnant. I will call in the debt.'

That's where the steel comes from, thought Lady Claire with a faint smile. 'Very well. Today is the sixth of October, I suggest she stays until the bonfire night party on November the fifth. In the meantime Eve, Jocelyn, and I will commence Operation Edward. He must be persuaded to see sense. It is that simple.'

*

In the matter of the murder of Dunstan Green, Constable Burrows found himself working alone. To his surprise neither of his partners turned up to a planned meeting and when he made enquiries, the answers he received were rather vague. He mentioned it to the colonel but was simply told to, 'Carry on with your enquiries on your own for the moment Burrows and report any developments to me'.

But as he set out on his police bicycle, Burrows had other matters on his mind as well. He and his wife had had their first significant row.

The previous evening, presented with an unappetising plate of charred sausages and soggy potatoes, he had finally grasped the nettle and had a word with his nearest and dearest. The difficulty was compounded by the fact that he was a fair to middling cook himself. Growing up with just his father, they had shared the meal preparations in their little terraced house in Cowley and from his early teenage years he had often been the one getting tea ready for when his father returned from work.

So when he remarked in some frustration that, 'It really isn't that difficult to cook up a few sausages and some spuds,' to his exhausted wife, he knew he was speaking the truth.

However, in the ensuing conversation it became apparent that his wife knew a few home truths as well, and within ten minutes a new set of arrangements had been established in the police house. From now on Burrows would be doing the cooking, wouldn't be going to the pub so often and, as a matter of fact, should also consider himself extremely lucky that he wasn't sleeping on the sofa.

But the following morning after a chilly, wordless, breakfast, Laura was full of regret over the events the previous evening. In particular, she knew she shouldn't have appeared in the kitchen wearing her husband's police helmet and shouted, 'From now on, I'll be the bally policeman and you can stay at home and be mother'.

Her beloved Burrows had been outraged at this desecration of his uniform and harsh words had been exchanged. But she had to admit that that her overreaction had been because she knew that her cooking was a weakness and was at a loss to know what to do. She'd simply always been hopeless, despite her mother's best efforts.

Unaware of his wife's reflections, Burrows pedalled thoughtfully over Tan Hill and through Little Tew. His plan was to travel onwards along a good track to the reed bed that marked the southern edge of the Langford Estate and, coincidentally, the boundary of his jurisdiction. It was reed harvesting time and he thought a general gossip with the men working down there might prove beneficial as he sought to build up his knowledge of the circumstances surrounding Dunstan Green's death.

Ten minutes later as the valley widened he crested a rise, and the river came into view. Thousands of years earlier the Cherwell had created a great wide sweep of bend that cut into the gentle slope of the hillside, but in more recent times the force of the flow had slowly cut through the isthmus and created an ox-bow lake in the old bend. The low lying area between this and the new channel formed a dense reed bed roughly half a mile square and this was Burrows' destination.

The reeds were a vital resource for thatching, not just for houses and cottages but also for the many hay and corn ricks that needed to be watertight through the winter, so they were carefully managed. The marsh was also a source of wild game and over the years a number of channels had been cut to allow the various Lords Langford and guests to hunt ducks and geese in the quiet waterways and on the old lake.

Reed cutting commenced after the end of the cereal harvest. It was back-breaking work using curved razor-sharp hooks and the men carried whetstones in their pockets and paused to resharpen the blades every minute or so. When they had an armful of five foot long reeds, they raked out the bundle to remove all the dead growth and 'knocked it up' on a three foot square board in the bow of the flat bottomed reed boat. This evened up the end to give a nice straight edge for thatching. Then the bundle was tied and piled in the stern. A good man could cut around fifty bundles in a day and after the requirements for the estate had been brought back to Home Farm, the remainder were sold by the bundle to other farmers.

Burrows leaned his bike against a tree and walked across a grassy field to where a group of the cutters were unloading one of the reed boats at a wooden jetty next to a small hut. 'Good morning,' he said cheerfully. From where he was standing he could see down the main channel to the other reed boat about fifty yards away.

'And to you Constable,' a thick-set man wearing a cap replied, as the others looked up and nodded at him. Burrows took him to be the man in charge.

'I saw you working and thought I'd come over and say hello,' he said.

'Oh yes?' said the foreman. The men had all stopped now and were looking at him. Down the channel he noticed the occupants of the boat were also peering back towards the hut. He sighed and reflected, not for the first time, that to be a police officer in a tightly knit rural community was to be a man apart.

He smiled encouragingly, 'There's no trouble gents, but I am making enquiries about the death of Dunstan Green. Just wondering if anyone had seen him or met him before he killed himself. It's for his parents really. They're decent people.'

'Oh yes?' the foreman repeated. In the ensuing silence a pair of shots rang out in the distance, quickly followed by a third. In answer to Burrows' raised eyebrows, the man in the cap added, 'That's Lord Langford on the lake, missing with both barrels I'd say, and Mr Stafford doing the necessary.'

A faint smile showed on his face as he added, 'a rare shot, is his Lordship.'

Seizing on this the young constable asked, 'Are you much of a shot yourself?'

'I'm not too bad if the quarry's wearing a German helmet, but you don't get many fowl on the lake like that.'

The men guffawed delightedly, but Burrows ignored them. Raising his eyes to encompass all of them he asked, 'Did you all serve?'

'Apart from Harry and Joe in the boat. They were too young. The rest of us were all in the Oxfords. We left a lot of men out there too. Decent blokes. There's not a lot of good feeling for Dunstan Green around here.'

Burrows nodded. 'I understand that. So no-one saw him on the night before he was found in the leat?'

The foreman shook his head. 'It was Wilfred's birthday.' He gestured to a slim man in his thirties wearing a waistcoat and cap. 'We had a little party for him down here. Lighted a fire and cooked a duck or two.' He met his eye and challenged the constable, who felt duty-bound to oblige.

'Lord Langford's ducks?'

'They were dead when we found them. We reckon they must have flown into each other. Seemed a shame to waste them.'

'What remarkable luck. And on Wilfred's birthday too. You were all here were you?'

'We were. Twelve of us.'

'That's a lot of ducks,' Burrows observed.

The foreman nodded and glanced upwards. 'It must have been carnage up there.'

Seeing the little semi-circle of men smirking, he decided to let this provocation go unchallenged and continued, 'And no-one saw or heard anything of Dunstan Green. We know he was down by the river you see.'

'No they didn't.' He gestured up the channel. 'Kenneth on the boat brought down a flagon of metheglin. That slips down like milk, smooth and mild, but it's sly. We all nodded off in the end. Woke up with dew on us and the fire out.'

'What time did you fall asleep?

'Well past midnight. We heard the chimes from St Bridget's in Leyland and sang Wilfred happy birthday, then sang a good few more songs.' As the foreman finished speaking another three shots sounded across the reed bed, the pattern and timing exactly the same as the first.

'And again. Makes you wonder why he carries on,' he observed with a slight note of wonder.

For elimination purposes Burrows noted down the names of all present at the party then retraced his steps across the field. The reed cutters had been drunk on pear liquor at midnight and still awake and singing later than that. And the reed bed was at least two miles downstream of the leat.

He thought it unlikely any of them were the culprits.

Chapter Nine

When Burrows got back he found the names of three of the reed men on his list and put a line through them with some satisfaction. He was also delighted to find that Laura was in an apologetic mood regarding the helmet incident so with mutual relief they put the row behind them, and the fair winds of married bliss returned to the police house.

Over the course of the following week, with regular reference to the Oxfordshire police instruction manual, he worked diligently and alone on further investigations and made considerable progress. One family was headed by a middle-aged father who suffered from severe arthritis and was looked after by his wife and teenage daughter, another by other a deeply religious man who occasionally helped out as a lay preacher at St Mary's. They too were crossed off, as were three families that were together at a violin recital in Oxford.

More names followed, so by the middle of October, he had just five names left: Mr Reeve and Mr Bennett, and a Mr True and his two sons. However, as it turned out, he was able to delete the latter three from his list as well, as the whole family had been staying with Mrs True's mother in Birmingham on the night of the murder.

One tea-time as he was silently contemplating a cheese omelette that would have soled a boot, the door knocker sounded and with some relief he answered it, to find Wilfred, the birthday boy from the reed bed, standing there.

He was looking a little shifty and Burrows brought him into the room with the counter and took up his position behind it. 'What can I do for you?' he inquired.

'When you came over you were asking about the night Dunstan Green was murdered.'

'That's correct.'

Wilfred nodded and twisted his trilby in his hands uncomfortably. Burrows waited. The silence stretched on, but the constable had learned a thing or two in his dealings with the villagers of Great Tew and said nothing. Finally, the man in front of him spoke.

'Frank Eales, the foreman, lied to you. And he knew he did too.'

The policeman raised his head in surprise. 'Oh yes?'

'Yes. He was right when he said we were all drinking and singing and then fell asleep. But Eales arrived much later than the rest of us. We were well into it and had eaten the ducks by then.'

'Really? What time did he turn up then?'

'Just before eleven.'

Burrows pursed his lips, thinking hard. 'Are you sure about that? You had been drinking.'

The man nodded. 'Maybe, but I heard chimes from St James's in Leyland at eleven and thought, well that's nearly your birthday over for another year Wilfred.'

Burrows' mind whirled at this new development. According to the post mortem Dunstan Green had entered the water by nine p.m. at the earliest. Eales could easily have walked down the river from the leat in an hour meaning that, if he'd arrived at Wilfred's party just before eleven, he would have had at least an hour between nine and ten p.m. to carry out the murder and dump the body in the Cherwell.

'Why didn't you say something when I was there?'

The other man shook his head. 'Eales is a bully and hard man. You'd be a fool to cross him in public. He's got his finger in a few dodgy pies they say, but he's clever about it.'

'So why are you telling me now?'

He shrugged. 'I don't owe him no favours.'

When he thought about this later the constable decided that Wilfred had probably suffered under Eales and thought he'd get his own back. 'What sort of dodgy pies?' he asked.

'He was conscripted then invalided out quite early. No-one is quite sure how he managed it, or what was wrong with him. They say he was involved in black market trading during the war, and he's carried on in that line, stolen goods mainly. He's always got plenty of money. Too crooked to lie straight in bed, some say.'

Burrows smiled at the image. 'Any family?'

'His wife left him, and his son was killed in the war.'

Burrows wondered how he didn't know of him, but this question was answered by Wilfred as he continued, 'He lives on his own, beyond the edge of the estate, but works on the reeds when they need cutting. I think he spends most of his time in Leyland.' The policeman nodded. The village was down river, where the Banbury and Oxford roads met, and off his beat.

'Is there anything else you want to tell me?'

'No that's it.'

Burrows showed him out and returned thoughtfully to the kitchen.

'Everything alright?' Laura asked.

'Yes fine, just some unexpected news that's all.'

'Your omelette's stone cold, do you want me to re-heat it in the pan?'

'No, no don't go to any trouble. I'll just have some bread and cheese.'

She looked at him suspiciously. After the recent rapprochement his wife had resumed cooking duties, but the issue continued to create an undercurrent that swirled around the kitchen.

Sensing danger he added, 'You have a seat and I'll put the kettle on,' and it appeared the moment had passed as her husband made a pot of tea. But disaster struck as he unthinkingly picked up the omelette plate and put it on the side, saying, 'Mr Perkins will enjoy that.'

They had recently acquired an Old Spot piglet from Mr Trotter and christened it Mr Perkins. It lived in pen in the back garden. His remark was innocent enough, but hideously open to misinterpretation. And his wife duly obliged.

'It's only fit for a pig? Is that what you're saying?'

'No, no. I'm just saying it won't be wasted, that's all.'

A wail sounded from upstairs, and Laura rolled her eyes. 'There she goes. Awake and hungry again. At least she enjoys the food I provide, Burrows.' And with that unanswerable truth she left the kitchen. He heard her climbing the stairs and shortly afterwards the crying stopped abruptly. He took the omelette out to Mr Perkins where it was received with enthusiasm and after a short discussion with him on the unfairness of women, went back to the house and gloomily sat down alone with a hunk of estate cheese and some bread.

*

The Times newspaper of the 20th of October 1920 was a routine issue with little news of great importance, and many people who bought it flicked through the pages reflecting that the previous day had been remarkably uneventful.

But in London, Great Tew, and Paris, certain individuals studied it with great interest.

In the Foreign Office Halley checked that the advert had appeared as instructed, circled it with a pencil, and took the paper through to the permanent secretary, who nodded with satisfaction.

'Well the die is cast now. I imagine we will receive another communication laying out the arrangements for the exchange in due course, and at that point we can start detailed planning.'

'Indeed, sir. Do you want me to do anything in the meantime?'

Sir Anthony tapped a pencil on the edge of his desk and thought for a moment. 'Assuming the location is to be Great Tew, we will need a couple of competent men with us to keep an eye on the money and do whatever is necessary after we have the papers back. Put a call through to Hayden Riley at the War Office, will you? I'll have lunch with him this week and see who he can rustle up.'

In the village, Beatrice Wray appeared in the general store at eight o'clock just as the papers were arriving. The brown-coated shopkeeper was surprised, as she wasn't one of his regulars. Even more interesting was the fact that, after her purchase, she stood there and studied the personal columns on the front page while still in the shop. After half a minute she suddenly shuddered, and her eyes widened in shock.

Concerned and, far more importantly, sensing an interesting piece of gossip, the shop's owner inquired, 'Is everything alright Miss Wray?'

But she just stared vacantly over his shoulder, seemingly completely engrossed in a shelf full of tinned fruit. He tried again. 'Not upsetting news I hope?' he leaned forward, trying to see where on the page she had been looking.

After a moment she gathered herself, met his eye and whispered. 'Do you believe in ghosts?'

He was taken aback. 'Ghosts? No, I don't think I do.'

'Then I rather think you should start.' And with this enigmatic remark hanging in the air she turned and left the shop, newspaper clutched in her hand. As the door shut and the bell tinkled the shopkeeper reached for the top copy of the pile of papers, unfolded it and bent his head over the columns of adverts. *What on earth had she seen?*

Copies of the Times arrived in Paris mid-afternoon, having been loaded onto the boat train in London at seven o'clock that morning. The man with death in his heart was waiting at a café called La Belle Epoch, which was a haunt of British expatriates and, in consequence, provided the English papers every day. He took a copy and went back to his table. As his eyes ran down the column he saw the entry he had been hoping for.

Trixie, I love you, Teddy.

Like Beatrice Wray, he stared sightlessly across the room for a moment. He rarely smiled, but an observer hoping that this might be one of those days would have been rewarded, as a sardonic grin appeared on his lips. *That was it then. The game was on.*

Crossing to the counter he asked for writing paper, returned for a second time to his table and removed the expensive fountain pen from his jacket pocket. He didn't hesitate. The thing was clear in his mind, and he simply leaned forward and began to write.

*

After the disastrous evening at the Dances, Edward Spense had reverted to the bottle, although the effect was not the same as those first desperate months after his shell-shocked return from the war. To his chagrin he had developed a conscience which, while not strong enough to prevent his drinking to excess, persistently nagged away at him through the haze.

He found himself in a befuddled no-man's-land, between oblivion and self-chastisement and spent his afternoons sitting blankly in the corner of the Black Horse, observed uneasily by Stanley Tirrold and Beatrice Wray.

The villagers noticed this behaviour and drew their own conclusions. The most obvious clue being the fact that Edward and Innes were suddenly and conspicuously no longer seen together, either riding out, or walking the estate.

Lady Langford found herself torn between conflicting emotions. She loved her son dearly and felt for him. He had volunteered early, served bravely in the war, won a medal for gallantry, and then succumbed to a dreadful case of shell-shock. Just when it seemed he had recovered and found a delightful girl to marry, her inability to tell him her secret had led to the dreadful scene at Marston House. Innes had made a bad mistake and it was no wonder he was upset.

But, as she pursed her lips and stared out across the parkland, she also had to reluctantly acknowledge that self-pity came easily to him. Her remark to Mrs Knox about high horses was true. That had always been his weakness and he defaulted towards introspection a little too easily.

If only Colin was still alive. His father would have snapped him out of it one way or another.

She glanced at her watch. It was half past three and she wondered if Jocelyn was with him now. As planned, Eve had asked her friend to speak to him. She knew the bond they shared and felt if anyone could wrench him away from his alcohol-fuelled brooding it was the clear-thinking, straight-talking colonel.

Matters were no better at Marston House where Innes was a hollow shell of her former self. To Eve's distress, she had resumed wearing the dreadful horn-rimmed spectacles that were her own personal hair shirt. A self-recriminating reminder of the mistakes she had made. Even though her primary instinct had been to flee the scene of the disaster, at her mother's insistence she had not travelled back to Glasgow, and now worked mechanically through the days until her one month sentence had passed.

142

As time passed she became increasingly angry with Edward. The incident had reinforced the deep love she had for her charismatic child, who glowed with such a joyful and innocent light. He was adored by Mrs Franks and Ellie, clearly much loved by Eve and Jocelyn and she, she reaffirmed to herself, the complete and utter centre of her life. She had been distracted by Edward, but Jaikie was her responsibility and her priority, and woe betide any man that tried to make her feel guilty about that.

It was against this loaded background that Jocelyn Dance entered the Black Horse, noted with satisfaction that his friend slumped in the corner was the sole customer and having collected a couple of pints of cider, joined him at the table. He had reflected long and hard on the best approach to take and had his strategy in place.

Behind the bar Stanley Tirrold picked up a tea towel and a glass and settled down to listen. Edward Spense was his friend too.

'Have you spoken to her?' The colonel's opening remark had a virtuous simplicity to it, which was received with a brief shake of the head by the man opposite. 'Can I ask why?' he followed up.

'What would be the point?' Edward answered.

The colonel sipped his pint. 'Do you still love her?'

'The best description of my feelings for Miss Knox would be angry indifference.'

Ignoring the logical inaccuracy of this remark, the colonel replied, 'So you have no desire to clear the air? Even if matters are over between you.'

'I am the aggrieved party. It is not for me to initiate any further communication.' His friend sighed inwardly and stared out of the window. Bert Williams was standing in the street talking to Ada Dale. The sound of their voices carried to him, something about Noah's ark, he realised to his surprise.

'You're right to feel upset, the girl made a mistake. I think that point is generally acknowledged.'

For the first time in the conversation Edward met his eye. 'You're on my side? I assumed my mother had sent you to tell me to make it up with her.'

Jocelyn grinned wolfishly at him. 'Oh she did, but I am on your side, you know that. However, in the time Innes has been with us I have grown very fond of her, and she is hurting grievously. I find myself on her side too.' They both turned to look through the window as Ada and Bert roared with laughter and she punched him gently on the arm. Edward appeared surprised that normal life was continuing around him.

'So you are prepared to let the whole thing whither on the vine?' the colonel continued, 'Innes will return to Scotland, and you will never see her again. That is what you want?'

'What I want is for this whole damned business never to have happened. I was a fool. I've seen the pain love causes, but I fell for her anyway. And my bally mother pushed me into it. Waving a ring around and wholeheartedly recommending a girl who has the most basic of character flaws...' His mouth tightened as he added, 'She's a liar, Jocelyn.'

The older man leaned back and frowned. 'That's a harsh judgement. She made a mistake, but I wouldn't put it in the category of a deliberate lie.'

'A lie of omission is still a lie.'

'But she told you didn't she? Yes, she put it off, but she knew you had to know, and in the end she did it in the most difficult of circumstances. In front of her prospective mother-in-law and family. That seems pretty gutsy to me.'

It was a measure of Edward's essential reasonableness that he nodded slightly at this but could not bring himself to say anything. Nevertheless, the colonel felt he'd scored a hit to the body and soldiered on.

'Can I ask you something directly, man to man?' He lowered his voice and glanced towards the bar where Stanley Tirrold was seemingly lost in a world of his own, glass and tea towel in hand.

'You may.'

'The bottom line is that Innes is a mother and has shared a bed with another man. Does that mean marriage to you is out of the question? As she is no longer virgo intacta, as it were?'

'For heaven's sake, Jocelyn,' Edward stirred uncomfortably in his seat and looked away.

But the colonel maintained his steely gaze and said, 'I'm sorry, but we must get to the heart of this. Be under no illusions, your mother, Piers, Innes's parents, and to be honest Eve and myself would all like to see the pair of you back together. So the question is a valid one because, if that is the case, then the thing is truly over, and I will carry the news back from Aix to Ghent.'

He regarded his friend coolly, then continued. 'But, if you have the maturity and grace to accept that such mistakes can be made. Then I will assume it was Innes's inability to tell you about Jaikie before your engagement announcement that is the issue between you. That was undoubtedly a serious error of judgement. But is not, I'd suggest, a hanging offence.'

He sipped his pint and watched as Edward did the same. Out of the corner of his eye he could see the landlord had ceased all pretence of working and was blatantly eavesdropping at the end of the bar nearest to them.

'Keeping busy, Stanley?' Edward remarked, as he replaced his glass on the table.

'I hear a lot of things in my inn. And I know when to keep my mouth shut. You need not fear any gossip from me,' he answered firmly.

His friend's reply surprised the colonel. 'Come and sit with us for a moment.'

The big man poured three brandies, brought them to the table and eased himself down onto the bench below the window. 'Cheers.' He picked his up, nodded to the two men and sipped it. His friends did the same and Edward began to speak in a low voice.

'In confidence then, two weeks ago Innes agreed to be my wife. We were both on cloud nine, but in the moment when we announced the news to our families, she confessed a secret that she should have told me when I first proposed. It is a serious matter, and I was shocked enough to withdraw from the arrangement. Jocelyn is here to see if there is any prospect of a rapprochement.'

146

'I see.' Mr Tirrold knocked off the rest of his brandy. To his credit he did not ask what the problem was, but simply said, 'Do you still love her?'

'Good question.' The answer was flat and gave nothing away.

'It is indeed Edward,' the colonel said gently, 'as was mine earlier. Is making up out of the question? Or is it Innes's dreadful timing which is the problem?'

'She made me look a fool you know.' Edward slugged back his brandy.

The landlord laughed. 'If you marry her she'll likely make you look a fool on more than one occasion. That's the nature of wives, in my experience.'

The colonel grinned at him. 'He's right you know, Edward. I believe Innes adores you, but it won't always be an easy ride. Marriage never is, but if ever I saw a couple that are supposed to be together it's you and Innes.'

'She's a fine girl,' Mr Tirrold observed. 'Smart and devoted to her patients, and very easy on the eye too. It would be thought of as good news in the village if you two got wed.'

There was a silence, then the door rattled and Bert Williams appeared, peered at them and nodded. 'Afternoon all, prayer group meeting is it. Do you need this?' His face cracked a grin as he waved a bible at them, and the tension around the table dissolved. The colonel stood up. He was pleased with his progress. Edward's pride had been piqued, justifiably perhaps, but the moral issue was not uppermost in his mind. Perhaps a reconciliation was possible.

'Bert, come and have a drink with us. Let's see if we can address your many moral failings,' he said with a smile.

'What would those be then, Colonel?'

'Well we could start with Mrs Sutton, I suppose.'

'Oh no, she don't think I'm failing, I can tell you that. Least she didn't last Tuesday.'

The door opened again and another couple of men entered. As Stanley Tirrold made his way over to the bar the colonel turned back to Edward, 'I'm glad we've spoken. Let's talk again soon, but in the meantime I would urge you to remember two things. Innes undoubtedly still loves you, and your life would be much happier with her than without.'

He glanced up as Bert came over and sat down, placing the bible rather obviously on the table.

'How are the fish biting in Dipper Pool these days?'

'I've absolutely no idea, Colonel,' came the robust reply. 'I'm not a fisherman myself.'

Chapter Ten

Dear Sir Anthony,

I saw your advert. You are a wise man. The letter I have is dynamite. The exchange will take place at Langford Hall, in Lord Colin's study at nine o'clock on the evening of the fifth of November. You will bring ten government bearer bonds, each to the value of five thousand pounds, and I will bring the letter. Ensure Lady Langford is present as well. Just the two of you. No tricks or there will be consequences.

I will leave this unsigned.

In the corner office on Whitehall, the foreign secretary and Halley poured over the letter, trying to extract every bit of information from it.

'Bearer bonds?' Halley queried.

'Like cheques from the British government. Once issued they cannot be cancelled and are cashable by the possessor in any bank in Europe or America. They're a lot easier to transport than cash. It's a sensible choice.'

'It's a great deal of money.'

'Indeed it is.'

One thing is clear, sir,' the young aide observed, 'the man knew Lord Langford. Only a local would call him Lord Colin.'

'Yes that's true and the fact that he wants Lady Langford there as well confirms it in my eyes. We are dealing with a man with a grudge against the Spense family and I'm increasingly inclined to believe that he did murder Lord Langford. If the matter wasn't so damnably sensitive we could ask the local police for advice, but the risk of things getting out is too great.'

'Do you intend to pay, sir?'

'As a last resort we will exchange the money for the letter, but I'd like us to have other options available. Whatever happens on the fifth, we must end the night with the letter in our possession. At any cost.' He looked at his aide. 'Do I make myself clear?'

'You do, sir. I'll ensure the men are armed and fully briefed.'

'Good. We can deal with a body, but we cannot deal with the world knowing a British agent started the Great War.'

*

As Burrows set off to interview Frank Eales on a chilly, misty, late October morning, he exchanged a few words with Bert Williams and his wife who were walking up the high street carrying wicker baskets. He could see their labours had been rewarded.

'A good haul, Bert. All legitimate I trust?' he called with a smile

'Pickers rights,' came the brief reply. 'Our patch.' Many cottages had wide, flat, baskets specifically made for collecting mushrooms and figures stooping in the grey light of dawn were a familiar sight at this time of year.

There were blewits and field mushrooms in the pasture by the river, gathered with the dew still on them, and big white puffballs that the villagers cut thick and fried in butter. In the woods they picked oysters from the stumps of fallen trees and highly prized penny buns from the foot of beeches and oak. Good places were jealously guarded, long-held 'rights' to parts of the woods were argued over, and scuffles and the occasional black eye were not unheard of – amongst both the men and the women.

And it wasn't just mushrooms. As October drew to a close the rich landscape of the Cherwell valley was heavy with natural bounty and the villagers of Great Tew headed out en-masse to collect free food. Some was for eating straight away, the rest would be preserved for the coming winter. And it was important work. Many families were only just making ends meet so any contribution to the table was welcome.

Perhaps the favourites were wild plums. Small, fat, and juicy, they ripened later than the other berries and made a fine jam or jelly that would last all winter in a cold larder. Alongside the plums the women gathered crab apples and rose-hips to make syrup. And, after the first frost, sloes from the blackthorn bushes to flavour home-made gin and chutney.

On the common land near St Mary's, walnuts were gathered by generation after generation. Wet and young, the milky-white nuts were a prized delicacy, and most households had a large sack that slowly matured and hardened through the dark months. Stanley Tirrold always collected a bucketful while they were still in the green, which his wife pickled and then sold over the bar. The Reverend

151

Tukes was a familiar sight in the Black Horse, a pint of cider in his hand, his lips blackened by their inky juice.

On the far side of the three-acre common, a line of sweet chestnut trees provided nuts to roast, and a large thicket of hazelnut trees was plundered for filberts.

In short, not a thing was wasted. All the edible produce in the autumnal landscape was eaten or preserved. Knowledge of such things ran deep, and memories were long. In lean times many families had been kept alive by ingrained foraging and preservation skills passed down through the generations. Rough bread made with chestnut or hazelnut flour, wild berry jam, hard brown walnuts and pickled mushrooms provided life-giving nutrition in the harsh, cold, months.

It took Burrows some time to find Frank Eales's cottage. The news that the man had lied to him about his movements during the night of Dunstan Green's murder had placed him front and centre in the young constable's mind, and he was intent on interviewing him with all despatch. But it proved oddly difficult to establish exactly where he lived. In the end he cycled to the village pub in Leyland, where the landlord confirmed Eales was a regular patron of his establishment and lived at the end of a stony track on a hillside half a mile up the valley.

When he arrived at the thatched single-storey building he was out of breath from pedalling up the slope and paused for a moment to admire the view. From its elevated position the cottage overlooked the oxbow lake where Lord Langford had unsuccessfully hunted for ducks. A stiff autumn breeze rippled the dark water with silver and made the huge reed bed beyond it hiss and flex as it blurred away into the distance. Burrows thought that the tops of the reeds looked alive, like the back of a huge animal. On the far side of the lake a wide channel ran directly into the marsh, and he guessed it led to the little jetty and the hut where had first met the foreman. He couldn't see them from where he was standing.

'Not bad is it?' A voice jerked him out of his reverie, and he span round to see Frank Eales standing four feet behind him. 'I see it in all the seasons, but it's best when the wind brings it alive.'

Burrows nodded. 'Yes, I can see that.' He eyed the stocky and pugnacious man for a moment, then said, 'You lied to me about your movements the night of Dunstan Green's murder. Why was that?'

This direct assault had the desired effect, and a momentary flash of concern crossed the foreman's face before his eyes narrowed. 'Now who told you that, I wonder?' he replied quietly. Burrows sensed the underlying threat in his tone and realised that Wilfred's characterisation had been correct. He ignored the question and carried on.

'You didn't arrive at the party until much later than the rest of the men. Eleven o'clock I've been told. So I'll ask you again, why did you lie?'

'So someone has been talking have they? What makes you think their version is truer than mine?' Eales met his eye. 'It's one man's word against another. I say I was there all evening. I served with those blokes in France and we back each other up.'

'Mr Eales, I have a list of the men at that party and am well aware of the minor transgressions that many of them commit in relation to the law of the land. If I choose to apply a little pressure, believe me, I'll have the truth out of every man jack of them. So for the third time, why did you lie?'

The Oxfordshire police manual was very clear on this point. When seeking an answer to a specific question, do not allow the suspect to deflect the line of enquiry.

There was a long pause while Eales stared out across the reeds. Finally he said with a smile, 'Alright, maybe I was a little flexible on the timings, but I was just protecting a lady's reputation, if you get my drift.'

'I see. A married lady?'

Eales gave him a man to man look. 'Her husband is in the navy, and she gets lonely.'

'And she can vouch for you can she, this woman of impeccable virtue?'

'Let's not rush to judgement now, you're a copper not a vicar.'

'I merely want to establish where you were, and when. Where does she live?'

'You're not going to see her?' Eales said in a wary tone.

'Certainly I am,' Burrows replied briskly. 'I'm going now. What is the address?' He got out his notebook and pencil.

'That won't do you any good. She's gone away. To her sister's, in Paignton.'

'How very convenient.'

Eales shrugged. 'Not for me. Short rations for two weeks. How's married life with you then? Very nice your missus. Popular too, they say, before she settled down.' He leered at Burrows.

154

Furious at the slur, Burrows glared at him. 'Watch your tongue, or it'll be the worse for you.'

'No, I don't think so, Constable. I really don't. You ain't got nothing on me. Now if you'll excuse me, I've got to read my bible.' With a smug grin he returned to the cottage and closed the door firmly behind him.

Burning with fury the constable stared after him. He had been bested. No doubt about it. Eales had stirred him to anger, deflected his questions and avoided giving out the name and address of his lady friend. If there actually was one. For a moment he considered going after him, but the thought of banging on the door in vain was more than his dignity could bear. He picked up his bicycle and pedalled off disconsolately down the track.

One nil to Eales.

*

It was half past four o'clock in the Black Horse and Nobby Griffin had set up shop in the snug bar, ready for the men coming in after work. 'A craftsman in wheels, ladders and coffins,' as the Reverend Tukes had once remarked, the carpenter was also the village barber and cut hair and shaved men for sixpence a time on a weekly basis. And he had an evil sense of humour. Many a youth nervously waiting for his first shave had been terrified when Nobby dipped his razor in boiling water and drew the back of the blade across the lad's throat. Indeed, a 'Nobby special' had become something of a rite of passage for the young men of the village, so there was no surprise when a cry of horror floated out from the snug.

155

'That's another one,' remarked Stanley Tirrold with a grin to the colonel who happened to be propping up the bar alongside Elliot Ramsey the estate's head gamekeeper.

'Aiden Wise's lad, I believe,' the colonel concurred with a smile. 'He'll be wanting a drink after that.'

'I'll put him on the beating list for Friday, that'll cheer him up,' Ramsey said. The two men nodded in agreement. The annual estate shooting weekend was always held at the end of October, when a small group of invited guests enjoyed the sport offered by one of the finest estates in southern England. The event was hosted by Lady Langford in memory of her husband who, unlike his eldest son, had been an excellent shot.

This year ten couples were attending, mostly members of the aristocracy, but with three government ministers as well. Guests arrived on the Thursday afternoon and left the following Monday morning, leaving three full days for their sport. Twenty men were needed as beaters and the work was highly prized. It was a decent daily wage with the chance of a tip and a bird or two if the bag was good.

'How about young Tommy Dunn?' the colonel said. 'He's big enough now and his mother will appreciate the money.'

The gamekeeper nodded. 'I'll make sure he's brought in. The guests are arriving tomorrow, so I'll drop by the cottage and let them know on my way home. Are you shooting, Colonel Dance?'

'No, but I tell you what, I'll beat myself on Friday and take Tommy under my wing. Tell him to come to the house at nine in the morning, will you?'

'That's very good of you, sir. He'll be all the better for a bit of guidance. I'd better be on my way now. See you at the shoot, if not before.' He nodded and walked to the door, meeting Burrows who was just coming in.

The constable crossed to the bar. 'Afternoon Colonel, Stanley. I'll have a pint please.' When this had been served he remarked, 'I'm about ready to bring you up to date, sir, when convenient.'

'Are you? Well not in here, come round after dinner.'

'Of course, sir.'

'Definitely an accident was it? Or suicide?' asked the landlord.

The chief constable glanced around. They were alone. 'They are the most likely explanations Stanley, but not the only ones,' he said carefully. 'You wouldn't have heard anything would you? Over the bar?'

Mr Tirrold shrugged his large shoulders expressively. 'To be honest few people were unhappy at his demise, not that anyone's really come out and said it in the open.' He thought for a moment and said, 'I did notice one thing. It is my habit to occasionally take a pint of beer at the Kings Head. To see if there's been any improvement,' he clarified.

'And has there?' the colonel couldn't help himself.

There was a long sigh. 'Mr Davison tries, but he has no natural talent when it comes to running a public house. I'm afraid it shows in every aspect of his establishment.'

Faint smiles appeared on the faces of the men on the other side of the bar. 'Thank heavens we have the delights of the Black Horse and its estimable host then,' the colonel observed.

This calculated diplomacy was received with a benevolent nod, not unlike a papal blessing by the landlord as Burrows remarked, 'You mentioned you'd thought of something?'

'Just that Reginald Bennett was in there drinking and I had a bit of a chat. He lost both his sons of course, and only just had his eldest's personal kit back from France. It's a disgrace, it really is. Anyway, he was reminding me that they boys didn't go to war willingly.'

Burrows raised his eyebrows. 'How so? I thought they'd joined up before conscription was introduced, so they must have volunteered.'

'Oh no. It wasn't like that.' The landlord leaned on the bar and told the tale. 'The Bennetts got into a feud with another family over towards Banbury. Some girl was involved and got let down by one of the Bennett lads, after certain favours had been granted. The usual problem,' he rolled his eyes. 'Anyway it rumbled on for a whole summer as these things do round here. Then finally the youngest was ambushed and badly beaten up. The next thing he and his brother went over to the other farm and set fire to a hayrick that had just been built. But they didn't have the sense to keep quiet about it and in due course they ended up before Lord Colin. Him being the magistrate in those days.'

Burrows looked at the chief constable. 'Does any of this ring a bell, sir?'

He made a little dismissive gesture with his hand. 'Vaguely, your predecessor dealt with it.'

The landlord continued. 'Anyway, they were found guilty and as rick arson is a very serious offence Lord Colin gave them a choice. Five years in Oxford prison or enlist in the

Oxfords. They very reluctantly chose the latter. Although at that time no one new how bad it would be over there.'

'So both Bennett boys would have had a grudge against Lord Colin,' the chief constable observed.

The landlord nodded. 'And so would the father for that matter. But the point is Bennett was in his cups the other evening and going on about Dunstan Green and how he'd got what was coming to him. He's the only person I've heard really come out and say it. That he was glad he was dead. And he meant it too. Vicious he was.'

*

After the colonel had finished his dinner that evening there was a knock on the door and shortly afterwards Ellie announced that Constable Burrows was waiting in his study. With a word to his wife, the chief constable put down the Times crossword and went to see him.

'Evening Burrows, take a seat, will you have a snort?' The older man gestured with the glass of Scotch he was carrying.

'That's very kind, sir. I don't mind if I do.' As the colonel busied himself with the bottle and glasses, he added, 'Something smells nice sir'.

'Mrs Franks excelled herself this evening. Roast duck in orange sauce. I must say, it was delicious. Soda?'

'Just a dash, thank-you.'

He took the glass, sipped appreciatively, and reflected on the dry, overcooked, pork chop and watery potatoes he had battled with half an hour earlier, as the colonel asked, 'Well, how are your enquiries going?'

'The first thing to say is that I have been working alone. Both Mr Edward and Miss Knox seem to have completely lost interest in the case.'

'Yes, well you're the policeman so I assume you can manage on your own if needed,' the man opposite pointed out.

Slightly stung, Burrows replied, 'Yes of course, I was just mentioning it, as you seemed keen they were involved when we first made plans.'

'I believe they're both concerned with other matters at present,' the colonel said blandly. 'So what's been going on?'

'I've pursued my enquiries, focussing on the families that lost two sons in the war. Before Miss Knox and Mr Edward lost interest...,' he paused for as long as he dared then continued, 'we had eliminated many of the possible suspects and decided that logically those who had suffered a double bereavement should be top of the list'.

The colonel sipped thoughtfully as he continued. 'We know Green entered the river between nine o'clock and one in the morning. Neither of the two men from the doubly bereaved families can fully account for themselves during that period. Mr Reeve at Spring Farm was at home with a daughter who was asleep by ten o'clock, leaving a clear hour before his wife and other daughters returned to the house at eleven. That is a big enough window to have done the deed.'

'Really? He could have left the house, met Green on the river bank, killed him, and returned within an hour?'

Burrows said, 'It's entirely possible, sir.'

'But is it likely?'

'I agree that is another matter, but at present I am just concentrating on who could have done it.'

The chief constable nodded, 'The groundwork must be done. Who is the other suspect?'

'The man who Mr Tirrold was talking about earlier, sir, Reginald Bennet from Upper Barn. He lost both his sons in nineteen sixteen.'

'Is that so? Stanley's tale brought it back to me. As I recall they were a right pair of tearaways. And there was a feud…' He thought for a moment then shook his head, 'Anyway the father is a possibility you say?'

'He was in the King's Head that night until eleven o'clock. No-one saw him after that, and his way home to Upper Barn could easily have taken him along the river bank.'

The older man stirred in his seat. 'What's he like these days?'

'A drinker I think and comes over as a bitter man.'

The colonel tapped his fingers on the desk for a moment. 'Of the two I'd have thought he's the more likely, wouldn't you? Especially after what Stanley Tirrold heard in the King's Head. I mean Reeve is a partner in a firm of solicitors. A man with a reputation and a wife and daughters.'

He's one of us you mean, thought Burrows.

'I take your point, sir,' he said, but the fact is that Mr Reeve cannot provide an alibi, and at one stage in our interview I saw real anger on his face, although he tried to conceal it.' The young constable frowned. 'In fact, there's a great deal of anger in that house, and not just with Green.' He recounted the story of the shooting lessons, concluding with the observation that, 'When the younger son volunteered out of

161

the blue, his brother reluctantly felt he had to do the same. So the parents and the older Reeve boy had good reason to bear a grudge against Lord Colin.'

'Like the Bennett boys and their conviction for the rick fire?'

'I hadn't thought of it before, but yes, neither family holds the Spense family in high regard.'

He finished his glass and put it down hopefully on the table but, as no offer was forthcoming, he moved on. 'So until recently Reeve and Bennett were looking like the two main persons of interest, but then I received news that warranted further investigation.'

He told the colonel about his decision to meet the reed cutters and the subsequent visit by Wilfred to his house. 'Yesterday I went to Frank Eales's home and interviewed him. He admitted that he had lied to me and that he wasn't present all night at the birthday party. His story is that he was with a married woman, but he flatly refused to reveal her name, in the interests of protecting her reputation.'

'Do you believe him?'

'I think he's a very slippery character, sir, and he has not provided a supportable alibi for part of the period when Green was killed. He has to be a possibility.'

'I don't know much about him, the colonel mused, 'If I remember correctly he was conscripted and served in France but arrived back early, claiming he'd been invalided out, although he seemed to be unscathed. They say he's not a man you ask too many questions of. Does that sound like him?'

The policemen nodded firmly. 'It does, sir.'

162

The colonel said, 'Yes, I remember now. His wife left him and took their son. Rumours of violence and so on. She set up house in Banbury with another man, but I'm afraid the boy was subsequently conscripted and was killed.'

Burrows eyes widened. 'So Eales would have a grievance against a man who dodged the draft.'

'On the face of it, yes, he would. If he was up to some nefarious act that night it's also possible Dunstan Green was simply in the wrong place at the wrong time and was killed because he saw something. Either way, if he hasn't got an alibi then I'd say Eales needs to go alongside Reeve and Bennet at the top of your list, Constable.'

'Yes, sir. I agree.'

The colonel pushed back his desk chair and stood up. As they'd been talking he'd suddenly realised the solution to sixteen down and was keen to get back to the puzzle. 'Good. Press on with your enquiries Burrows. You've got three men that have a motive and all of them could have done it. You now need to find out which one did. Carry on.'

Chapter Eleven

A spiteful wind blew down the Cherwell Valley, stirring the trees and causing the men on the hillside to shiver and stare northwards into the looming grey sky. But Thomas Dunn barely felt the cold. He was beside himself with excitement as he climbed side by side with Colonel Dance and a group of beaters towards the bottom edge of a band of woodland a mile from Langford Hall. The men carried sticks and were dressed for rough country, in boots, old tweed, moleskin, and corduroy. Ahead of them, the trees were a mixture of oak, beech, and ash, with hazel in the clearings. They had been deliberately planted two hundred years earlier, high on the valley side where a fold in the land meant the shooting line was well below the trees.

The colonel pointed this out as they walked past the numbered pegs that marked the positions for the guns. 'Look up now Tommy, see how far the tops of the trees are above us. When we beat the wood from the far side the birds will come out high up. It's a challenging shot and more of a sporting contest.'

The boy nodded. 'My dad told me that when he used to beat, sir.'

'Yes, I remember him well.' He paused and nodded to Lord Langford who was standing with his guests by a pony and trap. A restless crowd of Springer spaniels and black Labradors were tied to one wheel. They were whimpering with tension and Tommy saw a big brown and white spaniel strain forward, roll its eyes, and lick the barrel of one of the guns.

'Morning Piers, the dogs seem keen. Nippy weather though, eh? Morning Bert.' His gaze took in the man standing next to him.

Bert Williams had a shotgun tucked under each arm, broken open to show they were not loaded, and was wearing a battered trilby with a long feather sticking out of the back. 'Morning Colonel, Tommy,' he grinned at them both and added, 'snow before long I reckon'

'It's certainly a cold snap,' the colonel agreed before addressing his young companion again. 'Each shooter works with two guns and a loader. As Lord Langford is firing one gun, Bert's job is to reload the other. Then they swap. The shooter watches the sky and passes the empty gun and receives the loaded one without looking. When the birds are flying it happens very quickly. Some of the guests bring their own man with them, because they're used to working in harmony,' the colonel explained. He looked up as Ramsey's voice carried over the group chatting by the cart.

'Ladies and gentlemen, the result of the draw is as follows.'

'To decide who gets which shooting peg,' the colonel whispered as Lord Langford moved over to the other guns.

'Peg one, The Duke of Ayr, peg two, Lady Dartmouth, peg three, Lord Bethell, peg four…' The draw was read out to gentle cheers and laughing commiserations.

'The middle pegs are the place to be Tommy, and you must shoot straight and not across another's line. Very bad form that.' He nudged the youngster and they walked on with the other beaters. 'I hope his Lordship has got his eye in, Bert,' he added as they walked past.

The countryman returned a smile of cherubic innocence. 'It'll be a lucky pheasant that comes his way. Very keen though.'

The beaters made their way up the steep slope at the side of the trees and, marshalled by one of the assistant gamekeepers, formed up into a line above the top edge of the wood. 'You go there next to me, about twenty feet away,' the colonel pointed. 'When we hear the whistle we set off into the trees. Make as much noise as you like and beat the bushes with your stick.'

'Yes, sir.'

'Quiet please, gentlemen,' the gamekeeper's voice carried to them, and they stood still and waited for ten minutes, until a faint whistle sounded in the distance. 'On we go then, try to keep in line,' he called, and they set off into the woods.

They beat another two hanging woods that morning, both high on the valley slopes, before re-joining the guns where Tommy counted fifty-two pheasant and a dozen partridge laid out by the pony and trap.

'Is that a good bag, sir?' he asked the colonel.

'It's not too bad at all. Lord Langford will be pleased with Ramsey I think, and his guests seem in good spirits in spite of this damnable wind.' The guns were standing in a little group sharing a couple of hip flasks and did seem to be in excellent spirits. 'Looking forward to lunch I imagine.' The colonel added. 'As am I. Come on. We all eat in the same building, at the foot of the valley.' He pointed to a roof showing amongst the hedges and fields a quarter of a mile away.

*

An hour later, Thomas Dunn was in a state of grace. He was sitting at a long table with the other beaters and just finished the best meal of his life. Roast estate venison cooked with chestnuts and blackberry jelly, with cheese to follow. The beaters were all in good heart, red faced from the wind and fortified by a barrel of cider and, judging by the noise, laughter, and clinking of glassware coming from the other room in the barn, so were Lord Langford's party.

'So Dunstan Green killed himself did he then, Colonel?' one of the men asked, emboldened by the cider.

'The evidence suggests that, although I won't enlarge on it if you don't mind.'

'Good riddance,' muttered another, to nods along the table.

'Now then, gentlemen,' the colonel replied firmly. 'Save it for another time if you please.'

But the brief exchange played on Thomas Dunn's mind and, as the beaters stood and prepared to set out for the afternoon's sport, he said, 'Sir, about Dunstan Green. I know something. I've been worrying about it since he was found, but it'll put me in trouble, see. We're hungry at home sometimes, and if I'm sent to prison it'll just be my mum and my sisters.'

The colonel had been steadily nipping away at a hip flask during the meal and, as a loud burst of laughter from the open door filled the room, he missed the implications of the boy's remark. But after a moment he caught up, looked at him and barked, 'Prison? What's that you said? What do you know?'

Intimidated by the sudden change in the older man Tommy hesitated. The room had emptied, and they were standing alone apart from a pair of servants collecting plates. 'What is it Tommy?' the colonel repeated quietly. 'You can tell me.'

The boy took a deep breath and began to speak.

'I found him the night before. I was tickling trout upstream from the mill. He was underwater, trapped by the bank. I pulled him up and he floated off downstream. I won't have to go before Lord Langford will I, sir? It was just a fish or two, for the table...'

He trailed off, tension showing in his face as he peered up at the chief constable.

'Good Lord. You found him did you? What time did you go out Tommy?'

He thought for a moment. 'Just after half nine.'

'And when did you find him exactly?'

There was another brief pause. 'I walked straight down to the river. It would have been before ten.'

'And he was definitely dead?'

'Oh yes.' The boy shivered at the memory.

They both turned as Ramsey's head appeared at the barn door. 'The guns are ready gentlemen, if you please.'

The colonel looked at the boy. 'Have you told anyone else about this? Your mother for example?' He was relieved to see him shake his head. 'Well keep it that way. And you've done the right thing telling me Tommy. Come to the house in the morning and you can tell Constable Burrows. And don't worry about the poaching, I'll overlook that on this occasion, but not a word to anyone else. Alright?'

Tommy nodded gravely and followed the colonel out of the door.

*

The following morning he knocked on the back door of Marston House and was admitted by Mrs Franks who took him through to the chief constable's study. Burrows was already there, in uniform.

The colonel beckoned to him. 'Ah Thomas, come in. Now, you're not in any trouble but you have to make a statement for the constable, so he can take the details. Then you'll sign it, so we have a fair record of what happened. You did tell me the truth yesterday didn't you, because lying to a policeman is a very serious offence.'

Shocked, the boy replied hotly, 'Yes, sir, I did'.

'Alright then. Tell your tale and do it slowly, so he can get it down.'

An hour later Burrows was sitting back at the police house sorrowfully contemplating the ruins of his suspect list.

There was no getting away from the fact that neither Reeve nor Bennett were murderers. Both were alibied for the period between nine and ten in the evening – the hour during which it was now apparent Dunstan Green had died.

That left only one man outstanding from his current enquiries. Frank Eales, the man who had comprehensively outmanoeuvred him at their last meeting. He didn't relish the thought of another encounter, but he simply had to know more about what he had been doing that night.

He heard movement in the hall and emerged to see his wife putting Matilda in the pram. 'Going out?' he enquired.

'Just for a walk with Ellie and Jaikie.'

'I'll not be far behind you, I'm late on my rounds.'

Half an hour later as he strolled across the common near the church he saw the maid from Marston House and flame haired Jaikie over by the walnut trees. The four year old climbed nimbly onto a low branch and hung on as Ellie rocked it to and fro. Laughter carried across to him as he walked over, passing a large pile of wood that marked the place where the November the fifth bonfire would be lighted.

'Good morning, that looks like fun,' he said, smiling.

'Will you rock us, sir?' Jaikie asked, and his wide-eyed charm did the trick. With a grin Constable Burrows nodded to Ellie and she sat down next to the boy, tucked her skirts in, and wrapped an arm around him.

'Ready? Here we go then.' He moved down to the end of the bough and pulled it far to one side before letting go. It catapulted back into place to screams of delight from both riders. Laughing himself, the policeman did it again and again, as Jaikie pleaded for 'just one more'.

Finally he stopped and they dismounted. 'I'm surprised Laura isn't still with you,' he remarked, 'she loves it up here on the common.'

Ellie looked at him. 'We walk with her sometimes, but we haven't seen her this morning have we, Jaikie?' She turned to look down at her charge and missed the flash of confusion on the policeman's face.

'Oh, I thought she was seeing you today, my mistake.' And with that he said goodbye and turned to head back towards the church tower showing above the trees.

*

Edward had reflected on his conversation with the colonel in the Black Horse and decided that he would forgive Innes. He recognised that this was a significant and generous gesture on his part, but his friend was right, he did still love her, and life with Innes would be indisputably better than life without her.

He also badly needed some relief from his mother, whose judgemental presence was haunting every hour he spent at Langford Hall. In fact the psychological pressure she had built up meant that he was seriously considering a move back to Holly Cottage. Meanwhile, his brother Piers simply refused to acknowledge him at all.

Matters had deteriorated during a conversation between the three of them the day after the dinner party, when his mother remarked that she had heard from Eve that Innes was very tearful and desperately upset over what had happened.

His naïve and foolish response was to quote a university friend whose amorous exploits up at Oxford had been legendary. 'In matters of the heart, a woman's tears are rarely spontaneous,' he intoned with an authority which he had not earned and which, in his mother's eyes, demonstrated his character faults only too clearly.

Jumping to her feet, she stared down at him and shouted, 'I could stand a son who was pompous, or even perhaps one who was an idiot. But why the good lord has burdened me with one who is both of those things, and cruel to boot, I

171

cannot understand.' With that she raised her hands to her face, burst into tears and fled the room, slamming the door behind her. The fact that she had then stopped, cleared her expression and put an ear to the keyhole was known only to Dereham who, as ever, was passing through the hall.

'Steady on, Eddie,' she heard her eldest son remark. 'I don't think Innes is calculating like that. She's a decent girl, you know.'

Stung by his mother, he hit out as only siblings can. 'I really wouldn't put you in the expert bracket where females are concerned, Piers, would you?'

The barb struck home. His face tight with emotion, Lord Langford quietly put his drink down and stalked out of the drawing room, barely giving his eavesdropping mother enough time to scurry through a convenient door as he passed.

At that point, having managed to infuriate his mother and alienate his brother, Edward had turned to the bottle and things had gone steadily downhill ever since.

So when he knocked on the door of Marston House he was hopeful that matters could be resolved quickly, and his life could go back to normal. Clearly, as the aggrieved party, it was for him to forgive and for Innes to fall gratefully into his arms. And he had to admit he was rather looking forward to it.

Eve and the colonel were in Oxford, so they were alone when she joined him in the drawing room. They stood awkwardly six feet apart, and there was a moment of silence as Edward wrestled with a sudden cascade of unexpected and confusing emotions at the sight of her. Struggling to maintain his train of thought, he said without preamble, 'I've got something to tell you.'

She raised her chin. 'Oh yes?'

'Yes. I've come to say that I forgive you.' He smiled and added, 'For your mistake. About the boy'. He saw a pulse appear in her neck and realised the emotional relief she must be feeling at this news.

'The boy? I presume you mean my son?'

'Of course. Jaikie. Whatever happened is in the past and we will find a way through it, I'm sure.'

'That must be a relief for you,' she said dangerously quietly.

'And for you, no doubt.' He beamed at her then, finally alerted by some instinct, added, 'I hope.'

But the pause had been too long, and his last chance had been used up.

'Tell me Edward, have you had much experience with the opposite sex?' she asked, her face expressionless.

He blanched at her question. 'Err…, well not particularly no, I suppose not.'

'No, I suppose not too. A boys' school. Two older brothers. A tight little group of fellows at university no doubt. Then the church and the army. I'd be surprised if you've ever managed to speak to one beyond bland observations about the weather.'

He thought for a moment, uneasily aware that he had lost control of the conversation. 'Well there's you, and my mother of course.'

Her bitter laugh was loud in the still room. 'Ah yes, motherhood. Well let me tell you something of that, Mr

Spense. The bond between a mother and son is unbreakable. It transcends everything, especially when the child is young and needs protection.'

With a sinking feeling he realised the enormity of the mistake he had made. And there was more coming. He stood and waited, as a red blush suffused Innes's beautiful face and deep anger showed in her eyes.

'Any man who places his own needs above those of my son is no man for me. I will not marry you Edward, and your smug assumption that I am simply waiting for your benign grace could not be more wrong.'

This last sentence was delivered in a furious hiss that was so intense it felt like a physical blow crossing the space between them. Innes Knox was not a Glasgow girl for nothing.

He slumped, and a fractured expression appeared in his face. 'My mother accused me of being a pompous fool. I see now she was right.'

She laughed again. 'Oh I am sure you have tested your mother's love on many occasions, Edward. You should have listened to her more carefully. At least she might have suggested you come here when sober. You have lost the battle and you have lost the war. Today is the second of November and I return to Scotland with Jaikie in four days, on Friday the sixth. Frankly it cannot come soon enough. You will not see us again. Goodbye.'

She turned and left, managing to hold her poise until the door was shut, but as she ran up the stairs her face cracked and by the time she was in her bedroom tears were running silently down her cheeks.

174

Left standing alone in the silent sitting room, Edward wondered how he could have got things so wrong.

*

The following day Marston House received another unexpected visitor. Beatrice Wray was a confident girl amongst her equals in the public house, but she lingered uncertainly in front of the handsome façade, not at all sure she was doing the right thing, and nervous even if she was.

Finally resolved, she walked round to the back and knocked on the kitchen door. Mrs Franks fetched Ellie who showed her through into the immaculately furnished drawing room where Eve was sitting reading. She stood up as the girl entered.

'Hello. It's Beatrice isn't it?'

'Yes Mrs Dance, it is.'

Sensing her unease, the petite and vibrant blonde gave her a pleasant smile. 'Well it's very nice to see you. Would you like a cup of tea?'

'Thank-you, madam.' The girl almost curtsied. Eve nodded to Ellie who, if she thought a village girl below her own rank deserved such indulgence, showed no sign of it, and departed on her mission.

Beatrice perched on the edge of one of the sofas and looked around. The walls were painted pale yellow and decorated with seascapes. There were two dark crimson settees on either side of the fireplace and French windows gave access to the garden. Outside, Beatrice could see a well-kept lawn and beyond it, an old brick wall with a bench at its foot and climbing roses still showing the occasional apricot coloured bloom.

She remembered that her hostess was a notable gardener and observed, 'The garden still looks nice, madam. Even though autumn's here.'

'You're very kind. I do try to keep it up until the Winter really strikes home. And there's always the greenhouse, it's heated with pipes, and I can keep some things going in there.'

Eve smoothly kept the small talk going as they waited for Ellie to return. From time to time villagers came to her with their problems, and her instincts told her this was one such occasion. And she was right. When the tea had been served and they were alone again, she asked, 'And to what do I owe the pleasure of your company this afternoon, Beatrice?'.

There was a silence as the girl gathered her thoughts, then said hesitantly, 'No-one knows I'm here. I mean no-one sent me', to which Eve gently raised her eyebrows and nodded encouragingly. 'The thing is, they say that you can help people. Like you kept Innes Knox alive after she was poisoned last year. They say..., they say you're a witch, madam. And I do believe that I am in need of one.'

The older woman studied her for a moment, decided she was genuine, and said, 'I see. Well I am a follower of the old religion, as are many around here. And yes, there have been times when I have been able to provide some assistance to people. Do you have a problem Beatrice?'

'I've had a message from the beyond the grave. Well, a postcard actually.'

Eve struggled to control her expression. 'A postcard?'

'From France. From a man I thought was dead. But now I've had a postcard from him. And it said I was to look in the

176

Times personal columns, and so I did, and there was a message from him. Saying he loves me.'

'That must have been quite a surprise.'

The girl warmed to her task. 'Not half. Dead these past four years and a telegram to prove it. His mum showed it to me. Official and everything.'

'So he was killed in the war, this fellow?'

'That's right. At a place called Delville Wood. He was in the Oxfords. There was a lot of them died there and buried nearby.'

Eve's face clouded as she nodded and remembered. It had been dreadful. The agonising wait, as rumours filtered back that the regiment had taken a pasting. Then the shock and grief on the estate as the telegrams had started to arrive. The tension for those with loved ones over there had been unbearable.

'But now he's sent you a postcard,' she said.

'I recognised the writing Mrs Dance. I reckon it's him alright.'

'So why are you here Beatrice. What is it you think I can do?'

The girl met her eye. 'I've heard you can go…,' she hesitated and gestured vaguely, 'beyond. I was hoping you could tell me if he's really dead. Because if he is, then someone's playing a cruel trick, and for no reason I can fathom. But I wouldn't put anything past some in this village,' she added darkly.

Eve's mind was whirling. The place where she had witnessed the gunfire and the men in the shell crater was the battlefield at Delville Wood. And now, here was this girl with her curious tale. And then there was the wraith.

A chill ran through her. Something was happening.

'When did the card arrive?' she asked, more calmly than she felt.

'About three weeks ago.'

'And the entry in the personal columns?'

'On the twentieth of October. I brought it with me.' She rummaged in her bag, withdrew the newspaper, and handed it over. Eve studied the circled message for a long moment then handed it back, thinking that the poor girl looked at the end of her tether, which was hardly surprising.

'He was your young man was he? You were walking out?'

'More than that. We'd reached an understanding. In the Promised Land. Not public, but we were going to be together. But then he didn't come back.'

'Anything that I can do remains private between the two of us Beatrice. You understand that? No gossiping. Not to anyone.'

'Yes, madam.'

'What was his name?'

And Beatrice told her.

*

Later that day Bert arrived at the vicarage for his weekly bible class.

'Good evening Bert, I thought we'd read about the parting of the Red Sea today, and how Moses led the Jews towards the promised land,' the parson greeted him, a slight smell of brandy on his breath.

178

The poacher pricked up his ears and grinned. 'The promised land eh? I've bin there myself a time or two, back when me and Edna were courting.' He paused and added reflectively, 'And not just with Edna, now I come to think about it.'

He eyed the man next to him curiously and added, 'You ever done any courting, parson? Back in the day?'

Tukes cleared his throat. 'Never mind that. We are discussing the original promised land. The one God gave to the Jews after they were forced to leave Egypt. I will read the relevant piece.'

He was a as good as his word and when he had finished asked, 'What do you think of that?'

'I've heard it before vicar. It's just a bit convenient isn't it?'

'How so?'

'With these miracles, it just seems to me one comes along every time one's needed.'

'Surely that is God showing his power and his love for the people.'

Bert scratched his chest vigorously, peered inside his shirt, and scratched again. The vicar eyed the upholstered chair he was sitting on and wondered uneasily when he had last bathed. 'I've never had a miracle. Does that mean he doesn't love me?'

'That is why we are here. So you can open your heart to God and let him into your life.'

'And get the allotment. So it's a trade-off then. I let God in, and you let me have the plot.' Bert could see no reason not to remind the clergyman of his end of the bargain.

The man next to him stirred. 'That makes it sound a little mercenary. I would encourage you to see Christianity as a community of like-minded souls united in their love and worship of God. A good thing in your life.'

'Oh yes,' came the airy reply, 'perhaps me getting the plot is my miracle, Vicar.'

'Perhaps, but I would remind you that the decision will be reached by the church council after your sermon on Christmas Eve. So your miracle is not yet in the bag.'

'It would be harsh to say no though, Vicar. After I've come to these lessons to get to know God an' all.' The plaintive reply hung in the air.

'Then let us re-double our efforts, Bert, and go through this story line by line.'

With a weary sigh the poacher leant over the book. 'Alright, but if I don't get my miracle I'm gonna be very angry with God.' He glanced at the parson and added darkly, 'And anyone on his side.'

180

Chapter Twelve

The following morning Eve managed to drag Innes out for a walk. They turned down Stream Cross, past Holly Cottage, which the young doctor eyed in silence, and over the narrow foot bridge that led to the track up Tan Hill.

The girl was utterly miserable, Eve thought. And it was no surprise, everywhere in the village must be full of reminders of Edward Spense. She had gone from deep joy to devastating disappointment, and that had now turned to barely suppressed anger. *When love turns to hate*, she reflected ruefully. Ellie had told her that Edward had come round and that she had heard the girl crying in her room afterwards, but Innes had refrained from raising the subject until now.

'What are your plans when you get back to Glasgow?' she enquired neutrally.

'Oh, doctoring of some kind. I'm still keen on psychiatry and I'll try to get a training post where I can practice and learn at the same time.'

'Will you live with your parents?'

'I think so. They've said they will look after Jaikie when I'm at work, which will obviously be a huge help.'

As they climbed up the hill, the view south down the Cherwell opened up to their left. It was a clear day and the slate grey river shone white in places as it flowed in wide bends through the autumnal farmland.

Down the slope she could see a farmer and two cattle dogs working a field. A large herd of Devonshire's were packed together by a gate that led into a wood. As the beasts slowly passed through it and disappeared into the trees the rust coloured backs of the diminishing herd reminded Innes of sand passing through the neck of an hour glass.

Like my remaining time in Great Tew.

Shrugging off the thought she lifted her head and looked down the valley. In the distance she could see a wide dark area that seemed to be flecked with white and black.

'The reed bed on the edge of the estate,' Eve remarked, following her eye.

'Last year I remember you telling me the land is resting now. In the spring and summer it glows like green crepe paper stretched over a bulb. But as winter comes it's fading.' She stopped, and they both looked out to the far ridge.

The older woman slipped her hand into her friend's and squeezed it. 'I'm afraid the light is fading in you too, my darling,' she said quietly.

Tears showed in her eyes. 'Oh Eve, please don't. Let's talk about something else.'

They walked on, hand in hand. Searching for a distraction, Eve remarked, 'I'm sorry you won't have a chance to learn more about my own work. I've been asked by someone who will remain nameless to try and establish if a person she believed was dead may, in fact, be still alive.'

In spite of her preoccupations, Innes was interested. 'Really? And can you do that?'

'I can certainly look.'

'Look where?' then, after a moment's thought, 'for what?'

The older woman gave a little laugh. 'That's rather a complicated question to answer. You need to understand that the soul and the human body are two different things. Here on earth they work in harmony, but our bodies are finite things that wear out, while our souls are not. They are pure energy, and infinite in that respect.'

'So the Catholics are right after all.' It was a naughty remark, and she knew it, but she couldn't help herself, knowing her friend's feelings about organised religion.

Eve duly rose to the bait and said tightly, 'No Innes, the Catholics could not be more wrong. Heaven and hell are invented places, the product of vengeful human minds intent on controlling an uneducated population through fear. I've told you before, there is no biblical God and there is no judgement when your body dies. I can assure you of that.'

'So if we're not promised redemption, what is the point of it all?'

Eve laughed again. 'Now that is your scientific brain craving a logical answer. I've come to realise that there isn't any point to it. Not in the sense you mean. Our souls, the eternal exchange of corporeal life and death, the great wheel turning, they are simply all elements of the natural world, a vast part of which is hidden to us while we are on earth.'

'But how can you believe in souls if you don't believe in a creationist God?

'Darwin was right about evolution, but he missed the most significant part of it. He limits his thinking to the development of our physical form. But our souls developed

183

in parallel. When life first began, it began with a spark of energy. The energy that powers our bodies is the essence of our soul. And when the body dies, that energy lives on.'

'Because you cannot destroy energy, only change its form?'

Eve nodded. 'When our bodies give up the ghost, quite literally as it happens, our souls pass out of it and in due course return to earth in a new one.'

'Where do they go?'

'Where I'm going to look for our undead friend,' Eve answered with an impish grin.

'But you're talking about reincarnation?'

'Yes. As I demonstrated to you on this very hilltop a year ago, not everything is explainable by science, nor is everything visible.'

Innes frowned, 'In my psychiatry lectures I was taught that our brains produce the sense of 'me' that we feel'.

'That might be the medical view Innes, but actually our brains do something different.'

'Really?'

'They don't create anything. Rather, they organise and manage what is already there, melding the world in which we live into something that we can understand through our five senses. Our souls are aware of everything all the time. They exist within the totality of all that has happened to us in past lives and has yet to be. But that cannot be allowed to happen while we are on earth. Put simply, we would lose all human perspective. So our brains limit our horizons during the times we are here. Almost like a form of censorship.'

She glanced at her friend and continued. 'Imagine your body as a very fine and brand new steam engine. It can go nowhere without a driver and so your soul arrives to set the whole thing in motion. But the engine is still restricted to certain tracks, and it is the brain that manages that.'

'But you can somehow detach yourself from that filter? You can go anywhere?'

'Not anywhere, but I can consciously free my soul from my body. And that enables me to see beyond the limits our brain imposes on us as humans.'

There was a long silence as the young doctor digested her remark. Then she said, 'Can I ask you something else?'

'Of course.' Eve was pleased that Innes was engaged with their discussion. Anything that took her mind away from the man who lived at Langford Hall was welcome.

'They told me I almost died. After the hemlock poisoning.'

'Yes, I believe you did.'

'You came to get me didn't you? I remember feeling that it was time to go. I was relaxed and could see a tunnel filled with warm white light. It was ready for me, and I sensed people waiting. But I heard your voice, and then you were there and took my hand.' She stopped and looked at her friend, half embarrassed. 'At least, that's what it felt like.'

'I did try to help you. We didn't want to lose you Innes, and people who are murdered are never ready to go. It wasn't your time.'

'So here I am.' She met Eve's eye.

'So here you are.'

They arrived at the top of the lane and walked across the cropped grass to the great monolith Eve called Litha, which stood on the summit of Tan Hill. In doing so they passed through one of the streams of energy that ran from north to south over the landscape.

Innes stared down at the ancient village. When she returned to Glasgow all this would fade away in the hard stone and background noise of the big city, but she already knew that the time she had spent with Eve would give her work as a psychiatrist a perspective not found in medical books. With a slight shock she realised that Innes Knox, the brisk and no-nononsense scientist who had arrived in Great Tew, had come to believe in ghosts and reincarnation.

And it had taken barely more than a year, in this enchanted place.

'Do you know how many times you've been re-incarnated?' she asked.

'No. I do know some things though. One is that I am bound to Great Tew and have returned here in many lives.'

'Really? For how long?'

Eve pictured the siege of Langford Hall. 'At least four hundred years,'

Innes pursed her lips. Sometimes she could barely believe the conversations she had with Eve, and yet she knew unequivocally that her friend had saved her from death and brought her back to earth. 'Why Great Tew?' she asked, after a moment.

'It's Creech Hill Ring. I know that now. I'm here to use it and to protect it. Almost like a guardian.'

'Protect it from who?' The question was inevitable.

'Swords can be used for good or evil,' she said enigmatically, almost to herself.

186

Rather reluctantly Burrows peddled back to the cottage where Frank Eales lived. He was not looking forward to renewing their acquaintance, so when there was no reply to his knock on the door he was relieved and disappointed in equal measure. Nevertheless, nothing if not resolute, he cycled along to the public house where Eales was a regular and asked the landlord if he knew where he might be.

Alert to the fact that this was the second time the constable had come looking for him, instead of answering his question directly, the publican asked, 'In a bit of bother is he?'

'Just a routine matter,' Burrows answered. 'He's a thatcher by trade I believe?'

'That's right. I think he's repairing the roof of old man Still's place on the Oxford road.'

Having received directions he climbed back onto his bike and peddled deeper into the beat of his neighbouring policeman, a taciturn and unpopular man named Brown. As he went he considered the best way to extract the name and address of the woman Eales claimed to have been with the night of Green's murder. The man was clearly too sharp to be tricked into it and Burrows reflected that he might be forced to arrest him, leading to all sorts of complications with Brown regarding in whose jurisdiction the matter fell.

These gloomy introspections were interrupted by the sound of faint female shouting coming from over his right hand shoulder. Pulling up, he put his foot down and turned to see the cause of noise.

Two fields away a plume of smoke was rising into the air close to the thatched roof of a farmhouse. As he stared it grew stronger, and then he heard pounding feet on the road. Two men carrying hay rakes dashed past him and vaulted the gate into the field next to the road.

'Rick fire!' one of them bellowed. 'Come on!'

Laying his bike on the verge the constable followed, his long legs eating up the stubble covered field. They vaulted another gate, and the picture became clearer. The farmyard lay between the house and a barn. Two large haystacks stood next to each other, both with chimneys embedded in the roofs. The one nearest them was smoking hard. No flames were visible, but the smoke was getting blacker by the second. He could see a middle aged woman and a young girl in a pinafore dress wielding rakes to try and break the rick open. A second girl appeared carrying a heavy leather bucket filled with water. The mother took it and threw it onto the hay, but the thatch was well made, and the water just ran off.

Then they were into the yard and the older of the two men was shouting.

'You women fill the buckets at the pump. As many as you can. You help them Constable. Willy and I'll break it open so we can get water on the seat of it.' And with that they went to work. Burrows grabbed the pump handle and started working it as the two girls and the woman carried the buckets over to the rick. As he pumped he saw the men lean a ladder against the stack. It was eight feet from the floor to the edge of the angled roof and as the younger man climbed the older one passed up a full bucket. Dragging it with him as best he could the man shuffled up the thatch.

'Down the chimney, Willy', his partner called, and he stood up unsteadily, balancing on the steep thatch and poured the bucket into smoking pipe. There was a thump from deep inside the rick and a powerful burst of black smoke shot upwards, like a train leaving a station.

'Watch out, she's too far gone. Come off there, quickly now,' the older man cried in alarm, and the lad slid down the thatch and off, landing in a heap on the cobbles as another thump sounded from the rick and a lump of thatch the size of a door flew upwards followed by bright orange flames. Thick smoke poured out, and the chimney pipe disappeared.

More men were arriving now, carrying pitchforks and rakes, and with a clatter of hooves a well-dressed man cantered into the yard. He bought his horse to a halt and took the scene in with a practised eye.

'We'll not save it now,' he bellowed. 'Break the next rick and get the hay out of the way. We can re-stack it.'

Burrows was pushed aside from the pump and a man in his thirties with forearms like ham hocks said calmly, 'Alright then Constable, I'll take over here. You get raking.' He set to in a fast and steady rhythm as Burrows ran across the yard, picked up a pitchfork, and joined the men pulling the stack to pieces as others furiously raked the hay away from the blazing rick. The heat was building and a plume of sparks and burning embers rose high into the sky.

'The house,' he heard the woman cry and turning he saw three blazing pieces of straw had landed in a triangle on the thatch near the chimney.

'Constable,' the man in the horse bellowed. He turned to face him. 'Get up there and deal with that.'

Dropping the pitchfork, he dashed to where the ladder the men had used was lying on the floor, carried it across to the farmhouse and leaned it against the wall. The thatch was slippery, and the ladder was two feet short, so he had the devil of a job gaining the roof, but he finally managed to jam his fingers in and lever himself upwards.

'Quickly, please,' the farmer's wife called.

'Alright, madam,' he muttered, sweat pouring off him as he wriggled up towards the small flames that were licking across the straw. With a sinking feeling he realised that he had nothing to beat them out with, so lying on his back he unbuttoned his jacket and pulled it off. Turning back onto his stomach he edged forward and started to flail away, feeling his helmet fall off and roll down the roof as he battled the flames.

With a sickening feeling he realised he was making no difference and the woman was in danger of losing her home.

'Watch out then!' A voice cried from behind him and the next moment a cascade of water splattered across his back and head.

He turned and glared. It was the lad, Willy, standing at the top of the ladder. As he watched he reached down below the roofline and took another bucket, braced himself and swung it. This time his aim was better, and the water landed fair and square on its target. Burrows beat furiously at the flames and within a few seconds they had disappeared. He raised his thumb in triumph, but the man just nodded and pointed to his right where more embers were landing.

'I'm on my way,' the constable cried and set off across the steeply sloping roof as the man on the ladder sent the contents of another bucket arching up and over the thatch.

Half an hour later the danger was over and only the mopping up was left. The fire cart from the manor had arrived and dropped a hose into the duck pond, and a steady stream of water was being directed onto the smouldering remains of the hayrick. Salvaged hay was piled high, and arrangements were being made to rebuild the rick the following day.

The man with the horse turned out to be the land agent for the estate next to Langford and he came over to thank Burrows. 'Sorry to order you about like that, Officer. But in the moment…, well, we needed to get down to it,' he remarked.

'That's alright, sir. All hands to the pumps, as it were. I was glad to be of assistance.'

'Your jacket's a bit of a mess, I'm afraid. Off your beat, aren't you?'

Yes, I was looking for Frank Eales.'

'Were you now.' The land agent didn't sound surprised. 'Well you'll find him here tomorrow afternoon. We'll build the rick in the morning, and he'll thatch it after lunch. He does most of the thatching on the estate.'

Burrows nodded vaguely as something clicked into place in his mind. 'Right, sir, thank-you for that. I'll be back then.'

Chapter Thirteen

On Tuesday afternoon, Burrows cycled disconsolately back from the scene of the rick fire, after another humiliation at the hands of Frank Eales. As he passed the reed bed and replayed the scene in his mind it did not paint a happy picture.

He had timed his arrival carefully, walking into the yard at four o'clock in the afternoon, having calculated that the stack would be rebuilt by then and Eales would probably be working alone. And he had been correct. The thatcher was two thirds of the way through his work, perched at the top of a ladder.

'Afternoon Mr Eales, I just wanted to follow up on our conversation the other day,'

'I've got nothing to say to you.' The man didn't even turn round.

He knew I was coming. The realisation swam into Burrows' mind, and he guessed someone had overheard his conversation with the land agent and warned him. As he stood there, Constable Brown appeared, uniform jacket unbuttoned, helmetless, and holding a jug of cider.

'Now then, Burrows. What's all this? You're well off your beat, aren't you?

The young policeman looked at him. 'Good afternoon Constable Brown, I'm just pursuing my enquiries and want to interview Mr Eales.' In the silence that followed, the thatcher climbed down the ladder, and he saw the two men exchange an amused glance.

'For the second time, I hear.' Brown was not an attractive man and the sneer that crept across his face did little to improve his appearance. 'I always say if you can't get what you want the first time, you're not much of a policeman.'

Eales sniggered. 'Not much at all,' he agreed and stared at Burrows.

'There's also the matter of procedure isn't there. Now you're young and inexperienced, but even you should know that if you're going onto another patch you need to let the local constable know. Etiquette they call it,' Brown intoned portentously, before lifting the jug to his lips and taking a long swig. He wiped his mouth then said, 'I'm in charge over here and I've got matters in hand. If Mr Eales says he was with a lady friend on the night in question, then he was. I'll vouch for him.'

'How did you know what I wanted?'

'He mentioned it to me. I make it my business to know what's going on around here. We know each other very well as it happens.'

Burrows eyed him, remembering Wilfred's words. *They say Eales has his fingers in a few dodgy pies and he's not a man to cross.* With a sickening feeling he realised that the two men were in cahoots.

As if he could read his mind, Eales grinned evilly and said, 'I think what he's really saying, Constable, is piss off.'

Burrows flushed and put his hand on his truncheon. 'Don't speak to me like that.'

But Eales just shrugged and re-climbed the ladder as Brown said, 'Just get back to your pals on the Langford Estate. You'll get nothing here.' The condescension in his tone echoed round the farmyard and with a face like thunder Burrows turned and stalked back to his bicycle.

His burning anger carried him through Little Tew and up over Tan Hill. Even the glorious freewheel downhill to the little footbridge at Stream Cross failed to cheer him. It wasn't just his abject failure to best Eales, and the gaping hole it left in the centre of his murder investigation. In addition, he was increasingly concerned about his wife.

Since the incident on the common, he was aware there had been two other occasions when Matilda had been left in the care of other women after Laura had departed with the perambulator 'for a walk'. The thing was nagging away at him, and he was starting to worry properly about what was going on.

As his trusty bicycle carried him up the high street the tower clock showed half past four. The afternoon had turned chilly, and he decided that day could only be improved by a pint of cider. Public house opening hours had been introduced during the war, and they were supposed to close between two o'clock and five, but as the chief constable enjoyed an afternoon drink from time to time, the rule was not enforced. In consequence Stanley Tirrold normally opened up at eleven in the morning and closed about ten in the evening.

The colonel's flexibility in relation to the law of the land, either for his own convenience, or to ensure village matters ran smoothly, was something Burrows had had to adjust to on his arrival from Oxford. He had been astonished at the inn's opening hours and had got off to a bad start with Mr Tirrold as a consequence, but his superior had been blithely unconcerned.

'You have to turn a Nelsonian blind eye to some things, Burrows. It's not Oxford here, and to some extent the villagers police themselves. You'll soon learn when to put your foot down and when to look away.' He'd paused and added, 'At least I hope so,' giving him a long gaze.

And the young and very keen constable had done so, with the result that, in general, he was a popular figure across the estate, not least because he was fair and incorruptible. The colonel had watched his development and marriage to Laura Bessing with approval and considered that his promotion to sergeant was a certainty in due course.

Inside the Black Horse a bright fire was burning, and the low hum of conversation seemed welcoming and comfortable after the cares of the constable's working day. And, inevitably perhaps, he stayed for another, sitting in silence in the corner. Sensing trouble, Stanley Tirrold took it over, and a half for himself, and eased down into the seat opposite.

'You look as though you've had an Irishman's raise,' he remarked.

Burrows flicked his eyes at him. 'Eh?'

'An Irishman's raise. A cut in wages.' He smiled man to man. 'Or something like it. Everything all right?'

The young policeman grimaced. 'I've not had the best of days, to be honest.' Knowing he could trust the big landlord, he quietly outlined the difficulties in the rick yard.

The landlord nodded sagely. 'You're as honest as the day is long, Burrows. We all know that, but Brown doesn't have a good reputation. 'If he's protecting Eales, the chances are they've cooked something up between them. Lives in a very nice house does Constable Brown, and always got a few quid in his pocket. I know the landlord where he drinks, I'll have a quiet word if you like. See if I can get you any leverage on him.'

'I'd appreciate that.'

Mr Tirrold looked at him. 'Is that it?' he asked, suspecting it wasn't.

'To be honest no.' And feeling considerable relief at the unburdening, he told his friend about his concerns over his wife's unexplained absences. 'The thing is Stan, my ma left me and my pa when I was young. After that he told me women weren't to be trusted, and I thought he was right until Laura persuaded me different. And now I find she's telling me lies.' A hot flush spread across his cheeks.

Three thirsty farm workers came into the pub, noisy and jostling good-naturedly as they walked over to the bar. Beatrice Wray welcomed them with a smile and picked up a pint glass, her eyebrows raised.

'Evening boys, the usual?'

'Pay your slates first,' the landlord called over. It was payday on the estate and the landlord only extended credit for a week to the working men. More banter was exchanged, but the money was produced and carefully counted by the barmaid before the board behind the bar was wiped clean.

Nodding in satisfaction, he turned back to the young policeman. 'I don't know what's going on, but I'll tell you

196

one thing. Laura Bessing was a fine straightforward girl when she worked for me, and I don't imagine a change of surname has changed her character. You've got a good one there and I'd let things lie if I were you. You've got to let your woman have a secret or two – it's just the way they're made.'

He paused and then added, 'Although they don't like us to have any. Not that they know about anyway.' And with a wink, he rose and strode back to the bar.

Unconvinced, Burrows watched him go in silence.

*

After supper, Eve excused herself from her husband and climbed the stairs to the attic. She made her preparations, then settled onto the cushion and started to recite the words she had been taught many years ago by someone very dear to her. As the rhythm of the ancient verses penetrated to every corner of the still room, she pictured the man in the photograph Beatrice had given her - a young man in army uniform, staring unsmiling at the camera.

'He had it done before he was sent off. As a memory for me,' she'd said.

When she saw the photograph Eve experienced a chilling sense that another connection had fallen into place. To make sure, she went back to the gunfire, back to Delville Wood, and back to the shell crater where the soldier cradled his dead comrade.

This time she lingered until she saw his face. It was the same man. No doubt about it.

So he was alive then, but it was quite possible he'd been killed later on in the battle.

But before she could interrogate the scene more deeply it dissolved to grey. Frustrated she drifted onward, higher and deeper, searching as she went, drawing a kaleidoscope of images into her view. What she saw was upsetting and without joy. Confused scenes of a hot French city, the turquoise sea, a moral battle lost, the worst of human emotion, and then death. Seven in all, starting with a man in uniform and ending with a girl on a train. Some of them had happened far away but with a shock she also felt a strong connection to Great Tew.

Distressed, she closed her mind to the images, held the photograph in her mind and simply asked, *Does he live?* And with sudden, startling, clarity, she knew the answer to Beatrice Wray's question. The postcard was genuine. The man had not died on the battlefield at Delville Wood.

She descended the attic stairs to the elegant landing, where she met Ellie who had just been checking on Jaikie. *She'll miss him dreadfully if Innes goes back to Scotland*, she thought. The pair were devoted to each other.

'Do you know where Beatrice Wray lives?' she asked.

'Yes ma'am, along Rivermead, it's the last cottage before the footbridge. A mile or so I'd say.' She glanced at the clock at the head of the stairs. 'But she'll be working in the Black Horse now.'

Thanking her, Eve descended and found her husband had gone to ground in his study. It didn't take much persuading to winkle him out and they strolled up the high street to the public house. She found an empty table and watched as the colonel ordered their drinks. The Reverend Tukes was at the bar, a dribble of pickled walnut juice on his chin. He and

Stanley Tirrold were leaning towards each other, talking. Eve thought it looked serious, and saw her husband become involved in the conversation.

After a few minutes he returned and placed the glasses on the table.

'What was that?' she asked.

He shook his head. 'There was a football practice on the common earlier this evening and Tukes offered to referee a proper match. One of the men had been in and out of hospital with shell shock and he only finally got back a day or two ago. They got him along to the game. He'd been a useful player and they thought it would do him a bit of good I suppose.' He pursed his lips for a moment.

'And?' his wife prompted.

'The fellow was standing right next to Tukes when he whistled to start the game. The blast went through him, and he collapsed clutching his head and screaming. The whistle was the order to go over the top you see. The last thing the men heard before the killing started,'

Eve stared at him. 'The poor man. Will it never end Jocelyn?'

Her husband shook his head. 'A lot of men who served look fine from the outside but inside they're melting like snowmen in a thaw. They took him to the cottage hospital and Innes had to sedate him for his own good while the others held him down. He's on his way to the Radcliffe as we speak. Tukes is pretty shaken up as well.'

'I can imagine.' She glanced over to the bar and saw the girl looking at her. She met her eye and beckoned her over. 'Would you give me a minute with Beatrice, Jocelyn?'

'As you wish,' he stood and passed the girl in the middle of the room as they headed in opposite directions.

'Sit down, my dear,' Eve gave her a pleasant smile and said quietly, 'I won't beat about the bush. In my opinion your young man is still alive. Given the time that has passed, I really don't know if you consider that good news or not. But I am sure it is the truth.'

The girl stared wide-eyed. 'So he wasn't killed?'

'No. I think his brother was, but he survived. There must have been some kind of terrible mix up. That's why his parents got two telegrams.'

'But where's he been then? Why didn't he come back? Or tell his ma and pa there'd been a mistake?'

Eve remembered the hot city, the turquoise sea and the dead bodies. 'I really don't know I'm afraid,' she lied. 'I have no idea where he's been, or why he would choose to contact you now after four years.'

Beatrice seemed struck dumb, and Eve realised that she had convinced herself that someone was playing a malign trick on her. *You might as well have all of it*, she thought and added, 'Actually, that's not quite true. The feeling I have is that he has got in touch because he is finally planning to come back.'

Hollow-eyed she stared. 'Coming here? Back to Great Tew?'

Eve smiled sympathetically. 'I think you have to ready yourself. At least you're not married. But I do think there is a distinct possibility that one day, quite soon, there will be a knock on the door, and he will be standing there. Or maybe he'll simply walk out of a wood in front of you when you're out and about.'

And there's something wrong with him, something terribly wrong.

The words ran through her head, but she couldn't bring herself to say them. Instead she just laid a gentle hand on her arm and said, 'I think you should be careful, Beatrice'.

*

Jocelyn Dance met Claire Spense in the knot garden believing that he had convinced Edward to make his peace with Innes. However, he was to be disappointed.

'She's refused him,' Lady Langford said. 'He hasn't told me directly, but I know he visited Marston House. Whatever he said didn't do the trick and he's been like a bear with a sore head ever since.'

The colonel clicked his tongue in frustration. 'Darn. I really thought I'd got through to him.'

'Oh I think you did. But I gather from Eve that Innes's feelings have turned from pain to anger. She thinks Edward has belittled the importance of the boy in all of this. And on top of that, I suspect my son approached her in the cack-handed way that appears to be his unique privilege in matters of the heart. We are approaching the deadline, Jocelyn. She leaves for Glasgow very soon and at this precise moment I cannot think of a way to bring them together.'

She gave a frustrated sigh and eyed a wizened gardener pruning a rose bush across the lawn. 'I will not be here for ever and I'm convinced that Langford could not have a better chatelaine than Innes Knox. She would certainly be a stalwart and loving companion to my darling and occasionally idiotic son. We also know she is capable of bearing healthy and adorable children,' she added as an afterthought.

The man smiled in agreement. 'It's ironic isn't it. If something happens to Piers then Edward's wife will become Lady Langford, one of the oldest and most notable titles in the peerage. And wealthy to boot. Many young women would crawl over broken glass for the chance of that, and yet Innes seems intent on demonstrating how irrelevant that is to her.'

His friend looked at him. 'That, Jocelyn, is exactly why I want her.'

*

In London final preparations were being made for the exchange. The bearer bonds had been withdrawn from the Bank of England with the prime minister's special authorisation, and now resided in a safe at the Foreign Office. The two hard men from the War Office would take control of them when they travelled to Oxford in a single car. Sir Anthony had decided that the party would consist of himself, his aide and the two men, one of whom would drive.

Everything had been checked and rechecked by Halley a number of times. They would arrive at the hall on the afternoon of the fifth and effect the exchange as planned at nine in the evening, at the height of the bonfire party.

Lloyd George had summoned them both to his office the previous day to reiterate the importance of success. No other aides were present, and the meeting had not been minuted. 'I'll make it very clear gentlemen, I have no interest in this man whatsoever. None at all. But that letter could bring down the government and plunge us into another war. We simply must have it. I expect you to return with the document, the money, and news that the blackmailer will not trouble us again.'

He held Kerr's eyes for a long moment. 'The British empire is the greatest the world has ever known, or likely ever will. We will not be knocked off course by a rural chancer. Do what you need to do. There will be no recriminations. Good afternoon.'

*

Early on the morning of the fourth of November the man in Beatrice's photograph finally moved. Carrying a light backpack and dressed in a brown gaberdine coat and cap, he left Gare du Nord station in Paris on the boat train, crossed from Dunkirk to Newhaven and carried on to London where he took a room in a slightly shabby hotel in the back streets not far from Paddington station.

With the door safely locked, he removed the letter from his pack and studied it for the umpteenth time. It wasn't much, just three short paragraphs on Foreign Office letterhead, signed by Lord Colin Langford, and dated 27th September 1912. But what made it worth fifty thousand pounds was the signature on a pre-typed line opposite the civil servant's name - Gavrilo Princip. The writing was neat, written in black ink, and clearly decipherable.

He looked out of the sooty window and smiled, because Princip was still alive. He had only been nineteen years old when he murdered the Arch-Duke and, because of his youth, he had been spared the noose and was currently serving a twenty year jail sentence.

Had he been dead Lord Colin's people could simply have claimed the letter was a fake. But it would be easy to obtain samples of the assassin's signature and his verbal confirmation that he had been working for the British. Even

203

an affidavit. There were plenty of ways to put pressure on a man serving a long jail sentence.

He had realised some time ago that Sir Anthony Kerr's priority would be the return of the letter and that he also probably intended to kill him. Dead men tell no tales. But the man had learned hard and well in Marseilles, and he had no conscience: None at all. By the sixth of November he would be a very wealthy man and, if things went smoothly, he would still be in possession of the letter and could come back for more whenever he liked.

There was a bottle of brandy on the table. He reached for it and poured himself a generous measure. He took a mouthful, letting the hot strong liquor linger in his mouth before swallowing; savouring the moment, as his thoughts drifted to Great Tew.

And then there was Trixie; delicious Trixie. He had enjoyed plenty of French and Arab girls in Marseilles, but his long term plan had always included her. He smiled as he imagined the consternation that his postcard would have generated in the cottage on Rivermead, and the advertisement in the Times that followed. When he was back in Great Tew he would see her before the exchange and tell her to get ready. The bonfire party would be in full swing, and the tipsy revellers would provide excellent cover for their escape.

He glanced out of the window. It was fully dark outside, and a full moon was rising over the tiled roof opposite. The last vestiges of decency had long been banished from his character and a restless urge moved him. He had killed seven times since the despatch rider near Delville Wood. The first two had been men. Robbed for their clothes and the cash they carried, then despatched because they had both seen his face. But then, in Marseilles, as he had started to make money in the criminal underworld, his motivation had been different.

The last four had been women, killed for pleasure. He smiled faintly as he remembered the most recent - a frumpy peasant girl on the train from Marseilles. Her last moments of terror as he had moved onto the seat next to her and looked into her eyes had been delicious. In Paris he had opened the compartment door and jumped down onto the platform before the train had come to a halt, leaving her lying on the seat, covered in blood and with the apple still in her hand,

And he had been fifty yards away before the screaming started.

*

Stanley Tirrold walked into the Fox and Hounds public house in the village of Leyland. The landlord saw him and nodded a greeting.

'Mr Tirrold, come to see how a proper pub is run have you?' he asked with a smile. The two men went back a long way.

'If you need any tips Mr Gentle, I'll be happy to advise you,' the big man countered. 'I'll have a pint of bitter please. And a quiet word when you have a moment.'

Catching his tone, the landlord called his wife to the bar and the two men walked to a table by the fire. An elderly man with a half of bright orange scrumpy was dozing on the other side of the mantelpiece, but there were no other occupants.

'Don't worry about old Duffy, he's deaf as a post even when he's awake,' Mr Gentle said, but nevertheless kept his voice low as he asked, 'What can I do for you?'

'Frank Eales and Constable Brown. What can you tell me about those two?'

'Not as customers, I'm guessing?' Tirrold shook his head. 'Well they're not popular. Neither of them. Eales managed to get out of the war early. When he got back rationing had just started and he got into the black market. Buying and selling, fencing for other like-minded souls.' The landlord rolled his eyes. 'There are rumours he's got a stash stuffed with all kinds of treasure hidden somewhere, most of it nicked.'

'What about Brown?'

The landlord shrugged. 'Paid off. And he's the law round here, so who's to say anything.'

'Does he have a woman, this Eales?'

'He was married, but his wife left him. And he hasn't replaced her, leastways not that I know of.'

'Oh really? So, if he gave the fact he was with a woman as an alibi for example...,' Mr Tirrold raised his eyebrows, inviting the response.

'Likely he'd be lying,' the landlord affirmed. 'He keeps it very quiet, and thinks on-one knows, but it's said he's a member of the same gentleman's club as Lord Langford if you get my drift. There's been a story or two. Lives alone up by the reed bed and not the marrying kind these days.'

Chapter Fourteen

Jaikie Knox screamed with pleasure as his mother flung the cupboard door open and cried 'Got you!'.

Aided and abetted by Ellie he had discovered the joys of hide and seek, although his range of hiding places was sadly limited to three – the hall cupboard, under the bed in the maid's room, and Mrs Franks' larder. The colonel, who was a keen hider and seeker, had been banned from the latter after an apple pie ended up on the floor following a spontaneous tickling match.

Innes hugged him, laughing out loud at his innocence and vitality, as he chortled and wriggled. 'Come on, it's breakfast time. Mrs Franks is doing you a scrambled egg on toast in the kitchen.' This news was met with less enthusiasm by the boy, but he allowed himself to be tucked in at the scrubbed table and set about a glass of milk as the egg was prepared.

Innes sat and watched him as he ate. He had grown three inches in the time they had been at Marston House, and they had both put on weight. She loved him with a passion that was frightening at times and was well aware that moving back to Glasgow would be a terrible wrench for the boy. He glowed with happiness and good health, having taken to the outdoor life like a duck to water, and was clearly well settled in Great Tew. The school mistress had said he could start coming to class in the mornings after Christmas and the support she received in the house had enabled her to carry on with her psychiatry studies in the evenings, while working a full week at the cottage hospital where she was now the sole doctor.

But only for two more days. A locum had been arranged and bonfire night would be her last time on duty. 'There'll be plenty of business for you then Innes,' the colonel had told her. 'Strong cider and fireworks don't mix.'

As these thoughts ran through her mind, she wondered if it was too late to patch things up with Edward. So much of her life in Great Tew was perfect. The fury she had felt after his bungled visit had eased but, although she knew the man was still deeply shocked by the war, she found she couldn't quite forgive him.

Eve had made a point of telling her that the Langford ring was still in the safe upstairs, and her mother's final observation as she had followed her husband onto the train at Oxford station had been direct. 'Not many girls get the opportunity that is sitting in your lap Innes and if you are sensible you'll bring him round. You and the wean can have a wonderful life here, think well before you walk away from it.' Then she had kissed her and pulled the carriage door firmly shut.

It had been an ultimatum of sorts and typical of her straight-taking mother. She smiled faintly. None of the women who were aware of events seemed to have any doubts that the decision to marry or to return to Glasgow rested with Innes, or that she could bend Edward to her will if she chose

208

to. She wasn't so sure – and crucially still didn't know if she wanted to.

As the love of her life carefully shovelled the last piece of toast into his eggy mouth and cried, 'Finished,' in triumph, she realised that she would still be dithering on the morning of the sixth and, as of this moment, had no idea if she and Jaikie would board the train or not.

*

Early on the fifth of November Stanley Tirrold called in at the police house and filled Burrows in on his trip to Leyland. They sat in the kitchen where the landlord drank stewed tea and eyed the constable's rubbery eggs and charred bacon with a distinct lack of enthusiasm.

Having cunningly censored his remarks because of the presence of Laura, he sat back, raised his eyes meaningfully and finished with, 'So there you are Burrows. It appears the man is a confirmed bachelor.'

'It's an odd alibi though, to say he was with a woman if it's widely known he prefers the company of men.' Laura's unsolicited remark from the far end of the kitchen was met with silent consternation by her husband and the pub landlord.

After a frozen moment, Stanley Tirrold observed uneasily, 'I believe he thinks that no-one knows Laura, and is therefore attempting to maintain a façade.'

She sniffed. 'Idiot. If he's a local he should know that nothing, absolutely nothing, is a secret in the villages around here. You just need to know who to ask.'

209

Shocked that his wife was aware of such matters, Burrows beckoned to the landlord, and they removed themselves to the room with the counter at the front of the house.

'The point is, you were wondering how to get a bit of leverage on him. Perhaps that's the way. A suggestion of exposure might bring him to heel,' Tirrold observed when the door was safely closed. 'It is illegal after all.'

The young constable nodded slowly, still stunned by his wife's casual acknowledgement of Eales's proclivities. 'I suppose you're right. And it means he doesn't have an alibi, even though he is claiming that he does.'

Left alone, he returned thoughtfully to the kitchen, where his wife remarked, 'I'm sorry if I surprised you Burrows, but we are all living in the same world you know. It's never spoken of publicly, but everyone knows that Lord Langford is a man's man. That's why Lady Langford is so keen to get Edward married off to Innes Knox. Surely you knew that?'

'Yes I did,' he admitted, fervently hoping that was an end to it.

But to his horror his wife continued, 'To be honest there were some very close friendships between the land girls on the estate during the war. Very close indeed.' She raised her eyebrows.

Her husband's mind reeled. 'That is the giddy limit Laura,' he barked. 'I'm off on my rounds, and I'll thank you to be a bit more….,' he struggled for the words, finally ending with 'wifely,' before turning and striding down the corridor.

Her face split with a broad grin, Laura turned back to the washing up.

*

210

Up on the common final preparations were being put in place for the bonfire celebration. Hardened as they were to outdoor conditions, the expected arrival of snow wasn't expected to put anyone off.

'She'll burn. Especially with a bit of petrol,' Bert Williams observed to Nobby Griffin as they pulled a tarpaulin over the weather side of the large bonfire. 'This'll keep the worst of it off and when we peel it back and light this side, the wind will drive the flames into the heart of it.'

Nobby grunted in agreement. 'No barrels in the field tonight though.' When the weather was mild the main celebrations normally took place by the bonfire, but given the bitter cold it seemed likely that, once the fireworks had been set off, a lot of the village would repair to the hostelry of their choice, be it the Black Horse or Kings Head. 'What time are we lighting it?'

'Same as normal. Seven o'clock and Mr Stafford's doing the display.'

'Watch out! Here we go then! Wheeeee...!'

Nobby chuckled and hopped about, waving his arms wildly. The fireworks were funded by the Langford Estate and the land agent jealously guarded his role as chief pyrotechnic officer. It was the high point of his year, and the village took as much pleasure from his own exuberant and childlike delight as they did from the display itself.

Shivering in the freezing wind, the two men secured the tarpaulin and walked across the common to the top of the high street, close to the lych gate of St Mary's.

'Fancy a pint then?' asked Nobby hopefully.

'Alright. My Edna is looking after Jaikie from Marston House all afternoon, so she won't be looking for me,' Bert replied with obvious satisfaction. 'You still got your beaters' money?'

'I do. Told my missus I'd only done two days, when I done all three. And she's a good tipper that Lady Dartmouth, so there's a bit of coin in my pocket.'

'Come on then.' A flurry of snow gusted over the pub roof and Nobby muttered and dropped his chin, but Bert glanced to the north with an experienced eye. 'Not sticking yet, but more's coming I reckon. And likely a lot of it.'

As they crossed the road, a large, dark, and highly polished car appeared by the market cross and turned up the high street. At first Bert thought it must be the Bishop coming to see Tukes, but instead it swung to the right through the wide gates to Langford Hall and disappeared.

'Visitors,' Nobby remarked, seeing no reason not to state the obvious.

*

'Just pull in at the foot of the steps will you,' Sir Anthony's voice sounded from the back of the car. 'It'll be nice to get into the warm, Halley,' he added to the man sitting next to him. 'Damn cold once you get out of London,'

'It certainly is, sir,' his aide confirmed, anticipating a warm fire and a cup of tea with some pleasure. He glanced at his watch. 'Just after three. We're right on time.'

Half an hour later the cup of tea and a plate of remarkably good biscuits had been served and the two men were sitting in the drawing room with Lady Langford and Piers Spense.

'I must apologise for my younger son's absence,' she remarked, 'he was told you were due around three, I really cannot think where he has got to. Piers, do you have any idea?'

'I'm afraid not,' his brother replied. 'He went out for a ride after lunch, but I'd have thought he'd be back by now. If only because of the weather.' All four of them looked toward the windows. Light snow was falling steadily, and the lawn was partially covered with a thin white layer that left it looking like a thickly woven green and white rug.

'Will it get any worse do you think?' asked Halley. 'I'm just wondering in regard to the exchange.'

'It's hard to say,' his hostess replied non-commitally, then turned to the permanent secretary, adding, 'perhaps you would outline the arrangements for later, Sir Anthony'.

He nodded. 'Of course. We have brought the government bonds, which are under the care of Mr Watson and Mr Bell who have travelled with us. They are currently in the servants' hall and will only part with the bonds at my direct order, witnessed by a third party. Our instructions are that myself and you, Lady Langford, are to be in your late husband's study at nine this evening. It is there that he insists the exchange takes place, but I have no idea why your presence is important to him.'

'Do you think my mother is in any danger?' her eldest son asked.

Sir Anthony hesitated. 'Logically, one thinks not. It must be the money that the man is after, and then a quick and clean getaway. I cannot think of any reason why Lady Langford would be imperilled in that scenario. But having said that, I will admit that I am uneasy about his request. I'd like to inspect the study and see what additional measures we might take.' He looked at his hostess and she rose.

'Very well, let's scout the field of encounter.' With that she led the men out of the drawing room.

'Fetch Watson and Bell, would you, Halley,' the permanent secretary said as they crossed the hall and, five minutes later all six of them were gathered in the study, where a low fire smouldered.

It was a pleasantly masculine wood-panelled room situated on the ground floor. A large desk and a handsome Adam fireplace were the main features, along with two comfortable looking armchairs placed on either side of a pair of French windows which opened directly onto the lawn. Outside, a large clump of laurel bushes lay to the left and beyond the snow-covered grass a statuesque group of cedar trees with white-clad branches were outlined against the grey sky.

The permanent secretary eyed the glass doors and then turned to his host. 'Well there we are. If they were open the night Lord Colin died our fellow could have simply walked in and surprised him. And it was late, no-one else would have had any idea he was in the building.'

Halley nodded. 'You're right, sir. Even if they were shut, if he'd tapped on the glass I imagine Lord Langford would have got up to see who it was.'

'But you still have no idea how he killed him? Or why?' Piers asked.

Kerr looked at him sympathetically. 'I'm sorry, we do not. It remains a mystery.'

Halley added, 'We've made the assumption that they knew each other in some way. The letter making the arrangements for the exchange refers to your father as Lord Colin. It seems an unlikely phrase unless they were acquainted.'

'From what you have told me, I imagine I will recognise him. Perhaps things will become clearer then,' Lady Langford observed calmly. 'And his choice of the fifth of November suggests local knowledge. There will be bonfire on the common later and a party afterwards that spreads between the two public houses. It's a tradition that the staff go, so the house will be more or less devoid of servants. That hardly seems a coincidence does it?'

'No, it does not.' Sir Anthony said thoughtfully.

'How do you think it will play out?' Piers asked.

'Your mother and I wait in here at nine o'clock in the evening. He appears, shows us the letter and we show him the bonds. One is exchanged for another and both sides retire in good order,' Sir Anthony replied. 'Of course we need to be certain we have the genuine document, that is the absolute priority.'

'And you're prepared to let him walk away?' Piers asked.

'I didn't say that, exactly,' the older man remarked in a steely tone.

'Will he come to the front door, do you think?'

'Like a regular visitor?' Sir Anthony shrugged. 'Perhaps, but then he might also use the back door, or even simply knock at the French windows,' he gestured in their direction. 'The only certainty seems to be that at some point he will be in this room along with the document we require. Until we have that letter he is in charge, once it is in our hands the dynamic will change.'

Halley asked, 'Where does that second door lead to?'

'Nowhere, it's a large cupboard used for storing family papers,' Piers replied. He crossed the room and opened it, revealing shelves of files.

Kerr glanced at the two men from the War Office. 'Watson, you'll be in the hallway by the main entrance. If he comes to either the front or back door you will escort him into this room and then wait outside. Halley, you stay with him. Bell, I can see no reason why you shouldn't lurk in that cupboard in case he comes in via the French windows. Leave it open a slight crack so you can hear what's going on.'

'Yes, sir,' the man replied.

'Beyond that I think we must remain flexible,' the permanent secretary concluded. 'Perhaps you would give us five minutes just to have a final briefing,' he smiled charmingly at his hostess who nodded and left the room with her son.

With the door safely shut behind her, Sir Anthony's expression hardened. 'Right, now you've seen the set up I trust we are all clear about the final outcome. Watson, if he wants to leave by the same door through which he entered, you escort him to it. And, once he is outside the house you shoot him dead. In the back, if necessary. Bell, ditto. If he goes out of the French windows, follow him straight away and shoot him on the lawn. No ifs, no buts, no hesitation. You have my personal order, given in front of Halley. Any questions?'

Both men shook their heads silently, their faces set, and the young aide shivered, knowing a man would die that night, within fifty yards of where they were standing.

The older man continued. 'The household will hear the shots of course but that cannot be helped. I'll deal with that end of things. When the deed is done, bring the car round from the stables and put the body in the boot and recover the bonds. Then we will return forthwith to London. A nice tidy job is what's needed gentlemen, and no slip ups.'

*

By six o'clock Edward Spense and been sitting in the Black Horse drinking for some time. It was dark outside, and he had no idea that the snow was falling steadily. Innes's departure the following day had settled over him like a damp fog and the morose introspection that his mother had correctly identified as his great weakness had him firmly in its grip.

Too late to speak to her now anyway, I was drunk last time, and I'm drunk again.

He had completely forgotten about the arrival of the men from London and was in fact musing on the odd appearance of a ghost in the woods. There had been no warning, no acrid smell and no sixth sense that there was an uninvited actor in the scene. In fact none of the normal triggers had been present. And yet the man he had seen slipping through the trees was dead, killed in the war, he was certain of it. On another day he might perhaps have wondered why a man who had died in France was haunting Great Tew, and had he pursued that train of thought it is possible that the appalling events of November the fifth 1920 in Great Tew might have been prevented. But as it was Bert Williams and Nobby decided to come over and the moment was lost.

'You want to help us light the bonfire, Mr Edward?' Bert enquired. 'We'll be going over in half an hour. Just time for one more,' he pointed out hopefully, and the youngest son of the current Langford generation duly obliged, nodding to the ever-alert Beatrice Wray that three pints were required.

'You're looking a bit down in the mouth, Trixie,' Nobby observed as she put the glasses on the table.

'Got things on my mind Nobby Griffin. Private things.'

'You in love again?'

'None of your business.'

The village barber and carpenter grinned. 'I think you are too, and there I was saving myself for you.'

'Thinking was never your strong point was it, Nobby? And neither was saving yourself, if I've heard right.'

*

As this exchange was taking place, Innes returned from her rounds and walked to Edna's cottage. The child minding arrangement had been in place for a few weeks, in recognition of the fact that Ellie had other duties at Marston House and couldn't look after the wean full time when Innes was working.

As she turned into Rivermead the wind drove thickly falling snow into her face and she shivered and hurried on to the cottage, looking forward to seeing her beloved son again and, like Halley earlier that afternoon, a warming cup of tea. But to her surprise there was no reply to her knock. After waiting for a couple of minutes she tried the door and found it was locked, a most unusual occurrence. Even more oddly,

218

when she walked round the side of the house and tried the back door, she found it was locked too. In the fading light she peered in through the back window, but the kitchen was dark, the range fireless.

Confused rather than alarmed, she retraced her steps to Marston House, assuming that Mrs Williams had returned the boy early for some reason. But Jaikie was not at home. Neither Mrs Franks nor Ellie had seen him all afternoon.

She explained in a few short sentences that the Williams' cottage was deserted and that she was sure the arrangements had not been changed. The three women stood and stared at each other in the kitchen. 'Well where can they be then?' asked the cook, giving voice to their common thought.

'He won't come to any harm, not with Edna,' Ellie remarked, although there was a faint frown of worry on her face.

'No that's true, it's just rather strange. If they're not at the cottage and they're not here, I really cannot think where they might be.' Innes said. 'I thought I saw his coat on the back of a chair and it's such a bitterly cold evening, they'd hardly be out for a walk.'

'He had his thick jumper on,' Ellie smiled gently and nodded to the cook who had spent some time knitting a bright red pullover for the winter. Its robustness had been a source of gentle amusement in the house and Jaikie insisted on wearing it every day.

'Bonfire night. They'll be up at the common. With Bert.' Mrs Franks clicked her fingers with satisfaction and glanced at the clock. 'Half past six. People will be gathering up there

219

now. The fireworks are at seven and they light the bonfire just before then. Ellie and I were going up shortly ourselves.'

Innes's face cleared. 'Of course. What a relief. Come on then we'll all go up together and find them.'

Ten minutes later, wrapped up against the cold and carrying a spare coat for Jaikie, they joined the throng heading up the high street to the common. As they passed through the gate a cheer sounded from the gathered watchers as Bert and Nobby peeled back the tarpaulin and poured a pint of petrol onto the branches, then threw on a blazing rag.

With a whump, the fuel ignited, and flames built rapidly. Innes, Ellie and Mrs Franks split up and pushed through the jolly, noisy, crowd, looking for the familiar figure of Edna Williams. Beyond the bonfire, Jaikie's mother could see Mr Stafford, torch in hand, dashing excitedly between racks of fireworks as he made last minute adjustments. Lady Langford and Lord Langford were standing nearby chatting to Stanley Tirrold and out of the corner of her eye she saw Bert Williams walking towards them, his work done.

She set a course to intercept and caught up with him just as he reached the little group.

'Bert have you seen Edna and Jaikie?' she asked without preamble.

Something in her tone alerted the others and they stopped speaking. Bert shook his head and answered, 'No I haven't. They'll be at home I suppose.'

'No they're not. The house is locked and dark. I think she must have brought him up to see the fireworks, but I can't see them anywhere. Ellie and Mrs Franks are looking too.'

220

The Dances arrived and, sensing the mood, Jocelyn asked, 'What's this?'

'We've lost Edna and Jaikie.' Innes briefly explained, for the benefit of everyone.

'Right, well we'll soon find them if we all look, there aren't that many people here,' the colonel said, looking over the crowd then muttering a curse as the wind drove a flurry of snow into his face. 'Split up and search. Everyone please.' The authority in his voice was unmistakable and without further ado they set off.

Seconds later, another great cheer echoed around the common as the first rocket rose screaming into the sky and within a minute the crowd was bathed in a cacophony of sound and coloured explosions as Giles Stafford worked his magic. The thickly falling snow and flashing coloured lights creating a confused, disjointed, picture and, as Innes walked more and more urgently through the milling crowd, she was reminded of a strobe light that she had witnessed at one of her medical lectures.

From time to time she met another searcher, greeting each with a quick and increasingly desperate shake of her head before pressing on. But after ten minutes, as the firework display rose to a climax, a hollow feeling that Edna and Jaikie were not in the field was consuming her.

Sick with worry, she found herself standing close to Stafford as he shouted to the crowd, 'And now ladies and gentlemen, the final firework for this evening. And as usual we've saved the best until last – the giant Catherine wheel!'

Climbing five feet up a ladder he held a lighted splint to what appeared to be an enormous circular Cumberland sausage fastened to a stout post. As the wick glowed, he hastily retreated back down the rungs and seconds later a burst of flame appeared and, with ever increasing speed, the firework started to rotate.

'Wooooo! Ahhhh!' the crowd cheered.

'Stand well back please,' called Stafford, almost dancing with excitement.

And indeed the crowd did move away a little as the great wheel powered on, roaring and throwing out a spectacular disc of vibrant orange and blue sparks some fifteen feet across.

Then suddenly he stiffened and shouted, 'Watch out back there!'.

A shadowy, stumbling, female figure had appeared behind the firework. Clearly oblivious to the danger, she staggered through the circle of fire and into the gap in front of the crowd, her bloody face shining in the garish light.

As women screamed and men stared open-mouthed, Edna Williams fell to her knees and, backlit by the roaring firework, screamed, 'He's gone. The boy's gone.' Then she pitched forward, face down onto the trampled snow and lay unmoving as the horrified crowd surged forward.

Chapter Fifteen

The man from Marseilles had hired a car in London that morning and driven to Oxford. Once there he left the main road and with the aid of a map and his memory followed quiet lanes to the little village of Leyland. Knowing that he was now in an area where people might recognise his face, he took care to conceal the vehicle on a heavily overgrown track that led into woods on the eastern slope of the Cherwell valley.

The weather was bitterly cold with lowering grey clouds and a vengeful north-easterly wind that penetrated the dense woodland, forcing the last of the foliage from the trees. Only the rust coloured beech leaves hung on, hissing their defiance high above him. He shivered and cursed, then wrapped his coat and scarf tight and set off to walk the two miles to Great Tew.

He passed to the right hand side of the great reed bed where he had toiled in his youth, and carried on up the valley, keeping parallel to the river. He knew the land intimately and avoided the footpaths that had been created by people walking to work in the fields over hundreds of years. The cold nipped at his face and made him think longingly of the hot and fragrant countryside of Provence, but there was an undeniable pleasure in being back among the familiar landmarks where he had grown up.

As he crossed a track, he was spotted by a man on horseback a hundred yards away. And the rider recognised him, and even said his name in his mind. The sighting only lasted for perhaps five seconds before, unaware he had been noticed, the man slipped back into the trees and continued on his way.

Motionless in the saddle, Edward Spense stared after him, then gave a mental shrug. Ghosts were a regular feature of his life and the sight of another dead man sharing the earth with the living was hardly an extraordinary event.

By early afternoon the man was in thick woodland on the slope above Rivermead and heading towards Beatrice Wray's house. He had a good view down the lane towards Great Tew's market cross and noticed an attractive woman with a long French plait enter the front garden of a cottage. She was holding a small red-headed boy by the hand. Edna Williams answered the door. From overheard snatches of the brief conversation, he deduced that the boy's name was Jaikie and that he and his mother lived at Marston House. Well aware that the chief constable lived there, he watched through narrowed eyes as the woman gave her son a kiss and turned back towards the main street. Head bent and talking to the boy, Bert's wife ushered him in and shut the front door.

Realising that fate had done him a favour the man crept forward to the edge of the trees and crouched, waiting.

Edna led Jaikie into the kitchen and sat him down at the table. 'Shall we make some currant buns to eat, while mummy's busy?' she asked, although it wasn't really a question, as the ingredients were already laid out on the table.

'Alright then.' Last time Jaikie had found the process rather boring, but there was no denying the excellence of the results, so he was prepared to give the woman his attention. For ten minutes they mixed flour, currants, and butter before Edna remembered that the range would need refuelling to heat the oven.

'I'll just get a shovel of coal Jaikie, you sit there.' She left the cottage by the back door and opened the shed. As she straightened up with the loaded shovel in her hand, the man from Marseilles delivered a vicious blow to the back of her head with a stone. With a sigh she subsided to the ground, out cold and bleeding.

He bundled her onto the pile of coal, tied her hands and feet with some twine and stuffed a rag into her mouth. Then he closed the shed door, dropped the latch, and entered the kitchen.

The little boy looked up. Expecting the comfortable and reassuring Edna Williams he was surprised and then alarmed at his sudden appearance. As he stared uncertainly the man said, 'It's Jaikie isn't it? Your mummy asked me to take you out on an adventure.'

'Where's Mrs Williams?' he replied, unconvinced.

'She's having a lie down.' And with that the man crossed to the table and slapped him hard across the face. Stunned, Jaikie fell backwards. The man quickly walked down the hall and bolted the front door, then returned to the kitchen and picked him up. He went out by the back door, leaving the boy's coat hanging on his chair.

Pausing only to turn the key in the lock and throw it into the bushes, he headed back to the riverbank, a decision made. Beatrice Wray could wait. The frightened and whimpering boy slung over his shoulder was just the insurance policy he'd been looking for.

As he moved silently through the trees, widely spaced snowflakes as big as half-crowns started to fall through the dark branches; the advance guard of a great army.

*

By seven fifteen a full blizzard was raging over Great Tew. Snow was building window-high drifts on north facing walls and laying a thick carpet elsewhere. In the high street it was a foot deep and getting deeper by the minute, and there was more to come. The storm had barrelled down the east coast of England leaving cities completely cut off, before veering to the west and running rampant over the central part of the country.

Edna Williams was still unconscious, carried to the cottage hospital by willing hands, where Innes, in a remarkable demonstration of her calling under the circumstances, had cleaned and dressed her head wound. She now lay unmoving under the care of a volunteer nurse. Bert Williams was at her side.

Up on the common, with no information other than the fact that the boy was missing, chaotic scenes reigned among the swirling snow and flickering light from the bonfire. Finally the colonel quelled the rising panic and despatched some men to the cottage, while he hastily organised parties of searchers with instructions to comb the area as best they could. As soon as she had finished with Edna, Innes followed.

226

Shortly afterwards, a message was received confirming that there was no sign of Jaikie at the cottage, but that his coat was still there.

This, of all nights, Lady Langford reflected bitterly as she glanced discreetly at her watch.

*

Half an hour later, only people with a desperate need to be outside were still abroad in north-west Oxfordshire. In the darkness, a howling, whirling, frenzy of snow cut visibility to a few feet and drove into every nook and cranny that was exposed to the wind. Out in the fields sheep turned their backs to the gale and slowly gave way, forced downwind until they reached a hedge. And there they stayed as the snow piled up around them until, one by one, they disappeared, buried beneath the deadly drifts, where suffocation and death waited.

But the shepherds knew the danger. From every farm, resolute men, women and children battled out into the maelstrom, waist and sometimes shoulder deep in the drifts as they pulled the precious beasts out by the horns and drove them towards the shelter of the woods and copses.

And the men and women searching for Jaikie Knox fared no better. It was exhausting work. Their calling voices were whipped away by the vicious wind and the drifts of snow made it impossible to search in any methodical way. Slowly they returned to the village as they realised that to stay out any longer would only endanger themselves.

Exhausted and disheartened, the Colonel, Eve, Claire, and Burrows, got back to Marston House having forged as high as they could go up the lane to Tan Hill before being driven back. Leaving the others, Lady Langford struggled through the snow to the hall and let herself in with a sigh of relief. Alerted by the unfathomable sense that butlers possess, Dereham emerged from the servants' door by the main staircase and hastened to help her out of her outer garments.

'Ask Lilly to find a pair of dry shoes and a warm cardigan, will you. Where's Sir Anthony?'

'He's in the drawing room, my Lady, with Mr Halley. Dinner is ready when you are.'

'Yes, tell cook I'm sorry I'm late, there's been an emergency.' She briefly outlined events at the bonfire, ending with, 'So inform the staff there will be no bonfire celebrations. As you can imagine Innes is in a terrible state and we're all frantic with worry. He's a good strong boy, but this is no night to be out.'

The butler was more than a servant. She met his eye. 'I fear the worst, I really do.'

Pain showed on his face but he had the experience not to offer platitudes. 'I'm afraid there's little to be done until the snow stops, my lady. Then we will rouse the estate. Let's just hope we're in time.'

'I'll see Sir Anthony now, come and serve drinks, will you. And make sure his men are fed.' She paused and added, 'There may be some skulduggery later. We're expecting a visitor at nine o'clock. A bad man. Although with this weather...' she shrugged her shoulders. 'Anyway, look out for squalls, Dereham. Tell the footmen to be on the alert too.'

He raised one eyebrow a minute amount and answered, 'I will, my lady.' With that he led the way into the drawing room where Sir Anthony and Halley waited. She brought them up to date on events and the news was received with a thoughtful frown by the older man, although he didn't comment beyond observing that he hoped the boy would be found safely.

'How is it outside, Lady Langford?' asked Halley.

'Frankly, it's grim. I wonder if our mysterious blackmailer will manage to put in an appearance at all,' she replied. 'The snow is knee deep at a minimum and much worse in many places. Dell Lane is blocked completely. Even if he is here already, I cannot see how he will get away again.'

'We will assume he is coming and await developments after that,' Sir Anthony said neutrally and Halley, who was an imaginative young man, had a sudden picture of a man lying in bloodstained snow, the case containing the bonds thrown to one side as he died.

'As you wish, anyway, I am starving so let's have supper.'

At twenty to nine Sir Anthony directed his players into position, then poured a whisky and soda for himself and another for his hostess and opened the curtains. They sat down and waited.

'Tell me, how is your family?' Lady Langford asked, with admirable sang-froid. Ever the diplomat, Sir Anthony dredged up an amusing story concerning his son's behaviour at Cowes week and the next ten minutes passed relatively quickly.

But by five to nine, all conversation had died away and four minutes later he looked at his watch and murmured, 'Any time now I'd say'.

Outside the window a fierce exhilaration pulsed through the snow covered figure as he saw Sir Anthony and Lady

Langford sitting in the two armchairs. They looked so vulnerable, and he felt an irresistible urge to kill them once he had the money. He stared, enjoying the voyeuristic moment. The civil servant was wearing a dark suit, white shirt and pale red tie, she a green dress and cardigan. A single shaded lamp illuminated the scene, although a blazing fire helped to throw light into the corners of the room. Behind them a leather portfolio lay on the desk. His heart raced as he saw it, but he waited, scanning the scene with the almost superhuman sense that he had developed.

He could feel fear coming from the woman and delighted in her discomfort, but the man just emanated cool anger. He let it roll around his mind.

There was no fear of losing. A trap had been set. Other men were close. Well that was no surprise. But he had a shot in his locker as well.

Bracing himself he stepped forward into the lee of the building where the snow was thin on the ground and rapped firmly on the window.

Lady Langford jumped in her chair, but Sir Anthony merely looked up and saw a shadowy figure standing outside. 'The garden route then,' he said, loudly enough for Bell to hear, then rose to his feet and walked over to the windows. He unlocked the door, opened it, and stood back as an icy blast flowed into the room.

The man's face was covered by a scarf and his hat was pulled well down. His coat and boots were covered in snow. They looked at each other for a moment, then Sir Anthony spoke.

'Come in then, if you're coming.'

Wordlessly he stepped over the threshold and looked at Lady Langford, his eyes showing in the narrow slit between hat and muffler. Lumps of icy snow fell to the parquet floor and lay, like toy icebergs, on a brown ocean.

'Will you show us your face?' she asked calmly.

'I don't think so. You wouldn't recognise me now. And anyway what would be the point? I died at Delville Wood, along with my brother.' His sardonic laugh sounded loud in the still room. 'I'll have a warm coat though. This gabardine isn't doing the job on a night like this.'

She hesitated, then gestured towards the door and said, 'There are some on the stand in the hall. Take one if you want.'

The man gave her a long look. She tried and failed to quell a shiver of horror as his dead eyes met hers. 'Oh yes Lady Claire, I can see right into your mind. And I can feel your fear. Now you run along and get one for me while Sir Anthony and I see to our business.'

Her face tightened, but with icy poise she rose and left the room.

In the silence the two men looked at each other.

'Have you brought it?' Kerr asked.

'You got the bonds?'

'You'll find them in there. Have a look if you like.' He nodded at the desk.

The man walked over, opened the portfolio and looked at contents: Ten five-thousand pound government-issue bearer bonds; as good as cash. Controlling a surge of excitement, he said, 'Very nice.'

Claire Spense returned, carrying a worn tweed overcoat with a high old-fashioned collar. He slipped off his soaking gabardine, dropped it onto the floor, and took it from her.

As he put it on he said conversationally, 'I killed your husband in this very room. In 1916. I came back from France especially to do it. Knocked on the windows one night when he was working. He wasn't half surprised to see me. And he was even more shocked when I squirted a whiff of cyanide in his face. A nice little gun thing I'd bought in Marseilles. One squeeze and it was all over. He died in agony, watching me laughing at him.'

'You'll swing for that,' muttered Sir Anthony.

The man laughed. 'I doubt it. You can't kill a man who's already dead. But you can kill one who's still alive.'

With that he pulled a revolver from his trouser pocket and fired three shots in quick succession through the door of the cupboard behind which Bell was concealed. The appalling noise stunned Lady Langford and Sir Anthony. Watson burst through the study door, gun in hand and, as they looked on in horror, the man calmly shot him in the chest. He coughed, stumbled forwards, and then lay still on the floor, blood seeping out from underneath his body.

In the shocking silence the man said, 'Two shots left. Maybe I'll see off the pair of you too, that'll keep it nice and neat.' He levelled his gun at Lady Langford.

'Oh, no you don't!' Halley appeared in the doorway, standing over Watson's body. He had a shotgun raised to his shoulder and the two dark rings of the barrels were aimed at the man with snow at his feet. Dereham was behind him, wide eyed and similarly armed.

232

'Oh reinforcements, is it?' the man appeared unconcerned. 'Well, I'm going to take the bonds now and leave by the window. And I think I'll keep the letter as it happens. With all that talk about reparations going on the Germans will pay handsomely for it. It'll be very awkward for you when they find out the British started the Great War.'

Sir Anthony called out, 'Shoot him Halley.'

'Just before you do, let me tell you about a little lad called Jaikie who lives at Marston House. I imagine he's known to you, Lady Langford. If I don't leave this room with the bonds and the letter, he will die. I took him and I hid him. When I'm safely away I'll telephone and let you know where. You might just be in time to save him before he freezes to death. A nasty way to go that. All on his own in the dark.'

As Lady Langford gasped, a note of genuine amusement sounded in his voice. 'Yes, it's a bit of a bind isn't it? Kill me and you'll be murdering him.'

Sir Anthony agonised for a long moment as an image of the German delegation brandishing the letter flashed though his mind. Then, with his face set in stone said, 'Shoot him Halley. There are too many lives at stake. Do it man. On my orders.'

'In God's name don't! Not if it means Jaikie will die,' Claire Spense ran over to stand in front of the aide.

And as the three of them stood in a frozen tableau, the man with death in his heart picked up the case, walked quickly to the French windows and wrenched the door open.

'Halley!' bellowed the permanent secretary, and with a look of despair the aide shouldered Lady Langford aside and fired both barrels in quick succession.

233

But the man was gone. And as freezing air tumbled joyfully into the study, the sound of laughter echoed faintly from the lawn.

*

The eye of the storm was over the Langford Estate. Stars were visible high overhead, although towering dark clouds showed on the horizon in every direction, giving the impression that the village was cut off by a huge black wall that rose without limits into the sky.

The wind had dropped completely and starlight reflecting on the deep snow created an eerie blue luminescence. Stillness and silence reigned; the contrast to the storm serving only to emphasise the unworldly atmosphere and bitter cold.

At this break in the weather the searchers emerged from their houses, and the single set of tracks in the knee-deep snow that led out of the gates of Langford Hall and down the high street was quickly obliterated as the teams were marshalled by the colonel and Burrows down by the market cross.

This time the organisation was better, and with clear directions and a communications chain in place the men and women set off again. The going remained dreadful, particularly where deep drifts blocked the lanes and footpaths. Rivermead was filled by a drift a hundred yards long that rose to the level of the hedge tops, ten feet above the sunken lane. The only way round was to clamber up into the field and skirt it. Other searchers experienced similar problems and after half an hour a familiar feeling of hopelessness began to permeate through the villagers. If the boy was out in the snow he was buried and, unless there had been a miracle, he was dead.

But Innes Knox forged on across the silent, eerie, snowfields, searching desperately for any sign: a mother in a living hell. No one had the heart to tell her what they were thinking and when every other group had returned exhausted and disheartened to the market cross, the people with her carried on, somehow finding the strength to match her superhuman efforts.

Down at the power house the man with death in his heart pulled the scarf off his face and waited under the trees, as a search party moved along the bank. They had crossed his tracks but dismissed them as being far too fresh to be the boy's.

'And an adult's anyway,' he heard a woman observe, 'probably someone out looking on their own.'

When the coast was clear he waded through the snow to the mill leat, crossed carefully via a little footbridge to the river bank. Below him the rowing boat and the punt that he had noticed earlier, were now lying heavily in the water under the weight of eighteen inches of snow.

Glancing behind to make sure the coast was clear, he slid down to the water's edge then pulled the mooring rope to bring the boat within reach and began to shovel snow out of it with his hands.

Chapter Sixteen

Eve climbed the stairs to the attic at Marston House, her feet sounding clearly on each wooden step. When her preparations were complete she knelt on the cushion, leaned over the scrying bowl, and tried to calm her mind. But as she stared into the motionless water a persistent feeling of dread built and built and she struggled to overcome it. There was a deeply malign presence in the village. She'd felt it getting closer over the last two or three days and now it was here.

Finally a picture of Jaikie appeared, as though she'd turned a page in a book. He was alone in the dark, his small body weak with cold. She reached out and tried to wrap herself around him, giving him comfort and strength. But with a sickening feeling she realised that whoever had taken the boy was shielding him from her reach.

She redoubled her efforts, sending him light and warmth as he lay curled up in a ball, his red jersey knitted by Mrs Franks offering scant protection against the cold. Then suddenly she was bounced out of contact so brutally that she felt a searing pain behind her eyes. Laughter sounded in her head, and she moaned with horror.

It was stronger than her. And it wanted Jaikie's soul.

She sat silently for ten minutes then descended the attic stairs, her face sombre. Down below she heard the front door open. It was Innes. She had finally returned and was alone. The colonel met her in the hall, helped her out of her snow-covered coat and ushered her into the drawing room. By the time Eve joined them she was sitting with a glass of brandy by the fire, shivering violently. Her haunted face looked beyond tears.

Her husband glanced up and gave her a brief but expressive shake of his head.

Eve sat down next to her friend and took her hand. 'There is still hope. Jocelyn thinks the wean has been abducted and not is out in the snow.' Her quiet voice reached Innes who turned and looked at her, unable to speak. 'Bear with me, there is one last thing to try.'

She left the room, re-climbed the stairs, and retrieved the Langford ring from the safe. Returning to the attic, she took a deep breath, slipped the ring onto the third finger of her right hand, and began to chant. Low, clear words; sometimes unique, sometimes repetitive; ancient words; in a forgotten Norse language, spoken with resonance and power. Words that carried way beyond the confines of the garret room and up into the night sky.

On and on she went, head bowed in fierce concentration, until her soul left her body and drove the spell higher and higher in a relentless, chiming, summoning that echoed around the clear, cold, light, where the Lords of the Air reside.

Eve Dance was a witch, and she was calling to her own.

Finally she came back into the room, shivering violently. She fell forward and lay comatose, candlelight glowing on her hair, her mind foggy and confused.

And at that moment a scream sounded from downstairs.

Cursing roundly, she dragged herself to her feet and hurried down the stairs, meeting Jocelyn and Innes on the landing. The screaming was coming from her bedroom, and they dashed to the front of the house.

The maid was standing by the window, her expression horror-struck. 'I was just drawing the curtains. I forgot because of the panic.' She gestured vaguely, one hand still on the drapes.

'What on earth is it?' The colonel paced to the window, peered down to the street, and reeled back. 'Ye Gods,' he said faintly.

Then Eve was beside him. She stared through the glass. Standing motionless in the middle of the deserted street, its baleful yellow eyes fixed on the window, was an enormous black dog. As their eyes met, the ring pulsed on her finger and the noise and violent chaos of the battle for Langford Hall cascaded through her mind.

'What is it?' whispered Innes, almost to herself.

Unable to resist, she smiled at her friend. 'You've met before, I believe.'

Ellie's eyes rolled. 'The black dog. It always predicts a death. Oh my God! The boy.' She lifted her hands to her face.

Eve gestured at her. 'No, I don't think so. Not this time.'

'What do you mean, madam?'

'I asked for help, and it's come.'

Two minutes later the front door of Marston House slowly opened. Eve, her husband, Innes and Ellie stood in a huddle on the step and eyed the great dog. At ground level the beast exuded a massive and malevolent power, as though raging at its summoning.

'There's no footprints ma'am,' Ellie whispered.

'She's right. The thing must weigh all of twenty stone but it's standing on the snow as though it's a fallen leaf,' the colonel said quietly. 'No tracks at all.'

Eve swallowed and said, 'Wait here would you?' She stepped out of the doorway and walked slowly down the garden path. Opening the gate with some difficulty, she waded through the snow and stopped six feet short of the dog. It growled and shifted on its haunches slightly.

'It's going to spring, madam,' Ellie's shrill cry gave voice to what they were all thinking.

'I'll get my gun,' the colonel said and turned, but his wife called after him.

'It's been dead for four hundred years, Jocelyn. That is not going to help.' She met the dog's eye and then slowly held up her hand, letting it see the ring and spoke, with all the command at her disposal. 'I know you Achilles, and you will serve me tonight.'

To the watchers in the doorway it seemed as if both the motionless figures in the street were glowing with a faint internal light that shimmered, unworldly in the silent eye of the storm.

She sent a picture of flame haired Jaikie deep into the creature's soul.

Find him. Where is the boy?

They stared at each other, and then the dog walked around her and down the street towards the market cross, moving lightly on the white crust.

As they rushed to find outdoor coats the colonel slipped on the icy step and fell backwards, cracking his head. Stunned, he lay there motionless for a few seconds as the three women reappeared clad for the weather. But when Eve called out in shock and bent to him, he gestured towards the street. 'Go on, go on. Mrs Franks will patch me up,' and with a backward glance, she led Innes and Ellie along the path to the front gate.

A hundred yards ahead, the great beast, as big as a bull calf, stopped at the market cross and turned to look back. Then it paced on past the garage and the King's Head and disappeared into the woods.

The three women, frightened, resolute, and frantic with worry, followed.

*

At Langford Hall Sir Anthony waited for the foreign secretary to return his call. He'd managed to connect with his private London number but had been told Lord Curzon was not at home. After a tense wait the telephone finally rang and, with no introduction or formalities, a simple question was asked. Halley who was standing next to him heard it clearly.

'Have you got it?'

'No, sir. I regret we have not. The man escaped with the letter. A pursuit is being prepared and there is thick snow here, meaning he will have great difficulty in getting any distance.' After another pause he added, 'Yes, Foreign Secretary, I am well aware of the implications.'

He listened some more and then responded, raw anguish on his face. 'No, we do not know who he is. He says he was killed in 1916 but is very much alive. He killed Watson and

Bell in cold blood and appears to have kidnapped a local boy to cover his tracks.'

At this point it became obvious that the call had been disconnected at the London end, and Sir Anthony quietly replaced the receiver. Halley thought he had aged twenty years as he listened to him.

'Lord Curzon was quite clear in his remarks. If we do not recover the letter my career is over, and you may as well join the church. I'm going to ask Lord Langford to rouse the estate as best he can. This damnable weather works both for and against us. But either way, I doubt very much that he's making a bid for it across the fields. My guess is he'll go to ground somewhere tonight. He knows the area. If we try to put some kind of cordon out we stand a decent chance of catching him. Come on, Halley, to horse.'

They left the room, seeking out a deeply shocked Lord Langford and his mother, who were talking quietly in the drawing room. The bodies of Bell and Watson had been removed to a downstairs storeroom.

But further frustration lay in wait for the men from London.

'I'm very sorry Sir Anthony, but the vast majority of those capable of searching are either already out looking for the missing boy or have returned exhausted and are not capable of mounting another expedition in the immediate future.' Piers Spense was apologetic but firm.

'Where on earth is Edward?' his mother interjected. 'A major emergency, two in fact, and he is nowhere to be found. I really despair of him sometimes.'

'I believe he went out alone to search for Jaikie, your ladyship,' Dereham, who had just entered the room, replied.

241

'Well it's ten o'clock now. Where is he?'

'Regrettably, I cannot say with any certainty.'

At that moment the front doorbell rang and two minutes later the colonel appeared, a large bandage wrapped around his head. Burrows was with him.

'I gather you've got problems,' he said shortly. 'I won't beat about the bush, Innes, Eve and Ellie are on the trail of the boy. The last I saw of them, they were going past the King's Head towards the footpath that leads to the river. That was an hour ago. It's a fifty fifty choice, but my instinct is that they'll head downstream. Unfortunately I cracked my skull but am fit to follow them now. We're here to borrow two of your horses, if that is agreeable?'

This simple statement of the available facts was received in silence then Kerr said, 'As it happens colonel, our aims are the same. To pursue and locate the man who kidnapped Jaikie Knox. We will come with you.' He glanced at Lady Langford who nodded.

'Of course. There are hunters in the stables, please take them. Piers, will you go too?'

But Lord Langford was already moving to the door. 'Follow me then, gentlemen. We'll saddle them up ourselves.'

*

In the icy, metallic, air beneath the black trees the three women from Marston House pressed on, the snow crunching with each step. They were deep in the woods moving roughly parallel to the river and, from time to time, they'd get a glimpse of the dog ahead of them, but it continued to leave no tracks.

242

Finally they emerged from the wood into a starlit, monochrome, landscape of gently sloping fields which stretched down towards the river away to their left and the dark line of the reed bed in the far distance. Innes forged out into the snow without pausing, but Eve held up her hand and called, 'I'm sorry, but I can go no further.'

Ellie, who had stayed close to her, said 'That's alright ma'am. You're a lot older than us two, begging your pardon. And I'm finding it hard work too.' She lowered her voice and added, 'I'll stay with her. She's driven, see. Won't stop until she's collapsed, or the boy is found.'

Her mistress nodded sadly, fervently hoping it would be the latter as snow flurries started to drift across the fields. Eve glanced upwards. Towering clouds were rapidly approaching. 'It's starting again,' she said. 'Look after her, Ellie.'

'I will, ma'am. You just follow our track back. Take your time. You'll get there.'

And with that they parted. Eve watched the maid cross the field in the thickening snow. A hundred yards away Innes was thigh deep in a drift and wading up the slope to where the top of a gate post showed above the white.

When Eve got back to Great Tew she was utterly exhausted. As she let herself in and removed her snow-encrusted outer garments Mrs Franks appeared wanting news, but in truth neither of them had much to report.

'The colonel went up to the hall, madam. Some search parties have come back up the high street, but I'd know if they found him,' she said, handing Eve a badly needed cup of strong, sweet, tea.

243

'I left Innes and Ellie close to the river above the reed bed. They're carrying on.'

'Ellie's a good girl.'

'Yes, she is.'

Miss Knox must be going through seven kinds of hell,' the cook remarked sympathetically. 'I've kept a good fire in the sitting room.'

'I think I'll have a hot bath. The cold seems to have got into my bones.'

'As you wish, madam. Will you have something to eat when you come back down?'

But Eve wasn't listening. Something unexpected had chimed in her head. An echo in the distance. A shield released. She stood in the kitchen frowning in concentration, then met the cook's eye. And it seemed to Mrs Franks that she was staring right through her.

Then she just said, 'Jaikie,' and turned and left the room.

She climbed to the attic, exhausted legs burning with the effort, and sat down on the cushion in the cold room. Then she closed her eyes, a thing she found all too easy to do, and tried to concentrate on the boy.

And to her surprise she found him easily. There was no blocking. He was suddenly just there, still, cold and nearly gone; hovering between life and death. She realised that he was willing to leave, and that the place he was going was ready for him.

Not yet my darling. Stay for your mother. Stay for all of us.

Summoning her last reserves of energy, she reached out and took his hand.

*

Innes and Ellie battled through the snow towards the next field. Up ahead she could just see the dark shadow of a hut. She thought the dog was standing next to it, staring over the marsh.

'What's that,' she asked the maid.

Ellie squinted through the darkness. 'It's the reed cutters' hut. They use it when they're harvesting the reeds. There's a little jetty where they moor the boats.'

As Innes nodded, a faint pop drifted through the night. It was an incongruous sound. They looked at each other. 'What was that?' she asked.

'Someone fired a gun, I think, madam, and some way off. But I don't know what direction.' The dog had disappeared.

'Come on Ellie, one more effort.' Without waiting, Jaikie's mother pressed on across the snowfield. The diminutive maid followed, scarf stiff where her breath had turned to ice. The hedges were the worst. Six foot drifts pushed up against a black, thorny barricade, with slight depressions in the snow where the gates lay. Gasping for breath they burrowed towards the wooden bars. Dark clouds arrived over them, and the wind and snow increased steadily as they crossed three fields and, at last, reached the reed cutters' hut and the little jetty.

A wide flat boat was there, with deep snow covering it from bow to stern. Beyond it the great black bed of reeds moved restlessly.

And they smelt wood smoke.

It was faint, diffused by distance, carried downwind from the marsh. 'Does anyone live in there?' Innes asked, gesturing across the valley.

'No.' Ellie's answer was assured.

'Well someone's in there now. And they've lighted a fire. Come on. We'll take the boat. At least we won't have to struggle through this cursed snow anymore.'

'Where's the dog?'

'I've no idea. But maybe this is where it's led us.'

Ten minutes later, they'd cleared most of the snow from the craft. They then set off down the main channel with Ellie poling from the stern and Innes in the bow. She found a snow-encrusted paddle under her foot and held it up in triumph and they made slow and rather erratic progress into the heart of the marsh. The smell of wood smoke got stronger, as the wind swirled confusedly around the high reeds.

'We're getting closer I think,' Innes called, scanning the banks.

Ellie said nothing. She was exhausted and the pole was very difficult to manage. She'd tried standing and had almost fallen in and had compromised by kneeling down and was doing her best to pole along from that position. But her arms and shoulders were aching in protest. Pushed by the wind, the boat drifted towards the right-hand bank of reeds and, as she flailed rather hopelessly with the heavy pole she noticed a narrow channel behind the thin covering of fallen reeds and smelt a strong gust of wood smoke. Looking closer she realised that some of the reeds had been pushed out of the way.

And she knew. She just knew. 'In here,' she called, poling backwards as the bow turned and edged towards the reeds.

She felt the boat move forward as Innes paddled and they broke through into the still black water.

By some instinct neither of them said anything, they just paddled and poled slowly through the high reeds, feeling oddly marooned from the storm raging above them. And their perseverance was rewarded because, as they swung round a bend, they were confronted with a small wooden hut twenty feet away. Smoke was coming from its chimney and, unlike the pristine snowfields they had crossed, in front of the hut the snow was rutted and piled high in places as though children had been playing there.

A rowing boat and a punt were pulled up onto the snow next to each other. But that wasn't what took their eye. In the shadowy gap between the two craft, close under the side of the boat, a man's body lay half in the water, its torso dark on the white blanket.

And Innes recognised him.

'Edward,' she screamed.

Chapter Seventeen

Edward Spense had not joined the search parties. Befuddled by drink he had returned to the hall directly from the pub and missed what had happened at the bonfire. It was Dereham who, well aware that he was lying drunk and fast asleep on a divan in the morning room, came to wake him, after his mother had returned to the hall and explained what was going on.

At the news he had hastily changed into outdoor clothing and set off alone to search for Jaikie as best he could. In so doing, he also contrived to miss the disastrous events at the hall, meaning he remained ignorant of the man's escape and the deaths of Bell and Watson.

He was still young and very fit. And he ranged far and wide in the appalling conditions seeking by instinct the ways under the trees where Jaikie might have gone; the routes of least resistance, the winding paths and tracks that led downhill to the river. Finally he emerged onto the bank at Dipper Pool. As the eye of the storm arrived over Great Tew and an eerie silence settled over the landscape he turned downstream, still scanning and calling the boy's name every few minutes.

When the power house came into view he decided with a heavy heart that he would climb the path under the chestnut trees to the bottom of the high street, and then home.

Perhaps there was news. Perhaps there had been a miracle.

To his surprise he saw movement on the river bank beyond the leat. It was the man he'd seen recently. The man he'd assumed was a ghost.

He stood still, made invisible by the thick covering of packed snow on his coat and hat, and watched the dark figure clamber into a rowing boat and head downstream. As the little craft disappeared, carried by an instinct he couldn't explain, Edward hurried to the bank. There were footprints everywhere.

No ghost then. But a man who'd died in France in 1916. A revenant.

Face set, he pulled the punt to the bank, reached into it, and started to mirror the other man's movements as he dumped snow into the river with his hands. Ten minutes later he was paddling downriver between overhanging, snow-laden, branches that formed a claustrophobic barrier on either side. The extreme cold had frozen the shallow water near the banks, and he noticed thin pieces of ice floating with him, reflecting the starlight like broken glass on black velvet.

There was no sign of the rowing boat. But from the old mill southwards the Cherwell twisted and turned as the valley slowly opened out, meaning there were few long stretches where he might have spotted him.

His mind was full of questions to which he had no answers. The man ahead of him was officially dead. But he was back in Great Tew. With a rush he remembered the nine o'clock appointment with the blackmailer at Langford Hall. And

Jaikie was missing. Somewhere, he reasoned, there must a connection between these events.

After half an hour he entered a long, straight, run of black water which led down to the reed bed, where the river split into a tangle of channels. He stiffened and stared, thinking he'd seen movement in the distance, but a second later it was gone, and he couldn't be sure. *Probably a bird.*

Feeling disheartened and aware he was steadily increasing the distance from hearth and home, he stopped paddling and let the punt drift with the current. On either side the woods had given way to open fields, onto which a featureless, undulating, white sheet had been laid. Drifts obscured entire hedges and on the hillside, clear against the white, he could see a group of dark figures digging frantically. The smallest was driving the sheep that they pulled out downhill towards a spinney, a black sheepdog flailing behind. Their faint cries carried across the silent landscape.

I should go and help them. I'd be more use doing that than staying on this wild goose chase. He hesitated, unsure what to do, then with a mental shrug paddled on. *I'll go to the reeds.*

*

The man with death in his heart knew the marsh well, having explored it thoroughly as a boy and then worked as a reed cutter when he grew strong enough in his mid-teens. But even with this intimate knowledge he was having trouble finding his destination. The combination of gale force winds and sheer weight of snow had bent the reeds over, meaning the entrances to many of the small channels were blocked. In the starlight the familiar network of little canals had disappeared, leaving a confused and chaotic picture.

He rowed slowly along the main channel looking to his right to try and spot the little break in the reeds that he wanted. He twisted round to look over the bow. Up ahead he could just see the hut by the jetty where the cutters based themselves during the harvest. The boat he had used earlier was still there. He narrowed his eyes, trying to judge the distance as an icy stirring in the air caressed his face and rustled the tops of the reeds.

He transferred his gaze to the sky. The patch of stars was no longer overhead. Instead a great wall of cloud was looming over the valley and he realised the eye of the storm was moving away. The second half of the blizzard was arriving.

Cursing he stared along the banks, redoubling his efforts to spot the blocked entrance to the channel.

Yes, there it was. His heart leapt. Some reeds had buckled over but beyond he could just see an inky black ribbon of water leading into the heart of the marsh. Turning the boat, he drove the bow at the gap and burst through. And at that moment, four hundred yards away, a low-lying punt with a single figure in the stern drifted into sight at the end of the main channel.

Even in the rapidly deepening gloom Edward Spense noticed him. In a still landscape any movement shows and the man's rapid strokes of the oars was enough for him to turn and catch a brief glimpse. Then to his surprise the boat simply disappeared. From his angle it looked as though one moment it was there, the next it was gone.

All thoughts of the comforts of Langford Hall forgotten, he drove the punt along the centre of the main channel. A few minutes later he arrived at where he thought he'd seen the boat, but to his frustration there was no sign of it at all. The starlight had faded, and a bitter wind was rippling the water so that it lapped noisily against the bow. Occasional snow flurries were combining into a rapidly thickening stream. With a sinking feeling he too realised that they were due another storm of the same magnitude as the first.

Like his counterpart earlier he turned, this time to stare back through the snow, trying to gauge how far along the channel the other boat had been.

And he noticed something.

Although at first glance the fallen reeds appeared to be lying chaotically, the general pattern was that they had all been pushed the same way by the wind. But as he stared at a particular section he saw that some of them did not conform to the overall picture. Instead they were bent away from the channel and into the marsh. It was the only inconsistency in the lonely landscape, and he paddled over.

As he got closer he saw that, while most of the fallen reeds carried a layer of snow on their stems, a cluster of them were bare. Increasingly certain that he was on the right track he nosed the punt into the reeds and paddled harder.

There was little resistance and moments later he found himself in a narrow channel about ten feet wide. Ahead the black water swung around a bend, and he paddled cautiously on. The reeds had not been cut for many years and formed a high and rather discomforting barrier on either side, but down at water level it was curiously calm, sheltered from the gusting wind which carried the snow clear over his head. At times he pushed the little craft through floating ice. In places it was half an inch thick in the channel and amongst the reeds he guessed it was thicker.

After ten minutes he rounded a corner and peered forward in surprise.

Well well. The marsh had a secret at its heart. He stopped paddling and drifted silently forward, studying the scene. And his concentration was his undoing, because seconds later a single shot rang out from his left. Edward felt a terrific thump in his shoulder which knocked him off the thwart. The punt tipped violently as he flailed desperately at the air to keep his balance, but to no avail.

With a despairing cry he tipped into the icy water and disappeared below the surface.

*

The old reed cutter's hut stood on a tiny island – the only one in the marsh. And although it was small it did have a title. One long forgotten by nearly everyone, but in certain homes on the estate if you mentioned Cain's Kingdom, the old men would smile and reminisce and tell their wives and daughters and grandchildren about the nights they'd spent there as young men, drinking metheglin and rhubarb wine, 'clear as claret,' when the reed harvest was over.

It had once been the home of an eel catcher's family, but Cain had renovated it and made the single room fit for human habitation of a kind. He'd even added a chimney, and gradually moved in to live full time there, eating eels and fish and occasionally paddling down to the pub in Leyland. And when someone realised that they hadn't seen old Cain for a month or two they'd come to look and found him stone cold dead one mid-summer's night in 1837. Two days later a young Queen Victoria had ascended to the throne.

That had been eighty years ago. But the man with death in his heart knew about Cain's Kingdom. And it was where he'd put the boy, poling up the narrow channel in one of the reed cutters boats.

He'd only seen the little punt for the briefest of moments, but it was enough, and he'd loitered, watching until its dark shadow slipped silently past in the main waterway. Even in the dim light he'd recognised the paddler's profile. With a surge of anticipation he'd scraped some snow off the fallen reeds, piloted his boat up the narrow channel and backed it into the reeds by the hut. There he'd waited, gun in hand, and when Lord Colin's son slid into his vision he had shot him from fifteen feet away. It had been a thrilling moment and he'd smiled with deep satisfaction as he had imagined Lady Langford's reaction.

Knowing that he'd hit him, and certain that the freezing water would finish him off, he had manoeuvred the rowing boat back into the channel, collected the empty punt and beached both vessels on the waterline below the hut.

But now something was troubling him. Edward Spense was still alive, he could feel him out there in the marsh. So he stood knee deep in the snow on the hemmed-in little island, ignoring the cold, and scanned the wall of reeds, searching for anything living or dead.

And his face tightened. Something else was moving in the frozen landscape; something ancient and powerful. And it was searching too.

Frowning, he turned, waded through the snow to the hut door, and disappeared inside. Shortly afterwards, as candlelight showed at the only window, a dark shape dragged itself one-armed from the water.

Edward thought he was dying. In fact he wished he was. At least then the pain would be over. He couldn't move his left arm at all, and a deep and powerful ache was rapidly developing down his entire side. In the reeds the ice had borne his weight and without its help the heavy coat he wore would have dragged him to his death. Somehow he had managed to remain unseen as his attacker stood motionless, head raised high, as though staring directly through the reeds. Edward had thought discovery was inevitable and braced himself for a second, and frankly merciful, shot.

But instead, the man had suddenly grunted and shaken his head, then disappeared inside the hut.

Do you want to die here? he wondered. Certainly, it was tempting. The little, high-walled clearing felt cosy and calm, and he was warm. Heavy snow was falling and he stared up into the night sky, marvelling at its chaotic beauty as images of Innes Knox swam through his mind. He smiled faintly as he pictured her laughing face and remembered sitting by Dipper Pool as she leaned against him. *Making plans.*

As his mind drifted he heard a child's cry. To his surprise he recognised it. Jaikie. The boy. Then he screamed again. It was a child's cry of surrender, a final gesture of defiance by a weakened soul. It reached deep into the semi-comatose man lying in the snow. And he remembered why he was there.

Rolling painfully onto his knees, he managed to get to his feet and stared around, trying to get his bearings. He saw the faint light in the hut window, staggered through the snow towards it and looked inside. The man from the boat was bending over something on the floor. Narrowing his eyes he moved a little to the left and craned his head. A rough tarpaulin had been thrown aside and the candlelight caught the flame-red hair of a little boy in a red knitted jersey who was moving weakly and crying. The man's face was inches from his, staring into his eyes.

Edward reached for the door and, with a roar of pain and anger, burst through it. He stumbled, fell forward and crashed to the ground four feet from the crouching man, who turned in surprise. Standing, he delivered a vicious kick to his stomach. Edward groaned and tried to rise but the man kicked again. He shrieked in agony and raised an arm, still trying to come to the boy's aid.

But there was nothing left. Smiling with delight the man with death in his heart reached into his coat and withdrew a stiletto with a needle-like blade. He knelt down by the stricken figure, grasped his hair and turned his face towards the boy. Despairing and wracked with pain, Edward saw Jaikie curled up and eyes closed. *He's dead,* he thought. *As I will be. I've failed again.* He felt the point of the knife enter his ear.

And at that moment a shadow fell across the doorway and a low, menacing, growl that seemed to come from the very bowels of the earth sounded in the hut.

As he faded into unconsciousness Edward saw the man stand and turn towards the door, the stiletto in his hand.

*

256

When he came to, Edward had no idea how long had passed. The candle on the floor was still alight and his entire body was wracked with pain made worse by the violent, uncontrollable, shivering coursing through his frame. He realised the hut door was wide open. There was no sign of the man but in the dim light he could see Jaikie lying curled in a foetal position in the middle of the floor. He'd pulled the tarpaulin half over himself.

Moving was agony, but he managed to make his over way to him. His skin felt ice cold but as he as he wrapped his good arm around him, the boy stirred, and emitted something between a sigh and a moan. *Still alive then.* Edward tried to rise above the pain and think clearly. Going back down the channel was out of the question. He simply couldn't do it with only one arm.

With a rising sense of panic he realised they were going to freeze to death. Then he suddenly noticed what he was staring at. A yellow box of matches lay on the floor next to a crude fireplace and a pile of old logs. Releasing the boy he crawled over and started to try and pile them up one-handed, but then sobbed with frustration as he realised that there was no kindling. They would be impossible to light. With a curse he crawled to the door, pulled it shut, then shuffled back to Jaikie.

The chimney would be blocked anyway, after all this time, he thought bitterly.

But as he cuddled the boy and tried to warm him, another thought drifted into his mind. *There would be a bird's nest up there. Almost certainly.* He edged back to the fireplace and lay on his back looking up the chimney. No light showed. He

257

struggled to his feet, head swimming wildly, and reached upwards with his good arm. But there was nothing. The nest was up near the top and beyond his grasp.

Desperate to lie down and hold the boy so they could die together, he forced himself to think. And inspiration came from somewhere. Holding on to the wall he edged around to the hut door and opened it. In the dim light the boat was still there, the punt in the shadows beyond it.

And so were the oars.

He knelt and swam crying with pain, one-armed through the snow to the bow. Without raising his head he reached in and grasped an oar and pulled it back towards him. It was heavy but it came and shuffling backwards on his behind, he made his way to the hut and shut the door again. He got over to the fireplace and sank to the floor, but that was a as far as he could go. He simply had nothing left to give. He could feel a dampness inside his clothes and guessed that the wounds had started to bleed again with his exertions. *So close.* He leaned back against the chimney and stared at Jaikie.

And to his astonishment, the boy stared back.

'Jaikie, are you awake?' he said, his voice sounding like a croaking whisper.

Extraordinarily, the boy replied, 'Eve came to fetch me.'

'Can you move? Can you come over here?'

'I'm cold,' he said miserably. Tears were running down his cheeks.

'If you help me we can make a fire and get it nice and warm in here. Then we can wait for mummy to come. Please help Jaikie, I can't manage on my own.'

He watched with relief as the wean slowly got to his feet and walked stiffly to him. Between them they managed to lift the oar up into the chimney and rammed it upwards until a shower of debris crashed down. A treasure trove. Twigs, dry moss, feathers.

They piled it up and put some of the smaller logs on top. But the effort had finally seen off Edward. His shirt was soaked from his freely bleeding wounds. He picked up the matches, but searing waves of pain caused him to scream out loud, and with a despairing moan of 'Sorry Jaikie,' he fell forwards in front of the fireplace, hit his head on the rough wooden floor and passed out.

The little boy in the bright red jumper sat next to him and cried at being left alone again. Then he reached out and picked up the yellow box. A forbidden item. He'd watched Ellie light the fire many times and always listened carefully to her firm instruction that he, 'mustn't play with matches'.

But now here they were, in his hand. And the fire needed lighting, he understood that. It took a long time to open the box and he ended up spilling the matches on the floor when the little tray fell out. Then he couldn't pick them up with his numb fingers. But at last he got one. And he knew what to do.

Frowning in concentration he picked up the box and put the lump end against the rough side.

*

Innes and Ellie frantically drove the nose of the boat into the snow next to the punt and the maid felt Innes push past her. 'Careful, madam,' she called, but the young doctor was already stepping onto the snow, her face slack with despair.

259

As she reached the prone figure a thrill of relief ran through her. She could see thick black hair. 'It's not him,' she cried then added wonderingly, 'but he's wearing his old coat'.

She pulled back the collar and horror pulsed through her. The man's face had been torn off and his throat gaped open.

The maid screamed and raised her hands to her face. 'What's happened to him?'

Innes shivered and said quietly, 'The dog?' Instinctively they both stared out at the wall of reeds that surrounded the little island.

'Shall we get into the hut, miss?' Ellie suggested.

They crossed the snow and Innes opened the door. As warm air and firelight flowed out into the night, she took in the scene in a single glance.

Ten feet away Edward Spense was lying on his side with his back to her, facing the glowing fireplace. She rushed over and knelt down next to him. Even in the faint light of the fire it was clear he was badly injured. Dried blood had pooled under his head and shoulders, his knees were drawn up and both arms were clenched across his stomach. Matches were strewn around an empty box at his feet.

'Edward?' she whispered, then gently touched his neck. There was a faint pulse. 'Can you hear me?' She asked, louder.

'What's happened?' Ellie said, kneeling with her.

'I think he's been shot.'

Ellie looked around, noticing a pile of cases in the corner of the room, and a document case on the floor close by. There was nothing else. She said quietly. 'Jaikie's not here, I'm sorry.'

260

And at this simple sentence, Innes finally broke. To Ellie it seemed as though her face just dissolved. She knelt forward, put her head in her hands and howled; a searing, keening, wail that rose above the storm and sounded over the desolate, snowbound, marsh. Ellie reached out and hugged her, knowing there was nothing else to be done. Tears ran down her cheeks as she cried with her, sharing the pain and misery.

The boy was dead. This had been their last hope.

And as their exhausted grief filled the little room, something stirred beneath the man's coat. For a moment neither of them noticed. Innes's eyes were closed, and Ellie's were raised to the roof.

But the movement caught her eye and, as she looked down, a small arm wearing a red knitted jumper appeared. Seconds later, Jaikie's head emerged between the arms curled protectively around him. He stared at them with sleep-bound eyes and said, 'I'm hungry.'

With a scream of joy his mother reached for him.

Chapter Eighteen

At the colonel's suggestion, the party from Langford Hall, followed the elevated old track along the valley side. It was a more direct route than the riverbank path and gave a clear view over the Cherwell as it meandered southwards. The horses managed reasonably well in the knee-high snow and were prepared to be led by Piers Langford on his seventeen-hand hunter through the deeper drifts.

Happily, the noble lord was a much better horseman than he was a shot. Burrows, by far the most uncomfortable of the party on a horse, brought up the rear by a distance.

They saw no sign of Eve, Innes and Ellie across the snowfields until they breasted a rise, and the reeds came into view through the falling snow. Piers reined in and called back, 'There's a boat in the channel. I can just see some figures but that's all'.

They pushed on and arrived at the reed cutters' hut as the boat came up to the jetty and its passengers were revealed; Innes and Ellie, exhausted but still somehow wielding the paddle and pole, Edward, lying prone between the thwarts and the flame red hair of Jaikie Knox just visible under a fold in his coat.

'We've got him,' Innes cried as they rushed to help. 'And Edward. I think he's been shot but I have no idea how, or what's happened. Jaikie is unharmed but nearly frozen. They were in a hut in the reeds.'

'Thanks be to God,' the colonel called, more out of reflex than belief. 'Can Edward be moved?'

'I'm not sure we have any choice.' Turning, she lifted the coat away from her son and said, 'Come on wean, we'll have you home and warm soon.'

Piers dismounted and removed his snow covered coat and tweed jacket, then pulled his jumper over his head. 'Put this on him. Then he can come up in front with me. I'll take him back while you deal with Edward. Put him in the hut here, I'd suggest, and I'll bring some men back with a stretcher. If he can't ride, it's the only option.'

'Alright,' Innes said. 'There's a dead man by a hut in the middle of the marsh. I thought it was Edward. He's wearing his coat.'

Sir Anthony stared. 'What did you say?'

She repeated herself, adding, 'Edward was there with Jaikie, he must have found them somehow. I presume the other man took the wean, although I've no idea why.'

The permanent secretary was already moving towards the boat. 'Can we get Edward out? I'm sorry to hurry you but I must get to that hut. Burrows, will you come with me?'

The colonel gave him a brief nod. 'Go and have a look. See if you can work out what's happened. I'll stay here with the others.'

With Jaikie now wrapped in his jumper, Piers remounted and held him secure under his Ulster. Innes stood next to him and reached up and stroked his face briefly. 'Mummy will be home soon, I promise.' With that, Lord Langford urged his horse up the field towards the track and followed the broken snow that marked their descent.

Working together they managed to lift Edward out of the boat and manoeuvre him into the hut, where to their relief they found the necessary resources for a fire. This was quickly lighted, along with an oil lantern.

As Innes and the colonel commenced an examination of the stricken man the firelight caught their faces. Ellie had once been to the art gallery in Oxford and remembered a famous painting of soldiers gathered around a night time fire after a battle. Looking at the others she thought they looked the same. 'He was cuddling Jaikie when we found him. He saved his life, we think,' she said.

The colonel held Innes's eyes in a long gaze, his face expressionless. 'Did he now,' he said calmly. 'Well there's a thing.'

She smiled back at him; the first time for a long time. 'Yes, isn't it,' she said quietly, then bent to her work. 'I don't want to expose him to the cold, but I need to see if he's still bleeding,' she explained, as she peeled the layers back. Ellie moaned and the colonel sucked in his breath as Innes opened his blood-stained shirt and the extent of his injuries became clear. 'Alright, we'll cover him up again for now. I think it's a bullet that's gone into his shoulder and come out above his shoulder blade. The arm is broken. There may well be more damage internally.'

As she gently pulled the clothes back over him his eyes opened, and he stared up at her as if in wonder. A muted croak emerged from his mouth.

'Is Jaikie all right?'

264

'Yes he is. Piers is taking him back to the hall. He's safe now.'

He smiled. 'I'm glad'

She bent forward. 'You found him, and you saved him.'

He nodded; eyes distant for a moment then looked at her. 'Please don't go to Scotland. Stay here and marry me. We'll raise him together,' he whispered, his voice barely discernible.

But Innes heard him, as did the others. And she put her mouth to his ear and whispered back, 'Yes. Alright,' then kissed him on the lips.

Ellie grinned delightedly and the colonel laughed and said, 'Congratulations.'

As Edward smiled gently and faded back into unconsciousness, she said 'Let's get him home safely then.'

*

Burrows and Sir Anthony found the narrow channel with little difficulty and within fifteen minutes of climbing aboard they were pushing the boat onto the trampled snow in front of the hut.

In curious mirroring of Innes Knox, the man from London pushed past the policeman and paced quickly over to where the body lay below the side of the punt. Shocked by the horrific injuries, he searched his pockets but found nothing. Cursing quietly he looked around and then led the way into the hut. Burrows, finding it difficult to tear his eyes away from the man's head, followed.

Inside, the fire still glowed gently and by its light they saw the blood stain on the floor, the scattered matches, and the pile of cases in the corner. Without speaking, the policeman crossed over and opened one. It was full of bottles of whisky.

But Sir Anthony only had eyes for the leather document case on the floor. Face grim with tension he walked over, picked it up, and withdrew the contents. The letter was with the bonds. His shoulders sank in relief, then he raised his head to the rafters, and said out loud, 'Thank God.' Putting it deep in his inside pocket he joined the policeman.

'Something important, sir?' Burrows asked.

'You might say that. What's all this, I wonder?' he asked, relief coursing through him.

Burrows remembered what he had heard about Frank Eales. *'There are rumours he's got a stash full of all kinds of treasure hidden somewhere, most of it nicked.'*

'I think it's a secret store for a local ne'er do well who's involved in the black market,' he replied.

'A good find for you then?'

In his mind Burrows revisited the scene of his humiliation in the rick yard and smiled. 'Yes, it is.'

'What do you want to do with the body?'

'We'll take him back to the jetty, I think, if you'd give me a hand, sir.'

Working together, they dragged the man out of the water and lifted him into the reed cutters' boat. 'God knows what's happened to him. Do you know who it is?' Sir Anthony asked, as they finished.

'It's impossible to say with his face like that. Not a local, would be my guess.'

'I'd beg to differ. He knew the Spense family. A bitter man, and from the estate I'd say.'

Burrows stiffened and looked at him. 'Do you mind my asking how you know that, sir?'

But the permanent secretary didn't answer directly. 'He took Jaikie, he told me so.'

Alarmed, the policeman said, 'You've met him? Tonight? What were the circumstances?'

'Affairs of state, Constable. I can offer you nothing beyond that, I'm afraid.'

Something gleaming faintly in the snow caught the policeman's eye. He walked over and picked it up. It was a stiletto. The vicious blade was less than half an inch in diameter at the hilt and tapered to a needle-like point. The handle was worn and fitted snugly into his hand.

'Nasty,' Sir Anthony observed over his shoulder.

'A killing weapon,' Burrows agreed shortly, trying not to let his irritation show.

But he was dealing with a skilled man, used to moving in political circles. 'Colonel Dance told me you're looking for a murderer, so I will say this. Our friend in the boat was here to carry out a scheme that he'd been planning as he waited for the war to finish. And there was something odd. He claimed he'd died at Delville Wood, along with his brother.'

The constable frowned. 'Do you know how long he'd been in Great Tew?'

'As far as I'm aware he arrived this morning, but he said he'd been here before. To surprise his girl. But something had happened, and he'd had to leave before he did so.'

The constable turned the weapon over in his hand. 'When was that?'

'He didn't say, but I got the feeling it was fairly recently.'

267

'And that was the only time he'd been back?'

'Yes,' Sir Anthony lied smoothly. 'Now, what do you want to do about these cases? I'd rather leave them for the moment, if you don't mind.'

Distracted, as he tried to put things together in his mind, Burrows nodded absently, but then saw Sir Anthony's mouth tighten, as though he'd made a decision. He watched him re-enter the hut, cross to the fireplace and remove an envelope from his inner pocket, placing it carefully in the centre of the embers.

The thick paper took a moment to light and the man from London stared stonily as it caught and flared, casting shadows onto the rough walls of the hut.

'What's that, sir?' Burrows asked, from the doorway.

'Perhaps, the saving of the empire,' Kerr replied enigmatically. 'Shall we proceed?'

*

Two days later a south westerly weather system had moved up from the Azores, bringing mild air and gentle sunshine. The snow was melting fast, and Dell Lane was passable. Down in the valley the Cherwell was in flood, running joyfully beyond its banks, and when it finally receded the flat fields would be covered with a layer of fertile mud that would slowly disappear, washed into the ground by the winter rain.

After breakfast Burrows answered the door of the police house to find Beatrice Wray and Eve standing there.

'Good morning, can I help you?' he enquired.

'Beatrice would like to view the body,' Eve said. 'She thinks she might know who it is,'

268

He raised his eyebrows and looked at her. 'Really? How is that?'

'I think it might be a friend of mine. An old friend,' Beatrice replied.

He eyed her. The tension coming off the girl was palpable. 'I have to warn you, his face is unrecognisable.'

She nodded. 'So they say. But I knew him well.'

'Even so…,' Burrows started, but seeing Eve's glare and rolled eyes, changed tack. 'Oh, I see. Very well. If you feel you can help'.

They crossed to the village hospital and descended the wooden steps to the cellar where the body lay, still and cold.

'What exactly are you looking for?' he asked, but Beatrice just stared silently at the outline under the sheet, clearly overcome with the moment.

'She says he has a mole at the top of his right thigh,' Eve said quietly, 'shaped like a triangle.' She took the girl's hand and led her forward. 'Will you raise the sheet Constable.'

Burrows did so, lifting it from the side to keep the mutilated face concealed. The mole was there. Beatrice reached out and rested her finger on it.

'Yes, that's him,' she said.

*

That afternoon Burrows called round to Marston House and sat down with his chief constable to try and work out what had happened. He hoped to have a collaborative discussion, but the colonel pre-empted this by asking him 'Right then, whose was the body on the island and who killed Dunstan Green?

269

The constable gathered his thoughts and said, 'I believe Theodore Bennett is the answer to both those questions.'

'The man with his face bitten off?'

'Correct, sir. He was formally identified by Beatrice Wray this morning, in your wife's presence.'

'Is that so?'

'He was armed with a stiletto and, according to Sir Anthony, he had been in the Great Tew area around the time of Green's death. It appears he was planning to surprise Beatrice Wray, who had been his girlfriend before he went to war. And it would have been a surprise, she thought he'd been dead for four years. I think the two men met by accident that night on the river bank. Bennett saw that Green had recognised him and, in order to stop word getting out that he was still alive, killed him and threw him in the river.'

'The stiletto would fit the wound, I imagine.'

Burrows nodded. 'Realising that there would be a fuss, he put his plans on hold and disappeared again to wait for things to quieten down. It's odd in a way. A man with no conscience murdering a man who claimed to have one.'

'Green tried to avoid the war while others went. His objections weren't principled, they were practical. He feared death.' The colonel frowned and tapped his fingers on the desktop for a moment then added 'I understand from Lady Langford that he killed two men up at the hall as well'.

'So I've been told, sir.'

'Heavens, what a night.' The chief constable shook his head and added, 'You're sure?'

'The only other serious suspect is Frank Eales, but of the two I favour Bennett.'

270

'Ah yes, Eales. What news of him?'

'Fled, sir,' the policeman said shortly. 'Once news broke about the hut in the reeds. By the time I got through the snow to his cottage yesterday there was no sign, and he's not been seen at the public house in Leyland or anywhere else. I never got to the bottom of what he'd been doing the night Green was killed, but I don't think he did it. Most likely up to no good with his black market trading.'

'And you say Brown's been corrupted?'

'He has a lifestyle above a constable's pay. There's a widespread assumption that he was being paid off by Eales to turn a blind eye to his nefarious activities.'

'Well, we'll deal with that. With more men being demobbed now there's a better pool to choose from. Tell me about Theodore Bennett.'

'He was the older of the two Bennett boys, sons of Reginald Bennett of Upper Barn. As you know, both men were convicted of arson and volunteered after Lord Colin told them it was that, or five years in prison. Their bodies were found together in a shell hole at Delville Wood and buried in field graves nearby. I've talked to other soldiers from the Oxfords who were back in a reserve camp when the news came though. There is no explanation as to how the mistake was made.'

'So who was buried with the younger brother?'

'I have no idea, sir, and we won't find out now. A lot of men just disappeared in those attacks, blown up, or buried under the mud. I imagine somewhere there will be a family with a 'missing, believed killed' telegram who will never know the truth'.

271

'So we're assuming Bennett faked his death by putting his identity tags on another body, deserted, hid somewhere in France, and hatched a plot to come back to Great Tew when hostilities are over. To what end exactly?'

Burrows moved uneasily in his chair under the chief constable's intense gaze. 'I'm afraid I'm not sure, sir. It's something to do with Sir Anthony and Langford Hall, but he nipped off back to London as soon as the road was passable. Also, I'm at a loss as to how Bennett received his fatal injuries. It's clear he kidnapped Jaikie, presumably in order to have some leverage in the other matter. But his face...' he shook his head.

The colonel said, 'Yes, well let's not worry too much about that.'

Burrows thought that his superior was oddly incurious on a matter upon which he had speculated at length and pressed the point. 'But it was like a wild animal, sir. The wound was noticed by the men who brought him back to the hospital. There was talk of a werewolf in the pub last night.'

'Well that's Great Tew for you. I think the official view is a nasty accident. Are we clear on that?'

'If you say so, sir.' Burrows nodded woodenly.

'Good. What about the bodies of the men from London?'

'I have no idea, sir,' the young constable muttered. 'I tried making enquiries at the hall but got nowhere. Taken back to London with Sir Anthony would be my guess.'

'So are there any outstanding matters?'

'Beatrice Wray had an interesting tale, sir...' He recounted the receipt of the postcard and the entry in the personal columns of the Times.

The colonel listened in silence, then as Burrows clearly had the bit between his teeth decided to open up a little. 'I'm going to tell you something confidential, Constable. Something that must stay in this room, but you're a decent man and a good policeman so I feel you deserve an explanation.'

'I went to the cottage hospital to see Edward at lunchtime. He was awake and weak from loss of blood, but the bullet is out. Innes has cleaned the wound and stitched him up. Edward identified the man as Theodore Bennett and mentioned he'd first spotted him in the woods the afternoon before bonfire night.'

'Really?' Burrows stirred.

'At the time he thought he was a ghost apparently. Anyway, I must confess that I was already aware of the man's identity. Eve brought Beatrice to the house after you saw her, and she told me then. I asked her to keep it to herself. Formally asked her. Warned her, in fact.'

As the young constable frowned and made to speak he held up his hand and continued, 'I was curious to see what you knew, and what you'd worked out, Burrows. What you certainly don't know is that I had a telephone call from Sir Anthony yesterday. Apparently the business up at Langford Hall on bonfire night was a blackmail attempt of some sort – and very serious. That was the reason for Bennett's return to Great Tew. He apologised but said he had been unable, for security reasons, to involve the local police. He was also very clear that no further investigations are desirable regarding the death of the man we now know to be Bennett. And if there are any suspicions about a connection to Dunstan Green, the

273

same applies to him. Put simply, I've been directed to shut the entire business down. And when Whitehall speaks, we obey Burrows. That is the natural order of things.'

Burrows sat up in his chair. 'Really? But we haven't got to the bottom of it at all, sir' A note of plaintive outrage suffused his response.

'Let the files show that Dunstan Green committed suicide and that the man who died in a nasty, but unexplained, accident remains unidentified. That will certainly be easier for Bennett's father, incidentally. The body will be taken to Oxford and incinerated. There will be no further enquiries beyond that. I trust I make myself clear, Constable.' The colonel folded his arms and leaned back.

Stung, Burrows drifted into dangerous waters. 'What about the fifteen cases of whisky, brandy, and cigars, sir?' he enquired tightly.

The colonel made a vague gesture with his hand. 'Hard to establish ownership. Donated to a worthy cause.'

'Might I enquire which organisation, sir?'

The chief constable gave him a long, cool, look. 'You might. I imagine it all depends on how you view your future career.'

'Case closed, sir?'

'Indubitably. Carry on.'

Reflecting on a valuable lesson learned, Burrows returned home. As he entered the hall a most delicious smell reached his nostrils. Head up and walking down the scent like a gun dog, he entered the kitchen where his wife was removing a dish from the oven.

'It's steak and kidney pie, Burrows,' she said over her shoulder. 'Wash your hands and sit down.'

Salivating heavily, he watched with considerable interest as she broke into the crisp brown crust and spooned a generous helping of pastry, meat, and rich gravy, onto his plate. 'I've roasted some potatoes in the oven with the pie. I'll just get them,' she continued. Her husband stared as she placed a bowl of perfectly cooked crisp potatoes next to his plate. 'Help yourself.'

'What...' he stared at her in astonishment.

She gave him a warm smile. 'I've been taking cookery lessons, Burrows. From Mrs Sutton up at the hall. She's told me how to plan a menu for a week, what to buy and how to cook the meals. I'm only up to four so far, but I thought I'd surprise you.'

He stood, walked round the table, and gave her a long kiss. 'I didn't doubt you, not really. I promise,' he said.

'Whatever do you mean, dear husband?'

But he just smiled and shook his head, then returned to his seat and tucked in with no further delay.

Epilogue

Five days before Christmas a pleasant afternoon tea party was taking place up at the hall. Edward, fully recovered from his wound, was sitting on the settee next to his fiancée and, arranged around the room, were Lady Langford, the colonel and Eve, Piers and the Reverend Tukes.

Lady Langford caught Innes's eye. 'Shall we leave them to it for a while?'

They left the room, climbed the main staircase and turned right along the first floor corridor, heading to a wing of the house that Innes had not explored before.

The older woman linked arms with her and said, 'An Easter wedding, I hear?'

'Yes, that's the plan. In Great Tew, not at the cathedral.'

'Lovely. Well we'll need to discuss the arrangements of course, but for now I want you to see where you and Edward will have your rooms. Just to make sure they'll do.' She led her past a wide bay window which lay above the knot garden at the back of the house. 'This side is not used very much these days, but there's a nice corner bedroom and I thought you could make a cosy sitting room next door.' She glanced at her daughter-in-law to be and delivered one of her devastatingly charming smiles. 'For when you're fed up with us.'

As Innes made deprecating noises, she led her into a large double aspect room, that overlooked the beautiful parkland to the rear of the house.

'You can decorate it as you wish of course and change the furniture and so on. It's really up to you. It'll be good practice for when you're in charge.'

'Part of me can still hardly believe it,' Innes said. 'It all seems rather daunting and at times I feel like an imposter. I know you married into the family, but you were born to the class. I'm just a wee sassy Glasgae' girl at heart.'

'Which is just what this family needs,' Claire said. 'I will be here to show you the ropes, and Piers will not marry, so in due course, you will be the chatelaine here. By the time I finally shuffle off you will be ready, I promise you that. And remember, although one must keep up appearances, and certain things are expected and necessary, you can also run the house as you wish.'

The beautiful young woman opposite looked at her. 'But can I? Piers and Edward are hardly pushovers All that history. All that bloodline.' She shivered.

Lady Langford laughed lightly. 'The neck turns the head, my dear. It's the woman's way. And once you have children they tend to become the most important thing and that'll be your domain.' She gave her hand a squeeze.

'What about Jaikie?'

'He will grow up as a Spense, at Langford Hall, with all that that means. But he will not inherit the title, that will go to your first-born. That has been the rule since 1066. As to the rest of it, surnames, adoption and so on,' she shrugged, 'that is a decision you and Edward must take together, although hopefully I'll be around for a while yet to help and advise'.

Innes nodded. 'I think we will maintain the deceit regarding my dead sister.'

'Very wise. It's widely accepted in the village, and no-one will ever suspect the truth beyond those that know already. And they can be trusted. Believe me there are plenty of secrets hidden in Langford Hall.' Her eyes glazed over for a moment. 'Some of them very recent. You're not the first new bride to arrive here feeling a little intimidated, look at this.' She led her to the bay window and pointed. 'In the bottom corner there.'

Innes craned forward. Some words were etched into the glass, and she bent her head. They were faint and difficult to read, but the date was clear, 8th July 1615.

'I love my husband. I miss my home. Pity Olivia.'

They both turned in surprise as a voice behind them read out the words. Eve was standing in the doorway. She crossed to them. 'Sorry, I wasn't eavesdropping, I just came to see what you were up to.'

'I didn't know you knew about this,' Lady Claire said, smiling at her.

'Olivia de Winter was sixteen years old when she married Sir Wyndham. She left her family in London and came to Great Tew.' Her eyes drifted to the view from the window. 'It must have seemed like another country.'

Innes stared at her, an intuitive thought suddenly and overwhelmingly in her mind. She reached over and placed her finger bearing the Langford ring onto the etching.

'Only a diamond cuts glass,' she said, then looked back and met her friend's eyes. 'This diamond perhaps?'

Eve looked at her, a distant expression on her face. 'Oh yes, that diamond. Without a doubt.'

*

King George the Fifth was in his private study in Buckingham Palace. At Lloyd George's request he had just completed a letter which would, later that day, be put on the mail train to Dover. Its final destination was a large manor house called Huis Doorn, near Utrecht.

It was hand written on the king's personal stationary and covered a single page. Laying his pen down he sipped a cup of tea and re-read it.

20th December 1920 London,

My dear cousin Wilhelm,

I trust you are well, and the family are in good health. I write to you in some haste as we leave for Sandringham later today.

Our Berlin embassy tells us that things remain very difficult for the Weimar Republic with great privations and civil unrest amongst citizens across the country. I gather Ludendorff is persisting with his rabble-rousing and intends to form a new populist political party. I sincerely hope this does not lead to more trouble.

My main purpose in writing is to advise you that the reparations committee in London has finally agreed the amount of money that Germany must pay in compensation for the destruction caused by the war. The figure is 132 billion gold marks which to my mind is an extraordinary amount, but the French have been resolute in their negotiations. This will be publicly announced early in the new year.

I understand Germany will be asked to make three bond issues to cover the sum, however, behind the scenes there is a recognition amongst committee members that, while the first two bond issues totalling some 50 million marks are expected to be paid, the third covering the bulk of the bill will not be enforced.

You have our British negotiators to thank for this concession. A large part of the share of the money the British Empire will receive is to be used to pay pensions to the widows of the fallen, so it will be put to good use.

Anyway, I hope this news will provide you with some solace, although I do fear for the long-term consequences of a bankrupt German republic at the heart of Europe and hope that the peace and stability return before further damage is done.

We send you and your family our warmest Christmas greetings and hope that under difficult circumstances you manage to have a peaceful festive season.

Your cousin,

George

*

It was Christmas Eve in Great Tew, and the church of St Mary's was packed to the rafters with worshippers. Edna Williams had fully recovered from her injury and had pride of place in the front pew. As he stood at the door and welcomed the congregation, the Reverend Tukes reflected ruefully that her husband was a greater attraction than God himself where the villagers were concerned.

'Good evening,' he smiled as a group of chattering jostling men and women squeezed past him, leaving a strong smell of cider in their wake.

The colonel and his wife arrived. 'Evening, Padre. A full house I see,' the chief constable observed.

'Indeed, and very nice to see you in the house of God, Mrs Dance. You are most welcome' Tukes replied.

'Don't worry, I won't burst into flames,' the petite twinkling blonde grinned at him. 'And I wouldn't miss this for the world.'

'Neither would we,' remarked Lady Langford who had appeared behind them with Piers, Edward and Innes in tow. 'Come and squeeze into our pew, there's a good view from there.'

At last, with every seat taken and the back of the church crammed with people standing, the Reverend Tukes climbed to the pulpit, beamed out across the grinning, expectant, and distinctly well-oiled crowd, and commenced the traditional Christmas service.

Half an hour later, as a spirited rendering of Once in Royal David's City concluded, he addressed the congregation. 'Well now it is time for our guest speaker, Bert Williams, who has kindly agreed to address us all on the subject of the importance of the church in rural life.'

The vicar descended from the pulpit and, in the lengthy pause that followed, a muted but fierce exchange could be heard taking place out of sight. Total silence fell in the church as every man and woman strained to hear the furious whispering drifting out over the congregation.

'It's out of the question, Bert.'

'No, it ain't'

'Oh yes it is. This is my church and I forbid it.'

'You said I have to give a sermon and I'm doing that.'

'Not like that you're not.'

'Oh yes I am.'

Astonishment and then delight appeared on the faces of the congregation as the sound of a scuffle and grunting carried from the shadows.

'Give me that.'

'No I won't.'

'They're having a scrap,' someone at the back intoned lugubriously. A crash and muted curse followed, then Bert Williams appeared in the pulpit, breathing heavily.

'Good God, he's got a dog-collar on,' the colonel whispered in delight to his grinning wife.

And the truth of this statement was apparent to all. Bert was wearing a clerical collar, or what passed for it, as the rear stud had become detached, and one half now extended upwards behind his left ear.

With a face like thunder, Tukes appeared from the shadows and glared up at him.

'Is he allowed to wear that, Parson?' It was the same nasal tone from the back as before.

'No, he is not.'

'Well I'm here now, Vicar, I might as well carry on,' the countryman glanced down and hastily gave him the sign of the cross. 'At this time of peace and goodwill.'

Shaking his head, Tukes crossed to a chair and sat down. Tight lipped, he nodded.

Bert raised his eyes to the congregation, fiddled with his stray collar and spoke out.

'Peace be upon you. Now as you all know, the vicar here asked me to say a few Christian words on Christmas Eve so that he can give me the allotment which I rightly deserve, being next on the list. I'm here to fulfil my side of the bargain and I'm sure, as a man of God, the parson will do the same. Won't you?' He peered towards the clergyman who said stared stonily back.

'Because if you can't trust a man of God, who can you trust?' he added, taking in the crowd with a sweeping nod. A low murmur of assent sounded across the ranks of worshippers.

The chief constable leaned into Lord Langford who was sitting next to him. 'Is that an old ploughman's smock he's wearing?' he said in a low voice.

Piers Spense gave him an amused sidelong look. 'Clearly he's had to improvise.'

Up in the pulpit Bert was getting into his stride. 'Now the parson and I have had many interesting talks on the church over the last few weeks and I must say I've come round to his way of thinking. I've bin saying my prayers every night and…'

'What have you been praying for, Bert?' a voice sounded from the left of the aisle.

'Trout rising and the keepers in the pub.' The reply from the back caused general amusement in the crowd.

But Bert held up his hand in admonishment. 'No, no. I'm a changed man. The holy book says, "Do not covet your neighbour's ass". And I reckon that applies to trout as well.'

'What about your neighbour's wife?' a voice enquired.

At this there was a stirring in the third row and Mrs Sutton rose to her feet, turned, and glared towards the crowd standing near the door. 'I heard that, Alan Farthing. I'd know your voice anywhere. Just you watch your mouth, or I'll box your ears.' She resumed her seat, sniffed, and said in a loud voice, 'I'm a widow anyway.' There was a cheer at this.

'I think he's got the crowd with him,' Lord Langford muttered to an openly smiling chief constable.

'Anyway, while I'm up here I've got a few things to say about miracles,' Bert said.

'It'll be a miracle if you get that allotment now,' a wag remarked.

'No no, that's the point. Everyone deserves a miracle and when you need one God hears you. Doesn't he, Vicar?' Bert leaned over the pulpit. 'That's what you said. If you repent your sins, I mean, and I've bin repenting like mad for weeks now. So I reckon I'm due one.'

An hour later Bert was the centre of attention in the Black Horse when the Reverend Tukes entered and crossed to the little group that surrounded him.

'A drink, Vicar?' Beatrice Wray asked him.

'Thank-you. A pint of cider would be most welcome.' He eyed Bert as conversation died in the room, and then addressed him in a clear voice.

'I have come directly from an impromptu meeting of the church council where the allocation of Mr Hawkins' plot at the Glebe allotments was discussed. I am pleased to say a decision has been reached and you may take possession on the first of January. Congratulations.'

284

As cheers erupted, he reached out and shook his hand and Bert felt a concealed note being pressed into his palm. He looked at the parson and closed his fingers around it. A minute later he managed to turn his back to the others and glanced down to read it.

It was unsigned and succinct.

Two good trout every fortnight. Delivered to the kitchen door.

The end

Author's note

The original inspiration for the plot of *The Death of Conscience* came from that fact that, during the Great War, around 160,000 British Empire soldiers simply disappeared. The Menin Gate memorial near Ypres records the names of 55,000 men and the Tyne Cot memorial nearby another 35,000 who were never found. These are the soldiers whose families received the 'missing believed killed,' telegrams and whose bodies are still being discovered every week across the old battlefields.

The Commonwealth War Graves Commission has a permanent staff in the region and continues to record and treat these remains with dignity and respect, whichever side they served on. They should be saluted. It really is a very fine organisation, that looks after war graves in 156 countries around the world.

The battle for Delville Wood was one of the major engagements of the Battle of the Somme and was subsequently noted for the efforts of the 1st South African Brigade which performed heroically to hold the positions they'd taken for six days, until relieved. Part of the area was brought by the South African government in 1920 and a permanent memorial to all the South African loses in the Great War was built there. Of the 776 colonial troops who died in the environs of Delville Wood, only133 have known graves. A sobering thought.

As described, the armistice that ended the fighting was signed in the Forest of Compiégne and the French subsequently built a memorial in the place where the railway carriage stood. When Hitler defeated the French army in World War Two he insisted the French signed the surrender document at the same location.

Between 1914 and 1918 the allied naval blockade of German ports was so effective that the country slowly starved. At the same time Ertzburger was negotiating with Foch and Wemyss in the railway carriage, armed crowds in Berlin were calling for the Kaiser's abdication. He finally went on November the 9th meaning the decision on whether to accept the Allied terms fell to the German supreme commander Ludendorff, as the country teetered on the verge of open revolution. He told Ertzburger to do the best he could, but to sign whatever happened.

The final page of the armistice document really was signed by all the parties at five o'clock in the morning on the eleventh of November without the rest of the document being attached, which seems extraordinary but is true. Hostilities famously ceased at eleven o'clock that same day.

The payment of war reparations by the losing side was an established practice in Europe, but the enormous bill Germany received from the allies was exacerbated by Berlin's decision to fund the war by borrowing. It is widely believed by historians that the financial impact of the settlement paved the way for the hyperinflation that destroyed the Weimar republic and led to the rise of Nazism.

287

A certain Corporal Hitler who served in the Great War was appalled by the terms of surrender. Writing later in *Mein Kampf*, he blamed the subsequent economic melt-down on Jews and Marxists.

The first daylight air raid over London by German Gotha bombers on the 13th June 1917, led to 162 deaths in the capital including a very distressing direct hit on a primary school. Six days later King George the Fifth finally changed his German family surname from Saxe-Coburg-Gotha, to Windsor, to general relief across the nation.

Regarding village life in Great Tew, I am indebted to a wonderful book called, *The Secrets of Bredon Hill*, by Fred Archer which chronicles life in Cotswold village a hundred years ago. It is a varied and authentic rural record, full of fascinating details of a world that seems very distant now.

Thank-you for buying and reading this book. I have tried to combine history and mystery and, as before, the supernatural aspects are inspired by my own experiences. If you enjoyed it please, please, write a brief review on the Amazon sales page for the book. It helps enormously with search rankings and it's a very competitive world out there for an independent author.

Finally, a word about Gavrilo Princip. He undoubtedly did murder Archduke Ferdinand and his wife, and the consequences of that action were appalling. But the decision to add to his woes by making him a British agent is mine and mine alone.

We will hear more from Great Tew.

Frederick Petford

Somerset, England.

288

Printed in Great Britain
by Amazon

87471968R00169